STELLA DUFFY

Born in London and brought up in New Zealand, Stella
Duffy is an author, actor, comedy improvisor and presenter.
She has written two other novels published by Sceptre,
Singling Out the Couples and *Eating Cake*, as well as
four crime novels, *Calendar Girl, Wavewalker, Beneath
the Blonde*, and *Fresh Flesh*. She now lives in London.

D0806633

STELLA DUFFY

Immaculate Conceit

SCEPTRE

Copyright © 2000 by Stella Duffy
First published in the UK in 2000 by Hodder and Stoughton
A division of Hodder Headline

A Sceptre Paperback

10 9 8 7 6 5 4 3 2 1

A CIP catalogue record for this book is available from the
British Library

ISBN 0 340 77002 3

Typeset by Palimpsest Book Production Limited,
Polmont, Stirlingshire
Printed and bound in Great Britain by
Clays Ltd, St Ives plc

Hodder and Stoughton
A division of Hodder Headline
338 Euston Road
London NW1 3BH

for Agent X-129 and the
Faerie Queen
for allowing the possibility

(Bear with me, it's been a big year.)
Thanks to my family and friends who supported my
desire to keep going even when most of them really
wanted to make me lie down and rest; the fantastic
email support network; Carole Welch and all at Hodder
for their love and understanding in a difficult time;
Stephanie Cabot, Eugenie Furniss and Yvonne Baker
for their constant support; the real Helen, Sandras and
Caroline – not lap dancers but great dancers; the amazing
Tartcity chicks; the Improbable Lifegamers for being part
of the process and giving me something wonderful to stay
well for; the men in white shining armour who beat off
the baddies and the women in red silk who kept them
breathing (and partying); Ruth Curson and Dr Buchanan
for their care and kindness; all at King's College Hospital
Breast Unit and the complementary alternatives who
generously went along with my plans and made keeping
going possible; Andy and Glyn for taking care of the girl;
and Shelley for protecting me when the world was too
scary to look at and for being beside me on those long
walks through the park.

When Sofia was a little girl she wanted to be a tightrope walker or a trapeze artist – swinging from the welcoming hands of one potential saviour to another, no safety net, thrusting her trust at strangers and the sky.

And then she was granted her wish.

One

Sofia should have known better. Sofia Anna Bridget Fisher, twenty-eight, resident of Crouch End, really should have known better. A strange man, sitting on the end of her bed, at four o'clock on a Tuesday morning. A man she didn't recognise and hadn't heard getting into her flat. A man who had found his way in past locked doors and safety-catch windows. And she didn't know why he was there, what he wanted nor, failing that, what to do with him. No idea.

Sofia worked late all week but kept Sunday and Monday nights for herself – Sunday was, if at all possible, exclusively reserved for an evening in, catching up on all the telly she'd taped over the week, with Monday nights free for whatever. On this particular night, a trashy drugs-and-low-life movie made in Hollywood by people who evidently thought all heroin addicts looked like Kurt Cobain three years dead, and dug up to pop over for a nice cup of tea. Sofia pictured her habit-run colleague at the club where she worked and wondered why nobody ever showed users wearing clothes from Voyage and tucking into a good steak sandwich, as Helen regularly did just after midnight. She'd been to watch the movie with her ex-boyfriend and downstairs neighbour, James. Unusually, they had disagreed as to the merits of the film, James loved every frame, she loathed it, and the ensuing discussion which rapidly turned into a fierce argument only marginally spoiled their meal. It took more than fighting with James to deter Sofia's enjoyment of her regular fried noodles and green chicken curry. Afterwards she had pulled him into the welcome doors of a last-orders pub and they'd shared three late lagers. Sofia's strategy for last orders was always to buy for a third person, just in case. The Elijah pint being her tacit acknowledgement that the extra half always tasted just that little bit finer for being another five minutes closer to magic midnight. They wove a delicate trek home and sat in the downstairs kitchen where they swift-sipped through a fifth of single malt and then moved on to James's sitting room for late-night telly and dope – too strong and heady for Sofia, she rationed herself to accepting the joint from him only every third time that it was offered. They giggled for a while at the inane screen, debated the pros and cons of the silicone-breasted presenter – too many cons for her, too much of a pro for him – and by the time the cuckoo clock squawked three, it was clearly time for bed.

Sofia had wandered slowly up the eighteen steps from James's flat to hers, taken off her make-up, locked the door, turned out the lights and gone to bed. Amused, fairly content and close to exhausted. She had fallen asleep the minute her head hit the smooth white-cotton pillowcase. Smooth because Sofia ironed her sheets and pillowcases. They were the only things she did iron. Ever.

Now, an hour later she was awake again, very confused and not a little frightened. She was certain she'd closed and locked the door to her own flat when she came upstairs, positive she remembered James double locking their communal front door. Thought she was positive, surely she remembered rightly; pissed yes, stoned a little, but she couldn't have been that bad? She wouldn't be this sober now if she'd been that bad then. She would probably have slept with James if she'd been that bad then. And yet there he was, a bloke sitting on the end of her bed in the middle of the night. And it wasn't James.

Suddenly completely sober, she thought about her options. Run for the door. But the man was sitting on the end of the bed. The door was beyond the end of the bed. She'd have to run past him. She could scream. She was good at screaming, it had been a well-practised art when she'd worked in Japan. And Sydney, New York, Berlin. And now. But despite her undoubted lung capacity, she was acutely aware that James wouldn't hear a thing. She'd slept beside, under and over him for more than three years, knew how deep James sank into the dream zone. And her bedroom was at the back of the house, his at the front. But she was going to have to do something. The man was watching her.

Deep breath, heart pumping tequila-slammer fast. With a cocaine chaser. Poor scared heart beating really fucking fast. Opened her squinting eyes properly. Sofia sat up – the man didn't move. She looked at him. He looked back, still didn't move, didn't acknowledge her at all. Like one of them wasn't really there. She looked again. Then, because she didn't want to be there herself, didn't want to be in that place and couldn't think what else she could possibly do, Sofia closed her eyes. Just for a moment. Except now she found that she was still looking at him. Even with her eyes closed. Lying back down, eyes closed, she could still see the man sitting on the end of her bed. Not in negative relief image, but really and truly, just the same as she'd seen him with her eyes open. And that was almost understandable. That she could see him with her eyes closed actually made it sort of all right. Because his appearance on the back of her eyelids meant he couldn't really be there and therefore this wasn't happening at all. Now that reasoning did make sense – Sofia certainly wanted it to make sense. It was the dope, the whisky, the beer. It was her overactive imagination, much praised as a child by eager parents. It was a flashback from an unremembered experience, it was a scene from the movie, it wasn't now. Not happening. Huge relief, big sigh and Sofia's tense shoulders fell three inches back into place. There was no man on the end of her bed. No tall dark man with his own backlighting. She was dreaming, tripping, whatever. She was off her face, it wasn't real and that was brilliant. Sofia snuggled down, pulled up the duvet, ignored the picture playing on the back of her eyelids, turned over, tried to sleep.

Then the bastard started talking.

And didn't stop.

Wouldn't listen to her protests.

Was surprised she didn't jump at the chance he was offering her, surprised she didn't believe him. Didn't want to believe him. But he wouldn't go away either. Leaving wasn't in his brief. He was staying until she said yes. Or no. Until she made a choice.

'You've got to be kidding.'

'Sofia Anna Bridget Fisher?'

'I already told you.'

'Sixty-three Hillside Gardens?'

'Sixty-three B. Maybe you want downstairs? James isn't busy for the rest of his life?'

'No. I want you. You're the one. It's you.'

'Listen mate, I don't know who's put you up to this, I don't know if this conversation is actually happening, but even if you believe what you're saying, even if I believed what you're saying, It's not real. It certainly is not me. You've made a mistake.'

'No.'

'But I'm not right.'

'Apparently you are.'

'I can't be the one.'

'Not for me to say, is it?'

'Look at me, look at my flat, look at my job. I'm a lap dancer.'

'I know. I've seen you.'

'Oh right, now I get it, you're some kind of stalker.'

'More of a guardian.'

'OK, fine. Then I'm a nutter and you're not really here at all.'

He shook his head, stupid grin, rueful grin, cute grin actually, but she wasn't going there. 'I think we both know better than that.'

'I don't.'

'Look Sofia, all I know is, it's my job to come and let you know. Ask you for your answer. It's what I do. You're the dancer, I'm the messenger. I'm just passing on the good news.'

'Yeah, brilliant. Thanks. But look, even if I did believe you – which I don't – even if I thought this was really happening, and I don't think I do – don't I get to be asked what I think? You can't just tell me this is going to happen. I must have some say in it.'

The man frowned, thought for a while, 'Maybe. I'm not sure. I mean, I suppose you could say no. If you really didn't want to do it. But it is a pretty big deal.'

'Big deal? It's impossible.'

'That's right.'

'It doesn't make any sense.'

'Doesn't have to.'

Sofia shook her head, unbelievably frustrated by his calm, 'Listen to me, will you? It really is impossible. It would have to be a bloody miracle.' He looked down at her, slight smile, slow nod, half wink, 'I think that's the point.'

'Oh for God's sake . . .'

Smug smile and bigger nod, 'That too.'

Sofia stood up and the man moved away. Back towards

the door behind him. Moved, except she didn't see him move, didn't see his feet make contact with the floor. Ignored the impossibility dawning on her. Kept playing the angry girl. It was easy, she'd done it before, indignant and furious, Sofia could play bad-mood-girlfriend for hours, she was well practised at it. Role playing in the bedroom. Again. It was a damn sight easier than believing what he was telling her. But the man didn't get the game.

'I need your answer Sofia.'

'Look, this is crazy. You're talking shite, you've broken into my home and you're asking me to make sense of it. I can't. So why don't you just go away, please? Otherwise I'm going to call James. The guy who lives downstairs. I only have to shout and he'll be up in a second. I mean it.'

'No you don't. James sleeps through anything. You know that.'

Anger subsiding, fear trickling in, dangerously close to tears and so not wanting this strange man to see her cry.

'Please go away. Please leave me alone. I don't understand what you want.'

He moved closer to her. No sound of feet on floor. No sound at all. 'I don't mean to frighten you.'

She was stunned to find that she felt calmer now that he was closer and hated herself for it, hated him for it.

'I'm sorry Sofia. But I do need an answer.'

'I can't answer you. You're not making sense.'

'As I said, it doesn't have to make sense. You just have to say.'

'What?'

'Yes or no. You have to choose.'

'What choice is there? How can I choose? You're talking rubbish. Or I'm going nuts. This isn't real. Your fucking feet aren't even on my floor. I don't know what's going on. For Christ's sake, I don't understand.'

The man nodded, held out his hand, 'I know you don't.

And I'm sorry. I understand that this is confusing. But you have to choose anyway. After you've made your choice, I can help, but I need you to decide. I have to have an answer.'

'You've asked me a question that doesn't have an answer, that doesn't make any sense and you want me to take you seriously?'

'I do.'

'And then will you go?'

'Definitely.'

'Promise?'

'Cross my heart.'

'Hope to die?'

The man smiled and shook his head, 'That doesn't work for me.'

'OK. Fine. Yes. If that's what you want. Or no. Whatever. I don't care. Go away. How's that? Will that do? Yes. Or no. Honest, it really doesn't bother me, I just want you out of my room, out of here. I don't know what you're on about, I just want you to go away. OK? All right? Please? Please will you just piss off?'

But the man had gone. Without Sofia seeing him leave. Eyes wide open and pleading, but she was begging thin air. She was talking to the light he'd left behind. The man had gone after she said yes. Given the assent. He never heard the no. Or the whatever. Left on wings of yes.

Sofia looked at her clock. It was still four in the morning. Just as it had been when she first opened her eyes and saw him on the end of her bed. She thought about going downstairs to tell James what she'd just been through, then rapidly thought better of it, couldn't bring herself to try waking him up. Primarily because she had no idea what she'd say to him once she did. Sat for a while, shivered for longer. She cautiously opened her bedroom door, checked the front door into her hallway. Still locked, undisturbed. Pulled the key from the lock and carefully made her way downstairs, hall lights blazing. Eighteen quiet and nervous steps down to James's flat. Main door double locked, windows closed and safety-caught throughout. She ran back upstairs, slammed and double locked the door behind herself. Turned all the lights on in her flat and made herself a cup of tea, shovelled sugar into it, sat by the window for half an hour, sipping at the sweet, sensible liquid. Eventually her racing heart slowed to a tired stumble and she dragged herself back to bed. Turned off the light after another ten minutes and lay in the fading dark looking at the nearly-morning shadows on her ceiling.

When Sofia closed her eyes, the man was behind her eyelids. Waiting. He smiled, 'Thank you. Thank you very much.'

'Yeah, fine, whatever. I'm tired. I'm clearly turning into a nutter. Go away.'

He held out his right hand to her, 'Behold the handmaid of the Lord—'

Sofia just shook her head, 'Oh fuck off.'

He did.

She slept. Immediately and long. And remarkably easy.

Two

Sofia is a dancer. A meant-to-be prima ballerina. From pre-planned vitamin intake to ovulation-day genesis right through to hospital rush, there were always strategies and schemes for this girl, the stated intention of nothing but the best. Whatever it was the little one proved to be good at, that was the course her parents would follow. She was the planned baby – their fantasy child born to make the dream come true. They wanted only the best for her. They wanted only the best from her. Had she been a mathematical genius, scientific prodigy, linguistic ace, it would have been the same. The mother and the father – conscious of the blessing in their new titles – were prepared to pave the path of guaranteed promise. They christened her Sofia, named her for Wisdom. They imagined the getting would be painless – as if the name itself might carry its own power.

When Sofia showed elegant poise as a swaying tree at tender three, she was immediately enrolled in every class available. Ballet and tap and drama and jazz and baby bouncing acrobatics to boot. And she did show promise, and she did work hard, and she took pleasure in rewarding the efforts and love of her home and teachers. Sofia was the star girl. All hope, all ambition focused in the stretch of her supple back and the arc of a perfectly poised arm.

Sofia's parents were not bad people. Nor were they, since Sofia had come into their lives, what society might call irresponsible. They had not smoked grass since their daughter was three. They owned a small house, with a carefully planned mortgage. There was a nice garden, tidy and well kept – particularly the herb bed. And if the kitchen and sitting-room walls were covered in tie-dyed scarves and the sayings of Kahlil Gibran, with obligatory Che poster for good measure, then Sofia's bedroom with semi-naked Barbie dolls, tired ballet shoes and pretty pop boys splattered across the walls and half the ceiling, went some way towards making their home look a little more like the rest of the street. They went to work, enjoyed a pleasant social life with both friends and neighbours, and cared deeply for their child. They were not bad people. But they were parents. Geoff and Sue had probably tried harder than many others to allow their child to develop at her own pace, to find who it was she wanted to be, by herself and for herself. They had read The Prophet. They knew their daughter was the child of life's longing for itself. They also knew that their daughter was the product of an inherent, biological, intensely human, and ultimately, inevitably, selfish longing to procreate. The all-human, egocentric drive to remake themselves in a better image. They meant to be only good and selfless and completely generous in their offering of life and love to the offspring. All through the planning and the pregnancy and the birth they meant to be perfect. Instead they were ordinary.

Sofia was almost seven when her parents revealed the sober colours of their truth. It was a ballet exhibition. Supposedly an event engineered for the pure enjoyment of performance, the competitive element was barely disguised beneath a pretence of art for art's sake. And a row of card-wielding judges in the front row. Each one perfectly illuminated with excess light falling from the stage. Each one scrutinising the legs, feet, arms and hands of every small child on view. Each child knowing, that no matter how the teachers told them just to go out there and play, that his or her heart was up for judgement. Not that any of the parents realised this. They wanted joy for their babies, the overspill thrill of lights and costume and applause. The enormous release of showing off. It didn't occur to them, sitting in the back rows and cheering wildly, that all the little ones would hear was the fold-back of overloud music on the stage. And all they would see, in the darkness of the small auditorium, its very ordinary size swollen to massive extremes by lighting and baby-fear, was the row of judges. Everything else disappeared into a black cavern behind the unscalable wall that was the judging panel.

The evening started well enough. There were the usual dressing-room traumas – lost tights, single shoes strangely missing, wild hair that refused to stay in place no matter how much thick lacquer poisoned the air. There were aunts and mothers admonishing nervous children to smile, smile, smile. There were best friends in the junior class falling out at the pivotal moment to reveal they had never really liked the other, and by the way, it doesn't matter whose clothes you dress her up in, everybody knows your Barbie is really just a Sindy. Normal, ordinary, chaos.

But none of this was for Sofia. Her costumes were clean and shining and perfectly ironed. Her shoe ribbons were sewn tight with mother love. Her two best friends were equally charmed, happy and smiling with not an unruly nerve in sight, and they sat in a corner talking through the Hungarian polka that was their own glittering showpiece. Sofia's parents had already been to the dressing room, checked her hair and make-up, supervised the hanging up of her five changes of costume, assured themselves of their daughter's calm and happiness, and then retired to the bar for a glass of wine. They neither fussed over her, nor pretended this was an ordinary occasion. It was special and exciting. But at the same time, it was simply a show. They were a model of parental perfection; a combination of self-restraint and enthusiastic encouragement. They kissed Sofia, handed over a parting good luck gift – Ballet School Barbie, complete with barre and plié knees – and left her to get on with it.

Geoff and Sue were lying. Acting. Performing as if born to it. Carrying on with the deceit they had maintained since the day Sofia was born perfect in every detail, and exacerbated daily by the continued shining starriness as she grew. They had kept up the lie that all they wanted from their child was her own happiness, that they wanted nothing more from her than her love. When in reality, just like every other parent in the building, what they really wanted was to see her outshine every other one of the pretty little girls in the dressing room. All they asked was that Sofia be perfect. All they asked was that she never, ever, put a foot wrong. They were asking for it.

The performance began. Auditorium lights dimmed. Crowd shifted and hushed. Curtain rose. Sixteen little girls and four brave boys flowed on stage dressed in their mother-made costumes of red and gold wind-blown leaves. Autumn. The Four Seasons. Vivaldi screeched through inadequate speakers, parents nudged each other in proud patronage and, from the big girls clacking in their full pointe shoes, right down to the tiniest three-year-old from the toddlers' dancing class, each one performed perfectly. Not a single forgotten cue, misplaced jeté, or inelegant glissade to interrupt the unblemished flow through sequin-sparkling winter, fresh green spring, and back to the golden glow of summer. Rapturous applause, frantic costume change, and then the babies were on for the Teddy Bears' Picnic. It didn't matter that not one of the seven remembered to lie down and go to sleep after their big tea on the gingham set, or that three more almost forgot to come on at all – they were all cute, all cuddly and all chaos. The big girls next, chiffon scarves and Pink Floyd backing track, serving up an intended Isadora Duncan tribute, unintentional Hot Gossip pastiche. The four boys completed a comedy hornpipe to butch Daddy laughter and clapping. Then another group presentation, this time the Twelve Dancing Princesses, complete with twin boatmen, flowing river of hastily reincorporated chiffon scarves, and an artistically inspired mountain of discarded, worn-down shoes. Then there was the interval and much back-slapping among the mothers and fathers in the foyer, quick changing backstage, while smiling, relieved parents downed warm wine and Maltesers.

Three little girls backstage downing warm wine and Maltesers. It had been a trying wait during the dancing princess piece, all three of them still marginally hurt they hadn't been considered princess material – despite the fact that their lack of royal blood meant they had been rewarded with a whole dance just for the three of them, an accolade not given lightly, but intended to show their youthful prowess and, more importantly, their great promise. Sofia's especially. After all, while all three girls had half-hoops of crêpe-paper flowers, dirndl aprons with rick-rack braiding, and heavy black patent-leather shoes, Kristen and Robyn were wearing matching coarse black joke-shop wigs – Sofia, who danced at pole position between the two of them, wore her own mother's going-out wig of real hair, shining blonde. The golden spotlights had given her an even more angelic beauty at the technical rehearsal, and her proud teacher confidently expected the seven-year-old to be the shining star of the show. She had confided as much to Sofia's parents on the night of the dress rehearsal. Unfortunately Sofia never heard the glowing report, Sue and Geoff thought it best not to tell her too much in case they came across as stage-parent pushy. Better that Sofia realise her own potential in her own good time. There was always the danger that if they told her all they believed her capable of, she might get too big-headed, fall unbalanced from her own strengths. Of course, there was also the chance that she might have taken the performance just that little bit more seriously.

All made up and nowhere to polka. Three little girls were bored. With everyone else either on stage, whispering encouragement from the wings, or out front watching, Sofia gave a little thought to alleviating the backstage agony of combined nerves and tedium. She whispered daring and dangerous enticements to her friends, posted them as look-puts at the back door and the stage entrance, and took off. A quick run down the side alley, out into the main street in Hungarian national dress, fake fair pigtails and plastic flower headpiece flying in a rush wind of illegal excitement, in through the front door and up to the store room at the back of the foyer. Three minutes later she was back with half a bottle of warm muscadet, three giant bags of chocolates, and two bottles of Fanta. Kristen and Robyn tried the wine but didn't much like it, settled for the, to them, equally illegal Fanta instead. Sofia drank half a glass of the muscadet, finished Robyn's Maltesers, took another four mouthfuls of the wine and sipped the end of Kristen's Fanta. Far more by accident than intent, all three were smiling and seemingly ready to go on when the teachers and mother-helpers rushed backstage to check they were standing by to get the second act going.

Into position behind the curtain, four bars wait, then one and two and the curtain swings up to reveal three little girls already moving, spinning, skipping in perfect counter-pointed time. Hop, skip, step, step. Step, hop, skip, skip. Skip, hop, step, step. Hop one, hop two, and turn, and bow. And hop and skip and stop and then Sofia is too hot, her shining wig is itching, and hop and kick and stammer and find it again, follow Robyn, watch Kristen, and turn and hop, but she's facing the wrong way now, and the lights didn't seem this bright before and why are those people staring? What are they looking at? Who are they looking at? Why are the judges looking so closely, too closely? Their pages flapping, notebooks slapping against each other. Kristen and Robyn grab her hands now, Sofia's hands are supposed to be on the half hoop, but she can't find the ends and crêpe-paper flowers are coming off in her tiny, sweaty fingers, and hop and hop, but the hop won't come, the usually light and clever little feet are weighed down with the patent leather, and Sofia can see herself spinning in the shine of the shoes, the glare of the lights, the terrified eyes of the middle lady judge as she and an arc of half-hooped vomit tumble from the stage into the front row laps. Robyn and Kristen try valiantly to carry on, but the audience are worried about the poor little girl and the music grinds down and the curtain falls on their hop, skip, step. Falls, but not as far as Sofia.

There are naughty little girls who ruin nice evenings for other little girls, lead them astray, spoil events that teachers and helpers have worked on for an entire season. Which is bad enough. Easily bad enough to mean taking back the new Barbie and cancelling the shopping trip to the city and having to stay indoors for the whole weekend. And then again, there is a naughty little girl who has not only done all that, but worse – far worse – who has spoilt things for herself. Who, at seven years old was clearly old enough to know better – has, apparently, ruined her own future. Damaged a career she didn't even know she was planning on. Certainly ruined her chances of the scholarship Mummy and Daddy's bank balance sorely needed. They didn't mean to shout so much, Geoff and Sue. Didn't usually shout at all, if they could help it, and mostly they could. But they'd had a couple of glasses of wine themselves before the show. Drank a little more than intended in the interval, out of nerves and excitement and the sheer thrill that it was now so close to the moment when they would watch their star-child daughter. Too much hope, too easily exploded.

The next morning, with varying degrees of hangover all round the breakfast table, Mummy and Daddy were stern but subdued. Sofia had indeed behaved very badly, but neither of her parents had meant to expose themselves quite so much. The punishment threats were carried out but lessened. The shouting never happened again. They all went shopping as planned. They ate lunch in a burger bar. They did not mention the performance and eventually were able to persuade the furious teacher to take Sofia back the next term. After a week or so, all the fallout swept neatly under the hand-woven carpet, they climbed Glastonbury Tor as a family and reclaimed it from the tourists.

It would take more than a make-believe happy family weekend to reclaim Sofia's innocence. One month after her seventh birthday, Sofia realised that the dancing she thought she did for fun and play and with, sometimes, a degree of hard work for personal satisfaction, was actually so much more than that. It was the thing she did to keep Mummy and Daddy happy. Being good at it was what made them happy. And because she was only seven, Sofia translated their happiness into their love for her. In her childish equation, being exceptionally good at dancing was what made her mother and father love her. And because her parents were just people, and therefore not perfect, in a way, she was right.

In another way, it sent her dancing after affection every day of her life.

Three

Sofia continued to work hard at her classes, and as she grew it became her desire as well as her parents', her wish that she become the ballet princess. But even the most careful nurture could not hold out against genetics, and stage mother was lapped in the final race by Mother Nature. Before her second blood-summer, Sofia's fine and smooth limbs had grown just that couple of inches too long. Then another Christmas brought gift hips clearly female, breasts that could no longer be eaten away by denying herself. At fourteen Sofia was already too much woman for the pointe of sugar plum confectionery – her centre of gravity slipped down from narrowed waist to grounded sex. The sad parents who had only wanted everything for their child realised their mistake and thought longingly of the binding bandages they'd rejected in the baby's infancy, their once-were-hippy leanings had allowed them to swaddle the child too loosely. Big mistake.

Sofia spent her early teenage years beating her body into submission. Semi-starving her traitorous flesh while simultaneously exercising her muscles into exhaustion – these were not the actions of a young woman in trouble, these were the actions of almost every girl in her class, every girl she knew. Sofia was simply following the well-worn path of body hatred that every other young woman she knew had taken. It wasn't unusual and because she still looked good, no questions were asked. With time, Sofia became more sophisticated in her self-harming, hid it better than the other girls, mutated her body traumas into other, more easily hidden phobias – and like everything else she turned her hand to, she became very good at it.

The first time Sofia was fourteen. Let down by her flesh, abandoned by her ambitions. Her parents attempted understanding but they were ill-equipped to help. And Sofia didn't know how to ask anyway. All she knew was that the closed bedroom curtains cut out the too-bright sunlight. Warmth burnt her eyes, laughter bled inside her ears. And Sofia hid her pain because she believed if she showed it at all, the force of presentation might crack her wide open. Sofia discovered cutting by accident. Tried and tested on half the bad-girl prison dramas in the land, it looked like a way out. Thin blade removed from her mother's pale pink razor entered and opened an inch-long hole in her wrist. Injured skin pulled away from itself and the initial single line became a stretched diamond. There was the thinnest layer of fat beneath. Soft smeared pool of yellow butter, she watched it spread over with red. Pale at first, soaking up through the gold, then darker, spilling out over the skin, pushing up through the wound, pumping in time with her terrified heart. The deep red persuaded Sofia that she wasn't looking for the way out – not the traditional exit at least. All she wanted was a way to claw back the light. The sharp slit cut into a clean air she'd almost forgotten how to breathe. Then the red, tangible blush. Something that really was her, was Sofia. A thing of beauty, in a place when what had become Sofia felt simultaneously leaden solid and insubstantial nothing.

Sofia's teenage depression was a dark blue cocoon, heavy blanket placed over her whole body, tight woven cloth weighing her down, laying her out flat, pathetic prostrate.

There were very occasional moments of respite, cool slits cut into the flesh of the poison blue, to let out a shade of red that might be light, might be life. This was never the cut of could-be death, simply a way of getting to the hope of another place. And even then, in the moment of swift blade, Sofia knew that, somewhere, reason and return were waiting. She proved this to herself by cutting thin and fine. Never the scraping, scabbing mess she had noticed on others. Somewhere in the dark blue she always knew she would be in the world again and therefore the body that was also career tool, her one vessel, must be preserved if at all possible. Now that Sofia works nightly in dim light and the dull reflection of plastic sequins, it is only possible to see her long smooth scars with careful examination. The fine slits were not made for show or exhibition, for a screaming help-me. These marks were simply the tracheotomy scars that lined her inner wrists and thighs – in the pit of heavy blue, they let her breathe. Connected disassociated body and soul in a way nothing else could.

Eventually, the parents realised what was going on, forced open the bedroom curtains, saw through the long sleeves in summer. They took her to see a man. And then a nice lady. And then another man. Sofia gave herself over to their search and finally she was chosen by the white-coated man from the long locked corridor. She would visit him twice weekly after school and wait outside his office. She'd hear a distant door slam and he would appear at the end of the corridor. Using two different keys in three separate locks the man would let himself through the reinforced glass door to the foyer where Sofia stood waiting. Over two months he offered a listening ear, then drugs, then a chance to join him on the other side of the locked door. Or did Sofia think she might possibly just get happy? And fairly soon if she didn't mind, he didn't have all the time in the world, not if she wasn't really unwell. Not sick enough to keep locked up.

And so Sofia got happy. Simple as that. Or rather she made damn sure no one else ever noticed again. It was years later that she realised the man had merely been doing his job when he'd terrified her. The aim was to get her better, the means were up to him. He was the professional. His offer was a form of shock therapy really. Be happy or we're locking you away in here. The problem was, it didn't work. Sofia made sure it looked like he'd been successful, but his shock tactics just drove the dark blue deeper in. No doubt he saved the NHS a fair bit though. There were small instances of nearly there, nearly gone, in the year or so to follow. But nothing quite as bad as the first, nothing that wasn't quickly alleviated by moving on as soon as possible, putting it far behind her.

Eventually, Sofia realised that she had also grown too big for house and garden, home and family. Her mother's silver dolphin wind chimes caught on her braced back teeth and sent irritable shock waves rippling down her long spine, while her father's loving hold hugged the breath from her chest. Only child of a single longing, their conditioned love was too heavy a blanket for Sofia to grow under. To the shock of the hot-house parents, the blessing-baby mutated into rancid runaway girl and, wide hips swinging wider, Sofia gyrated her way across southern Europe, America, South East Asia. Pock-marked post cards eventually made it home. Pinned carefully to the kitchen wall, they charted her global migration from West to East. Tall and pale girl to the squat Mediterranean men, finishing taller still, though deeply tanned now, for the shorter Oriental. Not accidental. Her non-specific desire to have and do it all, coupled with an abundance of youthful arrogance, meant that Sofia spent her travelling years consumed solely with the simple wish to dance, no consummation, at five pounds an hour less than the others. A troupe of twelve dancing princesses and Sofia the only virgin among them. Still pure at sixteen, virgo intacta at seventeen. Her choice. Not virgin at eighteen. Her choice again and well chosen. The journey was all, the magnificence of moment.

Five years later Sofia came home. New York had been fast but cold, Berlin decadent in a declining decade, and in Sydney, where the sun never set, she had eventually developed migraines from the constant requirement to laugh aloud, squinting into bright light, no ozone filter for the un/lucky country. She came home, reverted to youth in her parent's house, tried to fit back into the pretty little bedroom with the pretty little bed and the peeling pop star posters, soft boy faces fading into middle-aged men on the walls. Tried, tried again, tried once more, and realised success wasn't necessarily the only ambition. After a month at home it was obvious she'd already learned what most tribes take generations to understand – that happy families are happier still by airmail.

She ran away to the East again, tried London. Prettier this time, cleaner, and somehow warmer on the streets than it had been in her first excursion ten years ago. Sofia was fully adult – the city now had wide streets of opportunity replacing the fearful alleys of her extreme youth. It was worth looking into. It was worth getting into. By the time she finally settled in London as an adult, Sofia thought that maybe she'd left her unhappiness somewhere, the threat of lunacy dropped by accident in some foreign street, not needed, not even noticed missing until months later. At fifteen she had realised teenage body-trauma was common. And ordinary. And while she had little control over the demands her chosen profession made on her body, she did have a degree of power over which part of her life was most affected by those demands. Sofia couldn't quite rid herself of the pain and paranoia, but she could take the semi-anorexia she saw all around her, and turn it into something slightly more special when it manifested in herself. Teenage girls traditionally starve themselves to be lovely and love to shop. Sofia decided to swap. Temporary insanity mutated until it only surfaced as shopping-terror, an uneasy trade-off for an easier life.

There was no one traumatic incident that started it. No dog bite in the butchers' or department store flasher that allowed the impossibility to seep in. She simply never much liked shopping as a child, failed to grow into the regulation Miss Selfridge teenager and then, as an almost adult, Sofia eventually realised she had choice. She chose to avoid the mirrored halls of conspicuous consumption, and instead allowed herself to consume inconspicuously. Chew and swallow one mouthful, chew and spit the other. Retail therapy for the shopping bulimic, and a safe place to store her terror. Like the body-abuse before it, Sofia's shopping-phobia became a part of her life.

Simply to get a newspaper, Sofia would lean against the opposite wall for half an hour until she saw that the newsagent's was completely empty, then rush in to buy her newspaper, pint of milk, packet of overpriced digestives. She would have the exact money ready, hand it over in one, and leave the fluorescent-lit emporium as quickly as possible. Her process was the same in the corner shop and the dusty chemist that doubled as a Post Office. Sofia bought stamps from the newsagent, sent single-page letters first class and did not bother with airmail. Her foreign-land friends thought they were valued especially highly because Sofia graced them with telephone calls instead of postcards – they didn't understand that the call cost her far less than ten minutes among the old ladies littering the minefield between the pension book grille and the corn plaster posters, bristling with single-purchase shopping bags and dangerous eye contact.

Supermarkets were more bearable, though only under

controlled conditions. Sofia spent her working nights warm-ing up slabs of frozen meat, she did not choose to do so at eleven thirty in the morning as well. She shopped as early as possible, while the teenage checkout girls still had the crusted sleep of radiant youth stuck to their morning eyes, before the stench of customer-enticing hot yeast had a chance to permeate the toilet-roll shelves and the aisles turned rancid with fractious mothers and their child-heavy trolleys. Sofia shopped while other people were showering for work and the wide aisles were clear for grand jetés over stacked barbecue charcoal, an unwilling pas de deux with the store detective. Though she only danced in her head, toes pointed inside her more sensible shoes. When absolutely forced to visit the supermarket, she would walk in, grab two baskets, one for each arm – good for the biceps and deltoids, saving her five minutes of exercise time – fill them to overflowing and then make for the first free checkout. Sofia did not have a loyalty card, the promiscuity of her purchases was determined solely by need. And which bus route on what day got her fastest to whichever shopping hall. Sofia was a supermarket slut.

She did not frequent sales. She would not fight to buy. The young women lolling behind counters, ignoring her for not being nineteen, would flip a switch in Sofia's gut the minute she walked into a clothes shop. Her itchy fingers begging to slap the impolite sneer on their slept-in-make-up faces. But Sofia stilled her hands, strode through racks and found four things that might just do. She would try them on, two were fine, perfect fit, the others not quite right. A shade off perhaps. This was intentional. Sofia would walk out from the changing room and into the narrow body of the shop, plate glass window reflecting sheer audacity, wearing only knickers and bra. Maybe. Confronting body awareness and shopping phobia in one. And then the young girls formed a queue of their own to cater to the magnified beauty, refracted at every angle in the communal changing room, archaic robing room. Sofia was always happier semi-naked than fully clothed. Another woman might come into the changing room, and in the light of Sofia's beauty, she too would find her reflection more pleasing, her legs longer, waist narrower, hips finer. Perhaps it only happened because the serving girls were smiling approval. Soon though, Sofia would need to leave the shop, cramming smaller plastic bags into her large canvas one, the four or five purchases that would do her for another three months. Though clothes shopping was the least disturbing, the transaction wore her out all the same. Not strictly the exchange of money, but that of energy and time. Sofia conserved the best of her energy for the dance. Any dance.

A few months before she met James the unhappiness she thought she'd traded in hit her again. Another boyfriend, another job, another home, all apparently going well, but the bastard blue wriggled out from an open pore and spread its malignant weave across her face. This time though, she knew what to do. Or thought she did. Carefully as slicing at the flesh, she left the boyfriend and home and temp job in one swift, hygienic movement. Ran to the other side of London and holed up in a tiny bedsit. Took to her bed and blade. Kept back a hidden hope of the dance, blood reserved for only the worst moments, worst lack of connection between body and soul, the cutting careful and measured.

When help eventually came it was from the nice lady downstairs, on her way to work. To the white-fronted Georgian over the road where she had a nice office and a view of the green park and a list of unhappy people that visited her every day. Beth took Sofia on. First as part of a research project, then as her client. There were slow days and progressive weeks, some drugs, other therapies, but also many more words. Then some playing and a little laughing and the eventual retrieval of friends and lost telephone numbers. There was a reworking of old pain and a lot of Vitamin E cream for newer scars. Finally there was clarity and hope and, Sofia hoped, the heavy blue was folded up and put safely away. Not completely useless, possibly needed one day in the future, but never again without invitation.

Once she was no longer a client, Beth took Sofia on as a friend. Sofia in turn promoted Beth to best friend and discovered that everyone has their own horrors. Even the saviours. Especially the saviours. The two women of disparate age worked hard at playing harder and had an equality of secrets within six months. For over four years now they had been up and down and best buddies and pissed sisters and lots of Sofia laughing and much more of Beth crying, and Sofia had almost forgotten how they'd first met.

Until the beautiful man turned up behind her eyes, asking impossible questions and promising definite miracles. Then she was shocked and confused, this was not her blue blanket depression, this was still less sensible and the obvious diagnosis – simple shopping agoraphobia promoted again to adult lunacy – was horrifying to her. Which was, of course, assuming Sofia was merely exhibiting new signs of an optional lunacy. Because terrified though she was of being a nutter, it was at least something she knew a little of. If she wasn't crazy, though, then the man was real. In that case, what he'd told her was actually going to happen. Which was far more frightening.

Four

Sofia and James had been sharing a home for almost four years when she discovered her career forte. They met in the third year that she was living in London. The first year she spent co-ordinating Tube colours with destinations, learning City from West End, and discovering which side of the water appealed most. In the second she peopled her London with new friends who would become long-term, and newer lovers who stayed short-term. Then there was James. They found each other at a party where neither of them knew anyone else or were especially fond of the hosts. Polite party, friends of friends, and the right thing to do to turn up. Where they also felt no need to stay longer than a respectable ninety-five minutes. Time enough to down a pint or two of wine, discuss the Met's latest fuck-up and England's most recent football failure. Nothing wrong with any of the other people in the crowded flat, but still not enough of a draw to make either of them stay when there were American sitcoms to watch, and a mutual hint of could-be desire, might-be sex. If they headed for the Tube at the same time, if they chose to go in the right direction, get off at the same stop. By fortunate coincidence Sofia was sub-letting a gloomy attic in Finsbury Park and James was house-sitting his brother's slightly less dank flat near Seven Sisters. They went back to James's brother's place on the

Saturday night, moved their chafed and hungry bodies to Sofia's bedsit late Sunday afternoon. On Monday night they returned from their full-time passing-time jobs – he as a bartender in a private club and she temping for a tiny film company in Soho – and began to look for a home of their own.

The relationship went from strangers to full-on lovers immediately – irritating all of James's old friends and Sofia's friendly acquaintances. James had never lasted longer than three months in a relationship before now, how could he possibly expect to actually live with this woman he'd only just met? Sofia never stayed in one place long enough to make anything work, he'd soon discover she wasn't as sane as she made out. Nineteen disconnected people who vowed and declared that anything so hastily formed and obviously based on pure lust couldn't possibly last. The odds were twenty to one against them making it to six months coupled – James's brother lost forty-five quid. To Sofia.

The newly crowned lovebirds proceeded to conduct an uncompromising, highly charged, extremely sexual affair for three delicious years. Until one evening, in the middle of yet another fight, over yet another imagined slight, just as she raised her fist to smack James in the face one last time, Sofia finally took a good look at herself – in the long hall-mirror, half-price from James's brother's second-hand shop – and burst out laughing.

'What the fuck's so funny?'

James was not amused.

'Nothing.'

Less amusing still.

Sofia shook her head, dropped her poised hand, 'No. This. Us. We are. We're funny.'

James stared at her, didn't speak, wasn't happy.

Sofia continued, 'This is fucking ludicrous. Us. And it's

brilliant. And it's very, very stupid.' She paused for breath, 'We should stop it. Now. Tonight.'

Seven hours, three fucks, and a lot of tears later – all his own – James finally agreed. Without Sofia ever having to explain her real fear. That James was too close. That being with him was too good and therefore also too bad. That the brilliance of the good days could never make up for the pain of the bad, and bad day depression was something she'd trained herself to do without. Sofia didn't want to run away this time, so she had to send James away instead. But not too far, he was also her best friend. Which left them with the little matter of a shared bed and a shared home for two people who no longer intended to share their bodies. Except in the middle of the night, as a reflex reaction, by accident. Or when pissed. Or when desperate. Or just simply horny. Or bored. Two months after breaking up and the morning after another accidental fuck, the move out became imperative. But neither of them wanted to go too far, both loved the location, and each one insisted the other should be the one to relocate. Then the bloke upstairs announced he was buying a house in Edinburgh and would be gone by the end of the month.

They spoke to the landlord. James expressed his fervent belief that as he and Sofia had been such fantastic tenants of the downstairs flat, they should be allowed to take on the slightly more spacious flat upstairs for only half the current rent. Sofia offered her own reasoning that of course the landlord could easily let out the upstairs flat, it was a lovely place. They all knew that. But what if the new tenant was someone with whom neither she nor James could bear sharing a communal entrance area, five sickly spider plants and twenty more healthy spiders? Then both she and James would have to move out and the landlord would lose their money – which was more than the upstairs rent anyway. It wasn't exactly an argument designed to impress the bank manager. It wasn't much of an argument at all, but given that most of their energies were fully expended in maintaining the amicability of their breakup – and trying to remember not to have sex – neither Sofia nor James had much inspiration left over to create the perfect case. Unfortunately their lacklustre attempt didn't impress the landlord a great deal either.

James downed a double espresso and tried another tack. Slightly less subtle. He threatened to speak to a selection of relevant authorities. On the one hand there were the drains he and Sofia had been forced to fix themselves after the landlord failed to do so five times. On the other, there was the little matter of the landlord's falsified returns to the Council – more tenants, more rooms and more potential income than he'd admitted to. Then, placing the boot firmly on the other foot, and far more to the blackmailing point, he offered to give up the landlord's real surname so his ex-wife could trace him for maintenance payments. None of it very nice, but the last point proved extremely effective. Though James did realise he would now have to stay in that house for the rest of his life – friendly landlord references detailing his perfect record of ideal tenancy were unlikely to be forthcoming in future.

Sofia and James took on both flats, for just two-thirds of the rent the previous tenant had been paying. Not quite as cheap as they'd hoped but certainly benefiting them more than the landlord. Sofia moved upstairs to take advantage of the longer sunsets, the stripped floorboards, and the far better view of the bus garage, and James spread his bird skull collection over what had been Sofia's exercise area in the downstairs box room. Then, in a moment of smelly-drain-induced pique, James called the relevant snoopers about their landlord anyway, and the ex-wife demanded two years' worth of back payments. Two months later, tied in by a sitting-tenant clause but no less furious,

Sofia and James's landlord put up their combined rents by two hundred and fifty pounds a month.

In the time they'd been together, Sofia and James's semi-temp jobs had turned out to be permanent, but offered neither of them the financial or personal compensations that came with chosen careers. The rent increase was dangerously scary. James sold the saxophone he'd bought four years earlier and had never used other than the one time he toiled for six hours to learn the first four bars of 'Summertime'. That and a building society-to-bank windfall just covered their excess rent for a couple of months. Losing the saxophone also left a storage gap in his bedroom, rapidly filled by a forty-quid, three-quarter-size guitar. James had no musical leanings at all, but he appreciated the look of possibility.

Sofia and James continued as money-worried mates and occasional lovers, enjoying the semi-illicit pleasure of fucking a partner who didn't also part-own the bed. Particularly enhanced when, as in James's case, Sofia had taken her orthopaedic mattress upstairs and left James with the guest futon. When they weren't shagging on the stairs, they were always in Sofia's bed. At least James knew he'd get a good night's sleep there. Eventually. Within six months, though, they had almost retrained themselves and were left with a financially desperate friendship. A companionable association based on the sex, formed from the warm embers of a tired relationship, grounded in matching newspaper, TV and movie tastes. Very nearly the perfect neighbours. With major money worries.

As the idea of finding cheaper accommodation appealed to both of them only slightly more than moving back home to their respective families, a new job had to be found. And it was. Surprisingly easily. Unfortunately, James didn't approve of Sofia's career change. Didn't like the job at all. Hated it when Sofia came bouncing home to tell him about the great new vocation that was going to take care of all her money worries and half of his as well if he wanted. And she knew he wanted.

No she didn't.

'You're going to be a stripper?'

'Lap dancer.'

'Stripper.'

'Dancer. At tables, on laps, to blokes. The money's better.'

'Post-feminist stripper. The politics are worse.'

Sofia winced, waiting for the onslaught of his straight-boy feminist lecture. It wasn't to be. She got middle-class Marxism instead.

'The owner of the club is a man. The workers are all women.'

'Except the cleaners. They're men. I met them this morning.'

James ignored her, clearly the cleaners weren't an integral component of his analysis. He continued, pressing home his point with a raised beer bottle. 'The body-workers are women. So these strippers—'

'Dancers.'

'Lap dancers – are still being exploited by the owner. They do the work, he makes the money – if it's not an issue for modern feminism, it certainly has class action implications.'

James's father didn't lecture part-time in early Socialist theory for nothing. Sofia pointed out that the women did own the means of production – their bodies. They were merely leasing them to the proprietor.

James wasn't buying it. 'In giving over control of their own bodies, even in three minute lots, they are relinquishing any gains that female workers have made in the past hundred years. The boss is still a fat, white, middle-aged bloke, right?'

'Wrong. The boss is an early thirties, firm-fleshed, North London Sikh bloke.'

James opened another bottle, passed it to Sofia, and went on – long suffering, long winded. 'Whatever. The consumers are men with the spare cash to spend on luxury goods. The women don't have that kind of spare cash in the first place and until the workers have money to spend on a similar amount of consumer unnecessaries—'

'So my body is a consumer unnecessary now?'

'It is here. Anyway, until then, the situation will continue to be a classic case of worker exploitation.'

The argument was pointless. Sofia had spent three years attending James's private lectures. She didn't even really disagree with him. Though she doubted the revolution was likely to be kick-started from the fire of James's half-pissed indignation. But she did need the money. They both needed the money. James had just about spent all of his windfall cash, this was something she could do. Could do well. This was what she'd been trained to do. Albeit usually with slightly more clothes. She'd kept going to classes over the years. She still thought of herself as a dancer. Wanted to believe she could be a dancer.

Sofia and James drank on through the night and before she made the slow ascent to her own flat, Sofia wondered if perhaps just the tiniest bit of James's rage at her infidelity to the political cause might really have had more to do with his desire to keep her to himself. A knight in shining armour waving a crusading flag, who knew he didn't really want the treasure-tower girl, but nor did he fancy sharing her with the mead-swilling yokels in the tavern. Just a little something in his semi-drunken demeanour gave away his real motive. Like the way he leaned into her when she kissed him goodnight and his tongue lunged halfway down her throat.

That and James's slurred, 'Yeah, whatever, I mean, go for it, it's your body, right?'

'Thanks James.'

'Now look Sof, are you sure you don't fancy a shag?'

Sofia became a lap dancer, table dancer, silver pole prancer. Her free flesh on don't touch offer, trading nights in back-lit beatification. Sofia worked at her charms. But not all that much. In her late teens, when she had finally allowed her growing self to reject the harsh mask of balletic androgyne and reluctantly eased back into actual woman, Sofia realised she had been uniquely blessed. She had simply been unable to see her real talents through all those years staring in the teenage mirror. Not now though. She was delicious, still life still living in smooth, sweet, unattainable flesh. Sofia's presence was magnified by the desire of her patrons and then, their twenty pound patronage bestowed, she would take the swift kiss of the fresh cash and remove herself, back to the beginning, start all over again for another punter. Sofia danced through the night in individual moments of truth and at times she felt she knew almost half of reality, very nearly glimpsed enlightenment in moments of glitter-ball sweat. In starting to dance again she made herself a new life and grew happy playing in it. Then, at nearly dawn, she would go home again, shot through with heavy sleep until the morning. James didn't like it much, Sofia liked it a lot, and things went on perfectly well. Until the morning when she was woken unexpectedly by the man whose feet barely swept the surface of her floor.

Five

It was well after midday when Sofia surfaced from a deep and sweaty sleep. Woken by a combination of her phone ringing – her muddled mind eventually understood it had been ringing for the past fifteen minutes – and a pair of heavy fists pounding on the door to her flat. She grabbed the hand-held phone as she stumbled towards the insistent knocking.

'Yeah? What? Who? What?'

It was James. James shouting at her on the phone and James standing at her door when she finally persuaded her pins-and-needles fingers to turn the key in the lock.

'Are you all right?'

'What?'

'Are you OK? I've called three times and you didn't answer, and your key was in the door. You never leave your key in the door. I couldn't get in. I was worried.'

Half speaking to her face, half on the phone, James finally realised what he was doing and turned off the mobile in his left hand.

'Christ babe, you look like shit. Are you sick?'

'No. Not sick. Knackered. Come in.' Sofia held the door open for James, 'I'm going for a pee, make coffee.'

By the time Sofia had put on an old T-shirt and brushed her teeth, James had made something of a dent in the pile of dishes covering her kitchen work surfaces and created enough space to get out Sofia's old percolator and start grinding the dark roast beans.

'No wonder you and I didn't work out, look at the bloody mess in here.'

'James, we can't all be anally retentive kitchen queens.'

'I am not a poof.'

'Kitchen queens aren't poofs darling, they're merely tedious.'

James threw a filthy tea-towel at her head, 'And I don't know why you can't just use a cafetière like the rest of the world.'

'I'm not like the rest of the world, it's why you love me.'

'Loved you. Past tense. And you're wrong, your great body's why I loved you, your coffee-drinking pretensions don't come anywhere close to true affection. Anyway, you still haven't told me why the door was locked.'

'My door's always locked at night. And in the daytime come to think of it. This is London.' She shook her head, 'No. Fuck that, this is Britain. Europe. The World. Everyone locks their doors. I'd be a nutter if I didn't.'

'Yes, but normally you take the key out of the lock. So I can get in.'

'Yeah, well, perhaps those days of you sneaking into my bed in the middle of the night are over.'

'They've been officially over for months.'

'Mmm, I heard that one too. No, surprising as it may seem, this isn't about you. I had a bad dream. Woke up in the middle of the night completely freaked. I thought someone was in the flat.'

'We only went to bed in the middle of the night.'

'And I woke up soon after.'

'Man or woman?'

'Man.'

'Attractive?'

'Very. Gorgeous. Really classically beautiful. Tall, dark, just the way I like them.'

James flicked his dark curls away from his face and passed her a small cup of strong coffee. 'I thank you.'

Sofia sat back ignoring his smile, took a sip of the scalding liquid, 'Much darker than you, white boy. He was beautiful. And he was just sitting on the end of my bed. Talking bollocks.'

'Maybe it was me, sleep walking.'

'The talking bollocks part, very likely. The extremely attractive bit? I don't think so.'

James stood up to pour himself more coffee, 'How quickly they forget. And to think I was once your best ever.'

Sofia held out her cup for a drop of the milk James had heated, 'I was being polite.'

'You were being driven wild in an orgasmic frenzy of unadulterated delight.'

Sofia nodded, conceding. 'More or less. Anyway, after I finally chased him out of my dream I got up, checked everything, relocked the door and went back to sleep. By then it was about four in the morning though, which must be why I slept through your calls. I didn't hear a thing.'

'I think it's possible that the reason you didn't hear anything this morning is because you were well pissed last night—'

'So were you!'

'Yes. And you were completely off your face by the time you came upstairs—'

'You were too!'

'That's right, only I rose from the fetid pit of my bed at nine. I've been for a three mile run and a forty length swim and I feel fantastic, whereas you're still not especially sober even now. Which is quite possibly why your left breast is hanging so enticingly out of your T-shirt and you haven't even noticed.'

Sofia looked down at the torn scrap she'd thrown on. James was right. She shook her head at his mock leer and passed her empty cup for him to refill, 'Thanks for telling me James. Because really, as I'm sure you can imagine, I just so fucking care.'

James left an hour later, having deposited Sofia in a hot bath with rose and lavender oils, and left a rack of clean dishes draining by the kitchen sink. Sofia lay back in her bath and took in the relaxing clatter and hum of someone else cleaning her flat while listening to the lunch-time news. James was right, in many ways they should have been perfect for each other. Best buddies, easy playmates, and James was also the perfect homemaker – something she was never going to be. But they just didn't work. He had been her best ever sex when they first started. And she knew for a fact that she was his. But that was the problem. In many ways, though they had started their relationship and friendship at the same time, they were much more like best friends who had become great lovers. Too-good lovers. And bound to end in tears because of it. It was safer this way. Rather less chance that she'd stab him in a fit of fury induced by the fact that as both best lover and best friend, he knew, far more accurately than anyone else ever had, where precisely to turn the knife. How to get in and how to hurt badly. And if Sofia acknowledged that James knew how to hurt her, she further recognised that she understood exceptionally well how to damage him. And she'd rather not be more of a bitch than was absolutely necessary. She'd rather not be seen to be more of a mad bitch than was absolutely necessary. For now she'd settle for singledom. The shagging wasn't so good, but the hold on sanity was far more successful. She wrenched herself from the yielding warmth and sluiced soap and bath scum from her body with a swift, bitterly cold shower. Relinquishing the brilliant sex was definitely a major loss. But had they kept going as a couple, Sofia knew that one day she would have had to give up James entirely. And that would have been one sacrifice too far. At least this way he was still her friend.

After her bath, Sofia dressed, went down the road to the local shops, slowly and deliberately bought a few essential provisions – more full fat milk, more extra-strong coffee, a couple of bottles of wine to leave in her fridge for later. For whenever. For every time. Abstinence of any sort was not one of Sofia's chief attributes, and while James occasionally took a week or so off drinking – just to prove he could, just to give his liver a rest – the idea of denying herself anything had not yet become appealing. Sofia looked forward to the day when she might start to parent herself a little more wisely – looked forward to it and hoped it was a long time coming. And James was always so self-satisfied in his abstinence anyway. Besides that, while her job was art of a sort and the money was great and it was even fairly enjoyable most of the time – the whole lap dancing thing was also a damn sight more bearable when she was just a little pissed. Or even just a lot pissed. And a large glass of wine before she set out for the evening was almost routine. Like the exercise sequence she now launched herself into.

For ten years Sofia had performed exactly the same routine of twelve different exercises every single day of her life – no matter how hungover, exhausted, or otherwise occupied she was. Even fresh love couldn't stop her. A combination of the ballet of her youth and a few other tricks she'd learnt as she'd gone along – several of them from supposed mystics in India and South East Asia – the entire routine took her just eighteen minutes from start to finish. And kept Sofia gorgeous. That and the basic genetics. Not for her James's thrice-weekly run and every second day swim, nor the huge variety of endlessly changing classes that half the girls at her work seemed to go to, and certainly not ten hours a week breathing in the humid exhalations of other people in an overpriced, under-regulated gym. This routine was the shortest, least sweaty, and most powerful she could get it. It was also immensely portable and had been performed at home, in the park, in small alleyways and in waiting rooms and airport lounges across the world. And twice at work. Virtually naked. When the punters were especially weird.

When she'd finished, Sofia went into her bedroom, pulled back the curtains, opened the windows to let in the warm, mid-afternoon breeze. She stood in front of the full-length mirror. Ever since James had woken her three hours earlier, Sofia had tried to put the strange man out of her mind. But now, in the bedroom, looking at the crumpled duvet where he'd been sitting, she could ignore it no longer. She didn't really think her experience had been a bad dream. She did believe the man had been sitting on the end of her bed. She did think it had happened.

She studied her body in the mirror. She looked exactly the same as this time yesterday. The pale blue eyes were perhaps darker ringed than usual, but that wasn't anything out of the ordinary, not after a late night anyway, and nothing an extra smudge of make-up wouldn't deal with later in the evening. Her cropped black hair could probably do with a cut. She kept it as short as possible, partly to enhance the gamine features, the excessively high cheekbones, partly to make it easier to change the colour whenever she felt like it. Quite often once a fortnight. Spring would be easing into full bloom this month. Perhaps she should think about blonde. A bright daffodil-blonde. Though something as far from Marilyn as possible – blondes might have more fun, but not in her workplace. There they had a damn sight more to do and it always involved a tedious time catering to older blokes who still held on to their teenage Mansfield/Monroe fantasies, and really, the extra cash at the end of the night simply wasn't worth their attentions. Not in Sofia's terms anyway.

Full breasts beneath broad shoulders – all the better to hold them up, as the M&S measuring lady assured her at fourteen. There was no assurance to be had at fourteen. All Sofia knew was that her flesh and bones wouldn't stop growing, that her selfish body was defying her will. Smooth waist, gentle curve of small belly, silver setting holding a dark blue sapphire in the piercing. Sofia stood sideways to the mirror. Her breasts and stomach looked exactly the same, right breast just that tiny touch larger than the left, ever so slight curve of flesh slung between wide and prominent hip bones. The narrow stretch of pubic hair permitted, the rest of her body depilated to within an inch of her job. Then long, strong legs, wide feet, tall girl's feet, straight toes finally smooth after years of growing back new skin from the callused ballet claws. Sofia looked herself up and down, and again. It was her in the mirror, she was the same, nothing had changed, the man wasn't real, she hadn't been lying to James, it was just a bad dream, no one could have entered the flat last night, nothing was going on.

She turned from the mirror, rubbed her eyes and he was there. Where her fingertips rubbed light into the darkness behind her eyelids. She jumped back, startled, wide awake, moved her hands, opened her eyes. The man was sitting on the edge of her bed again.

'Sorry, didn't mean to frighten you. I just thought I ought to check up on you, make sure you were OK.'

Sofia looked at him, looked back into the mirror, saw him staring at her reflection. Looked at the impossible dimensions of the narrow window-frame and the size of the man. She saw that her bedroom door was still closed, had not moved since she'd come into the room. She looked at the man who was obviously waiting for her reply, polite conversation dictated she answer him. He smiled that half smile, expectant, and she made her decision. She answered him as she walked out of the room, closing the door firmly behind her.

'You are not real. I cannot talk to you. You are so very not real.' Sofia went straight into the sitting room and picked up the phone. She left a message for Beth.

'Babe, it's Sofia. Listen . . . I know it's been a while since we talked about anything other than your sex life and my lack of it, and I don't know how you'd feel about this . . . but I think I need help. Something's happened. Can I see you tomorrow? I'll come over to yours at eleven unless I hear otherwise. I'm working tonight, leave me a message if there's a problem and we'll arrange another time. But soon. Please?'

Sofia had a shower, got dressed in the bathroom, locked the bedroom window, downed a quick glass of wine, grabbed her make-up, threw keys and girl accoutrements into her bag and left the flat, double locking it behind her, every light blazing for her late-night return. The man was still sitting on her bed when she left. He had not moved. He was smiling still. But only just.

Six

Sofia got ready to meet Beth and then made one more phone-call. Braver still than the last. If dealing with shop chicks and shelf stackers was unpleasant, buying drugs was a way of confronting her shopping phobia head-on. Sofia did not have a coke habit, she had a coke hobby. Certainly her intake was not vast. She and James bought a gram between them – sometimes once a week, or once a fortnight, once a month, or not at all. They shared their purchase with others often. Thin lines after dinner on Sofia's nights off, more interesting than a cheese course and – taken at that point in the evening – less likely to spoil the perfectly cooked meal that James had slaved over for half a day. However, the anti-inhibitor still had to be obtained. In person. James mostly did the off-licence run, Sofia found the drugs. It was she who made the phone-call, went through the ritual requests of hello and how are you, and the wife, and the kids? When the only relevant question was what time, how much, and today or tomorrow? Johnnie batted back her questions with his stock answers of 'keeping going' and 'keeping on', finally they would arrange to meet in half an hour's time. Sofia walked from one end of the street, Johnnie arrived from the other, high noon transaction at four thirty-five. He kissed her cheek, she pressed cash into his pocketed palm, he passed over the wrap in an impossible-to-detect sleight of underhand. Unlike most people it wasn't the subterfuge that she found difficult nor the class-A paranoia of a street meeting. In some ways her usual fears were lessened. On the other hand though, this was shopping on an intimate and personal basis. Pure shopping. Purer phobia.

Every few months Sofia would wake from another particularly excessive night, synapses beating a dehydrated tattoo on the inside of her thin-papered skull. The desire to give up was as fleeting as the time it took her to drink a two-litre bottle of water and cold shower herself back into daylight. Sofia's alcohol-induced crises were occasional and quickly dealt with. Her drug-induced horrors, on the other hand, happened only when utterly sober, before any indulgence had taken place. She kept doing it though, hoping that eventually she might get better at it. Sofia would never be a shopaholic, but maybe she could find a way to hate it less. The intimate nature of the meetings with Johnnie should have been what made this buying transaction a good one to begin working on her phobia. It was a novel form of therapy – open with the hard drugs and work up to the post office queue.

Sofia left her flat for Beth's and went to meet Johnnie on the way. She purchased the coke and made her way to the Tube, tried to bury her multiplying fears in the bland faces of the other tunnel travellers, to stare blithely into empty space as they did, but her racing brain was having none of it. Playing flash-cut sequences of last night's conversation with the intruder one after the other until she was left with the stark choice, either it had been real, or she was really mad. Neither option offered much hope. The arrival of a strange man on the end of her bed in the middle of the night had brought all her old terrors flooding back. Having once seen herself as crazy, there would never be anything as terrifying as the thought that it might be coming back. That place of not.

Half an hour later, Beth opened the door and smiled up at Sofia, reached her arms out to offer a hug and almost at once bent over double, clutching both hands to her stomach, 'Oh, shit, bloody hell! Stop it you little fucker!'

Sofia bent down to her friend, 'What? Are you OK?'

Beth shook her head, groaned, then steadied herself. A moment later she grabbed Sofia's arm to pull herself up, 'He's been beating me up all week, but that was one hell of a punch, worst he's managed yet. Little bugger.'

'How do you know it's him?'

''Cos he's at the front, taking all the credit. She's at the back, typical bloody girl. Sitting on her arse. Sitting on my bladder.'

The diminutive Greek Australian turned her heavily pregnant frame in the door and waddled back down the hallway, shouting behind her with a voice astonishingly loud in so small a frame – now doubled widthways by the advanced state of her pregnancy, 'I tell you babe, if I'd have known it was going to be this much bloody trouble and this damn exhausting, there's no way I'd have gone through all that shit in the first place, that's for bloody sure.'

Sofia thought momentarily about maybe just going away again, this was obviously not an ideal time to be visiting, but another high-pitched yell from Beth convinced her otherwise. Perhaps listening to someone else's far more immediate troubles was the very thing she needed. She closed the front door quietly behind her and followed Beth into the kitchen, which, like the hallway, was in an upturned state of semi-renovation.

Beth's husband was a builder and decorator and, with the babies due in less than eight weeks, he was trying to make everything perfect. In the evenings and weekends when he wasn't working on his 'proper' job. Unfortunately his idea of perfect and Beth's vision of the same were diametrically opposed – or rather they had become so since the pregnancy, when she discovered she seemed to have changed her mind on pretty much everything – and work was seriously stalled while they fought furiously over colour charts and tile books. The babies, meanwhile, grew on in their own home, the walls of which were taking a beating as the confined space became increasingly cramped.

For the past seven years Beth and her husband Pete had been trying to conceive. Seven years of painful potential and inevitable disappointment. From the first ectopic pregnancy to the fourth miscarriage after the third IVF cycle. Through counselling of every description and tests both medical and psychological to homeopathic remedies and months of acupuncture and very long weeks of exceedingly strange diets. Until, after another impossible failure, Pete admitted that it was too much and neither he, nor Beth's body, should have to cope with any more. Beth, who'd decided the same herself about a month earlier, but hadn't had the heart to tell Pete, agreed. She consented reluctantly, exhausted and, somewhere in the morass of unhappiness, with a certain degree of unspoken relief as well.

They waited a few months to get used to the idea and then they tried the adoption route. And were told straight out they were too old. No beating about the bush and no need for delicacy of delivery – it was simply policy, nothing to be done. At forty-three Beth was too old to be considered for motherhood. Though of course, as she noted bitterly, Pete could go out and shag any fecund girlie he fancied within the next forty years, and if that resulted in pregnancy, no local authority was going to deny him his progenitive prerogative, whip the child away because he didn't meet the age criteria of perfect fatherhood. And the NHS would probably quite willingly give him prescription Viagra to help his sperm on their merry way. What's more, while Beth was Australian Greek, Pete had an even more mixed progeny – Jamaican, Scots and Jewish. Even if Beth hadn't been considered old, the chances of the PC police finding them what they termed an 'appropriate' child were less than nil. No less unhappy about the state of affairs, Pete – thirteen years younger than his wife – held his pain quiet beside hers and waited until they were able to breathe again.

After two weeks of extreme nastiness toward Pete and several more directed at herself, followed by many months of mourning, Beth eventually woke up one day and decided it was time to get on with it. Let go of the four unborn and try being in the world again. They went to Australia for the first time in eight years, Beth too scared to go home for all that time in case she missed an appointment, missed a cycle, missed a baby. She swam in the healing Pacific and blessed herself with the midnight Southern Cross. Then they drove out into the desert together. And waited. With no alcohol and no grass, it was the most hippy thing either of them had ever done – other than the weeks of homeopathy and acupuncture to try for a baby, they were firm traditionalists in terms of what made them smile. Two days later Pete decided they had communed with nature enough, Beth had finally stopped crying, and it was time to go back. They drove again into Alice, flew to friends with a new baby in Darwin – the first one they'd seen in years that didn't hurt to hold – and then down to Sydney just in time for Mardi Gras. They stayed with gay boy friends and partied for four days solid. While in London they had confined themselves to alcohol and a little grass; only at times when it wouldn't affect the baby potential and those occasions so rare in the past seven years. Now they were in Sydney, the conception race was over, it was finally time to let themselves really go. They traded folic acid for the real thing and ice-cold champagne and rough cheap coke and delicious Oceanic grass topped off with hundred-flavour vodka. And they fucked like it didn't matter and they didn't have to and the timetables were long gone. Fucked like there was no reason other than that they wanted to and no tests to take the next day or a week later, and no depressing period to wait for, terrified of the blood and pain, so much wanting bigger blood and more pain. And they had a fantastic time and fell in love again and very nearly forgot what it was they were running away from in the first place. And when they finally woke up, almost sober, in the burning brilliance of an ozone-thin sun, they fucked some more. And they didn't get pregnant. Which was extremely fortunate, because with all those drugs swimming in their veins, it would have been a bloody terrifying pregnancy.

They came home, calmed down, and got on with their lives. Pete put the money they'd set aside for potential medical and legal costs back into his decorating business and took on two major commissions. Beth finally agreed to a long-offered promotion at work which entailed her taking on another twelve hours a week, along with supervising several other members of staff, and committing herself to at least three conferences a year. They booked a midwinter holiday in Hawaii, knocked down the wall between their bedroom and what they'd hoped for so long would be the baby's room, giving them an open, modern, loft-style upper floor to their Thirties semi. And, just when they started to dream a new state, then they got pregnant. Twins.

Beth was not in any way unhappy with what was now her lot. And neither was Pete. They waited the requisite three months, and one more just to be sure, and then came clean at their jobs, dealt with the fall-out, made provision for new baby assistance where they could, and decided that an open plan space for a family of four was ideal contemporary living and likely to feature in half a dozen Sunday supplements within the next year. It certainly would if Pete could manage to sell the story often enough. It was all fine, even with the arguments over the half-finished hall walls and the still-to-be-tiled kitchen floor, everything was going to work out, they would get the gift that most people believed was theirs simply by virtue of being human after all. In fact it was perfect. Except for the reality of being a first-time mother. At forty-three. With twins. What was now driving Beth crazy was the reality of carrying two other people inside her. And she still had a month to go. She made tea for herself and strong coffee for Sofia, moaned a little more about the ludicrousness of using her body as a home for double the parasites she'd been expecting, complained briefly about money pressures, whined for just a little longer about Pete and then sat down opposite Sofia. She stared at the younger woman expectantly. Raised her eyebrows. Waited to be told the reason for Sofia's visit.

Sofia smiled. Took a deep breath. Then another. She looked around the room, noted the new windows. Looked back at Beth. Opened her mouth to speak and then shut it fast. She shrugged and looked up from her fidgeting, nervous hands, incomprehension scrawled across her face, unable even to begin

Beth's years of intensive training came into play and her caring, therapist, career-self took over, 'So, what's your problem, kiddo? Are you going crazy again or what?'

Seven

Sofia told the story and Beth listened. Then the questioning began.

'He was sitting in your room?'

'On the end of the bed.'

'What time was this?'

'I don't know, about four. All of it.'

'What?'

'It stayed four o'clock the whole time.'

'You were stoned?'

'A little.'

'And still pissed?'

'A bit I suppose.'

'A lot I imagine.'

'Don't let your jealousy make you rude.'

'Can't help it. I was born rude. And I am jealous. So would you be if you were reduced to waddling around like this, refusing every second glass of wine for what feels like a lifetime. What woke you? Was it him sitting down or did he say something?'

'I didn't feel him sitting down . . . and he didn't leave a dent in the duvet when he got up either.'

Beth ignored the physical improbabilities, 'Didn't you scream? Shout for James to come up?'

'He wouldn't have heard. You know he sleeps through

anything and anyway, he was in a worse state than I was.'

'But you didn't make a fuss?'

'Um . . . no.'

'Pick up the phone?'

'No.'

'Hit him? Beat shit out of the marauding intruder? Turn she-wolf when your den was invaded by an evil outsider?'

'No.'

'Good.'

'Why good?'

'Well, any of those actions would have made sense if this man was real. But because part of you already knew he wasn't, you didn't go overboard. You had the appropriate reaction to the situation. Didn't lose it. Ipso facto, not a looney. Having imaginary conversations with non-existent men, but not a complete nutter.'

Sofia thought for a moment and then discounted her friend's theory, 'No, Beth, that's not how it felt. I did think he was real. Maybe that's why I didn't do anything at first.'

'But you've been in difficult situations on other occasions and you've never frozen before.'

'I didn't freeze. I didn't know what it was. What he was.'

Beth nodded, 'Well, that makes sense too. Even though you were shocked, some part of you knew what you were experiencing wasn't actually happening. Not in reality anyway.'

'Because I was already pissed and a bit stoned . . .'

'Probably. And while what was left of your rational brain didn't quite get what was going on, it did at least understand that the guy wasn't really there. Not physically. So on some level you actually knew that you were dreaming.'

Sofia shook her head, 'At the time I thought so too. As much as I thought anything. But then I closed my eyes and he was still there. In my head, behind my eyes. That's what made me sure I was dreaming.'

'Or hallucinating.'

'If that's possible on several pints, a few whiskies and a little grass . . . yeah.'

'Well, it's not impossible. So, if you knew this bloke wasn't real—'

'But then I saw him again today. When I was getting dressed. And I was completely sober this morning.'

'Completely sober, but still a bit shaken up.'

'True.'

'And if you were that pissed you couldn't have been completely sober anyway. Not after five hours sleep.'

'True again.'

Beth sat back, adjusted herself in her seat, closed her eyes to think. Sofia waited, hoping for answers, explanation. Comfort.

Then Beth looked up again, pulled a few loose strands of her long dark hair into the ponytail they'd escaped from, put another couple of cushions behind her back. 'OK. So, starting from the premise that you know he's not real, this man that's just turned up and is sitting on your bed out of nowhere, but you've dreamed or day-dreamed or somehow manufactured him into your room twice now . . . what does that tell you?'

'That I'm a sad bitch desperate for a shag?'

'He's good-looking?'

'Very.'

'Tell me.'

'Tall. Six two or three maybe. Big body, wide. Nice hands. He's mixed race, mixed races really. I don't know what he is, he's got brown-black skin, but almost almond eyes, like Indian maybe, Southern India. Long black hair, really dark brown eyes, perfect eyelashes. Beth, he looks like a composite picture of my ideal bloke.'

'Doesn't he though?'

'What do you mean?'

'Just that you're describing your ideal bloke. The fantasy man you always say you want but never seem to end up with. So you've made him happen.'

'Based on the fact that I'm desperate for a shag?'

'Could be. Did he talk to you?'

Sofia grimaced, 'Ah, yes.'

'What did he want?'

'Oh God Beth, that's what's so fucking weird.'

'What?'

'He told me I was going to have a baby . . .'

'Yeah?'

'He told me I was going to have a baby . . . and it . . . the baby—'

'Spit it out girl!'

'He said the baby would be the next Messiah.'

'Oh. Right.'

Beth smiled, started to laugh, realised Sofia wasn't joking, and removed the grin with some effort.

'See what I mean? Beth, I must be a nutter.'

'And did he have wings, this gorgeous stranger?'

'No.'

'Halo?'

'No.'

'Long white gown?'

Sofia shook her head, 'For fuck's sake Beth, none of that. He was normal . . . ordinary. Except he wasn't. Blue jeans, black T-shirt . . . Oh . . .' She stopped for a moment, '. . . and no shoes.'

'You've only just realised?'

'It didn't seem strange at the time.'

'And he definitely said you were pregnant?'

'No . . . well, yes. But he also said I didn't have to.'

'Have to what?'

'Agree to do it. Be the mother. But that no one had ever turned it down before.'

'As far as we know. I don't imagine any other girls who passed up on the Virgin Mary job were all that keen to broadcast the fact. It's hardly the height of sanity as a reported statement, is it?'

'Beth, he said I was the one. I could choose for myself, but I'd already been chosen.'

'Mmm.'

'What do you mean "mmm"?'

Beth leaned forward, uneasily shifting her weight, 'Look, sad bitch desperate for a shag is certainly possible, but in my clinical opinion I'm afraid I'd have to lean more towards a diagnosis of sad-bitch-desperate for a shag and still more than that, begging for attention. Delusions of grandeur in a big way. I take it back Sofia, you are a nutter.'

'Thanks.'

Beth grinned, 'Alternatively, there's always the possibility that spending time with me has made you realise the extreme joys of motherhood and now your innate desire to procreate has come to the fore. The undeniable primal force, the mothering gene, the inbred nature of the species, has got to you after all.'

Sofia looked at Beth, her swollen stomach, swollen ankles, tired face, 'Ah, no. We don't do inbreeding in my family.' She shook her head, 'Not even the glories of your clearly perfect pregnancy could do that for me, I'm afraid. Motherhood's just not on my agenda Beth. Not right now anyway.'

'Why not?'

'No partner, no room, no time, no job.'

'You've got a job.'

'Not a lot of childcare options in the eight to four a.m. slot.'

Beth smiled, 'Fair enough, what else?'

'What?'

'What else is going on? Obviously this has got something to do with your desire – or not – to mother. What else do you feel about it?'

Sofia shook her head, lifted her hands to her face, 'I don't know. I don't think about it. I'm twenty-eight. I feel like I barely know what I want from my own life, let alone adding another life into that. I guess I've always expected I might do it one day, have a kid, but the older I've got, the further away that day goes. My parents weren't young when they had me, but they were together, they had a good relationship, still do. I suppose I've just always thought it would come with a relationship. I'd have a relationship that worked and then I'd want to have a baby. Probably. Maybe. Eventually.'

Beth sat back, 'So what if you are pregnant?'

'Well that's partly why I'm so freaked – you know, I don't want to think I was seeing things, because if I was, then I'm really a looney. But on the other hand, if I'm not seeing things, if this bloke was real, then maybe what he said was real too. That I am pregnant. And believe me Beth, I don't want to be pregnant.'

Beth shook her head at her younger friend, 'No. I don't suppose you do. Though I have to say – as your ex-therapist and current friend – that if you wait for the perfect relationship to happen, you may never be pregnant. Relationships don't do perfect, babe.' Sofia groaned and Beth continued, 'Still, I think we can confidently assume the pregnancy option is unlikely. We're far more likely to come to the eventual conclusion that you're basically just a nutter after all.'

'Bitch.'

'Yeah. I am. Sorry,' Beth patted her stomach, 'I blame it on these two. They've made me far less tolerant than I used to be. I don't give very good "there, there" therapy at the moment.'

Sofia finished her coffee, 'Bollocks Beth, you were crap at "there-there" therapy before. That's why I was happy to keep paying you for so bloody long. And you're probably right anyway. Frankly, right now, I think I'd rather go with crazy than pregnant.'

Beth stood up, waddled towards the sink, stretching her shoulders back and round, 'It's not all bad. And maybe it wasn't a dream. Maybe you are it. The one. Maybe they're going for someone a little less perfect this time. Fancy a cuppa, star of the sea?'

Sofia looked down at her own, barely-there belly, 'Yeah. Strong, black and throw in a double whisky for good measure.'

Beth turned to fill the battered kettle and thought for a moment, 'Why don't we both go for camomile, eh? Just in case?'

Eight

Sofia left Beth's house feeling slightly calmer. Of course he wasn't real, the man in her bedroom, floating behind her eyes. But that didn't necessarily mean she was seeing things either. There had to be some sort of compromise explanation. There was a time when it had been easier to see herself as slightly crazy. When to some of her friends, it had seemed attractive, even interesting, to be the girl teetering on the edge. Not that Sofia had ever been really insane, properly demented. Just depressed. Easy word, easily used.

Beth had a few theories. About attention seeking and relationship-pining. About baby making, or not making, or refusing to even address the question when it clearly couldn't be ignored for ever, left in the land of someday-my-prince-will-come. Two-point-four children loaded on to the back of his dashing white charger. About fears of heading for thirty with no aims, no plans. About what living in the pocket of your ex-lover did to the potential of ever meeting another. Of ever meeting The One. When part of you still wondered if maybe he had been it and you'd been too scared to admit the truth. About blithely continuing with a career that had no future beyond the next five years, and how Sofia consistently refused to wonder what might come after. How her long-held desire to go where the next whim took her might well have been useful, even ideal, for her twenties, but might not be so easily accomplished in her thirties – biology would show on the inside no matter how impressively Sofia held it at bay on the outside. Theoretical explanations of a real-seeming terror dream, explaining the midnight shock value in Freudian, Jungian and Gestalt terms. Any or all of which could well have been true, were perfectly plausible rationalisations of Sofia's night-fright experience. And none of which was likely to be dealt with any time soon. At least not while she was in running-away mode. Though she recognised that Beth's parting shot was even more likely to be the real reason for her vision – 'And for God's sake girl, stop drinking so bloody much and taking so many drugs. No wonder your brain's talking shit to you – give yourself a break from all that crap. I mean, I know I'm not one to talk, but even a week off wouldn't do you any harm.'

Sofia knew Beth had a point. Maybe it was a problem that she and James were still practically living together, maybe the idea of thinking about some sort of career structure to her life wasn't so stupid. Perhaps she was panicking about getting older and still not really doing anything, not yet having a proper job. Those were all definite possibles. The only definite definite, however, was that Beth was certainly right about the excess of chemical intake. And Sofia had already been thinking of maybe detoxing for a week. A weekend. A day even. Thought of it every morning when she woke with a hangover – and then ignored the concept again by mid-afternoon. She walked down the hill from Beth's house, on past three bus stops planning a month of self-imposed purity. Which she would absolutely do. As soon as she finished the vodka in the freezer. And the half bottle of white in the fridge. And the third of a gram in her credit card holder.

Sofia walked another fast fifty minutes across three A to Z pages, holding off the rising terror of might-be

pregnant/may-be crazy by mapping out the far more inviting possibility of an ordered life. The sun was shining when
she got home, illuminating the dust layers on every surface.
But there was no strange man, sunlit in her bedroom. When
she stretched out on the sofa for an afternoon sleep there
was nothing behind her eyelids but flesh-tinted light. She
gratefully kept her eyes closed and caught up on last night's
sleep. When she woke two hours later, the purity kick was
still in full force. She opened all the windows, dusted and
vacuumed the flat, and worked her way through another
pile of dishes that James hadn't loved her quite enough to
clear. It was true there were times when Sofia wondered if
she'd really done the right thing in breaking up with James,
when she marvelled at how well he knew her. But there
were other times, like this, when the bliss of ordering her
home reminded her of how much better she was in her
own company. How she was a much nicer woman when
she was single. The kitchen perfected, she flung open her
wardrobe doors and threw out a dozen old items of clothing
she hadn't worn for over a year. She tidied her knicker
drawer and made the bed. With crisp, cool sheets. Then she
showered, dressed, and – despite the four schoolchildren
lingering threateningly by the crisps stand – ran into the
corner shop for a two-litre bottle of water, drinking almost
half of it before she'd made the top of her stairs. And then
she did her exercise routine one more time just for the hell
of it. At seven she left her spotless flat to go to work, walking
her perfect and pure body down the street to the bus, with
a cereal ad spring in her step, finishing the water as she
walked. Feeling like Heidi, looking like Tank Girl.

An hour later Sofia walked down the stairs into work.
In forty-five minutes Joseph and Tony would take up
their positions on the door and they'd open the club to
the punters; fast music, soft lighting reflected in glittering
glass and chrome would welcome in the eager early risers.

She was greeted by the two cleaners, one of whom made it perfectly obvious that he'd now have to rewash the bit of floor Sofia had so carelessly stepped on, while the other sang out-of-key Tony Bennett over the whine of his vacuum cleaner. The place smelled of a combination of stale cigarette smoke and new sprayed furniture polish. Underlaid with the unmistakable tang of last night's sweat. Customers' sweat, not dancers'.

She opened the door to the dressing room and her wrinkled nose was assailed by a new force – shampoo, conditioner, deodorant, moisturiser, make-up, perfume – each one different. It was a smell she loved, the scent of Friday night – teenage girls, getting ready, remaking themselves. Other than the pleasure of counting up her tips when she finished work, this was definitely her favourite part of the evening. The intimate choreography of women preparing. An in-the-trenches dressing-room feel that was exactly the same as every other dancing job she'd ever had. Them and us. The opposition of ticket holders and workers uniting a handful of disparate women into a crack fighting force, no drill sergeant necessary. Most of her team were already there – four women on early, another eight to arrive for the post-pub rush, ten more later still when the late-night losers turned up. Staggered shifts keeping the girls fresh and alert, keeping the punters happy according to the boss. Keeping the punters paying, according to the women.

They were getting dressed. Undressed. Dressed up for dressing down. Immaculate fresh-showered bodies, sparkling clean teeth, perfectly manicured hands. Legs, underarms, forearms and pubes depilated to pre-pubescent smooth; disarming little-girl pudenda on woman-bodies so clearly readying themselves for adult work. Four naked women stalked the tiny space, self-caged tigers prowling back and forth from shower to mirror to lockers, perfect flesh rubbing easily against each other, an hour or so that any one of their punters would have offered double to sit and watch, for the women it was an hour of self-centred relief. The time each paid most attention to her own flesh, readying it for display, and yet were also least aware of it. In this time the skin moved merely for itself, not for effect.

In the real world Caroline was a runaway rich girl, hiding in Stoke Newington from Mummy and Daddy, supporting her Spanish musician boyfriend, Mariano – the boyfriend who had provoked the row that resulted in her leaving the family home in St John's Wood just six months ago. First time away from home. She'd sent two postcards since. One to say she was fine, the other to apologise for taking her mother's diamond when she left. She didn't send the ring back though. Sandra was a Danish au pair, supplementing her meagre wages with the dancing work and planning to use the money to run away with her employer's wife. One day. When she got around to telling the PTA-stalwart boss lady that she was in love with her. One day never. But she was saving anyway. Helen was a long-time heroin user, mother of two. The kids lived part-time with their father. She'd left Cardiff to break away and get clean. To become the good mother. Except that in London there were more drugs, more availability. More choice all round. Come to London to get a better job – and find a better habit, fund a better habit. Sofia was older than Caroline by a decade – though Caroline insisted she was twenty-one. Sandra had just turned twenty-two, and while Helen's tiny frame and wide baby-eyes made her look like a sixteen-year-old, she was in fact fast heading for thirty. The women discussed politics and TV and tabloid gossip. They shared each other's make-up and swapped shiny little pots of glitter, stick-on stars. Then they were ready and Danny came in to tell them the doors were about to open. Tuesday night, no doubt a quiet start, but he had a party of City boys lined up for around midnight. Someone's birthday and someone else's big bonus payout. They might well be expecting a late evening. And a busy one eventually. Big payers, big tips, big smiles all round.

The girls walked out into the room, lights dimmed, barely dressed bodies glowing. Sofia saw a couple of their regulars come down the stairs. Sofia saw two hundred quid come down the stairs if she worked it right. She went to the bar and asked for a vodka. Double. Straight. She'd start that detox thing tomorrow. For now, the music and the dance would be all the tonic she needed. That and the cash.

Nine

In the dance.

It is not about the man, though he is paying, his friends are braying, and he sits, fully dressed, tie still in place, just breath-touch inches from her thighs. It is not about the music, though this track was expressly chosen to suit the mood, mind his suit, to flow with her body and around it, covering her semi-nakedness in an armour of pewter sound. Nor is it about the venue, the dark corners hiding sticky stains no amount of cleaning will shift, plywood bars covered in chrome-effect plastic, morning tawdry. There is soft light playing on her skin and an audience and that will do. It was sufficient on childhood holidays to dance on the balcony of a cheap Greek hotel, plenty of illumination from night cars or the daylight swimming-pool reflection. Just making the dance is enough. The rest of it is not even there. Not if she chooses otherwise.

Sofia dances with and for herself. Actually Sofia dances for his cash, but only at the point where she first makes eye contact in order to have him call her over, and after that only in the dying seconds of the final bar. In between, the dance is for Sofia. It just looks like she's a lap dancer. Appearance is all. For the next three minutes forty-one seconds Sofia is white girl playing brown sugar black, sweet sixteen. She'd have chosen 'Wild Horses' herself, a slower beat to incite more anticipation, but Danny knows better than to offer a lengthy selection, too wide a choice is merely confusing, takes too long. As do too wide thighs. And anyway, these men vote for their favourites in recollected singles. This is not a place for them to exhibit traditional male dominance of dedicated music detail. At least not on the bottle after bottle of champagne the girls are encouraging them to buy tonight. There is no recognition of irony as English rose girl dances for London middle men while Surrey boys invoke movie-image New Orleans and hallows eve souls. It doesn't matter though. None of it does. Not in the dance.

The choice of Seventies music is no surprise either. It is the predominant theme of every night. While the resident DJ has everything in his ample stock, there's not a lot of call for the girls to dance to Boyzone. Or Oasis. Millennial Britpop offers only the beat of bump with no grind. Crossing the Atlantic for the real thing doesn't work either. Invariably these roaring drunken forties would choose Madonna if they could, but the more sensible dancers try to direct their punter selection to a safer bet. In reality, Ciccone's sanitised pseudo-slut simply doesn't work, not without lighting, cameras and action. There's no room for careful editing of these three minutes. The man makes his choice because he wants to be JFK and would have her be Marilyn, taking her clothes off just for him, happy birthday tea for two. Instead he finds that the real material girl makes him feel like tired Bill, while at the office door Monica is fighting Hillary for the right to wear the sainted blonde wig. Far better to stick to chick-strip music made by men wishing they were boys. This is the hall of fame for adolescent fantasy, not tabloid revelations, digitally-enhanced. Besides that, these girls know which songs give them the best moves, leading to the best tips. And the moss-encrusted, ageing Stones do it every time.

In the dance. The music is playing. And now, in the four foot square space before his table, it isn't about anything except movement. Not to Sofia anyway. Her mind is somewhere else, the punter can think what he likes, they all can. From the outside it looks as if it might be about the sex thing, the fucking, the playing of it all. Role play, role modelling, rolling through the music. Occasionally, there is a surface glimmer of real Sofia looking out, but her eyes do not connect, slack retinas pull nothing into focus, there is a film before her eyes. Sofia is projecting herself. She shines. On to him, on to the table, against the mirrored wall. Sofia is protecting herself.

One two three four one two three four one two three four. And again and again. The most basic of moves would fit this, it is a slow time two-step, studied polka, easied beat, the interpretation requires no special skill, not when semi-naked. Except that Sofia makes the rhythm bigger than it is. She refashions the ordinary beat into a more complex three-four, fitting four places into every three bars, basic multiplication factoring this back to a magic twelve. It makes it necessary to watch her, the feet tap involuntarily with the music, but she goes over it. This song is probably older than Sofia, but it doesn't matter. None of it does.

In the dance. Left foot moves independently in demi-pointe, perfect turnout. Twists the body round after it, twists her punter's gaze round after it. Other body parts are immediately jealous of the attention, individual limbs pull focus, snap the viewer to their perfection. Right shoulder slow turns from her torso into ether, uncoupled collar bone hangs empty, prominent above naked flesh as the thin blue scarf is discarded, then the arm hugs itself back into ordinary-lovely and right hand flirts with left breast. Sweep-down head turns to look over left shoulder at beckoning finger, smile rises from breast to lips, one step back, belly gently follows. Stomach muscles ripple beneath skin shined sweet, there is a shimmer which might be the falling seventh veil. Sofia wants Salome's head on a plate. Has his anyway, has them all – the punter, his friends, potential customers, even the other dancers – their pin-point eyes a combination of jealousy and adoration. High priestess giving of herself that the unwilling virgins may be educated into a more skilled sacrifice.

In the dance. Move from upper body to lower. Muscled, narrow thighs cross over, open wide, cross again. Rub each other, rub across each other, there is the backbeat, these are her bare feet. This is the place. Insistent music with shush shush of silk skin, hush hush of twenty-pound notes shifting in walleted palms, pocketed hands, rocketing glands. Sofia smiles out from inside her body, high tits and perfect teeth, welcoming hips and great arse, she would wear more clothes on a beach and still she does not feel exposed, not here, not covered by the music, shielded from his ineffectual desire by the cash she takes from him, two twenty-pound notes to line the narrow strip of cloth between bared teeth and barred cunt. Sofia is both in this dance and very far away. Her choice, his choice, her bank balance. His too, but that's not her problem.

The three minutes forty-three seconds are over. Sofia takes his money happily, takes his smile and applause happier. Just twenty quid for the dance, but another forty in eager tip. The third fresh twenty he thrusts at her heaving groin is curled at the edges, it wriggles round her fingers as she walks to the dressing room to stow it in her wallet. She'll watch this man now, mark the next trip he and his two friends make to the men's toilets and stand close when they come back, all three attacked with the sudden onset of a minor cold. Three minutes of her precious time, strategically placed just ten minutes after he's hoovered up another couple of fine lines, should net her a good night's profit. There's nothing quite like the generosity of a drunken cokehead, sixty quid for his evening's gram multiplying itself into double that for Sofia in his good-time adrenalin rush, chasing fun and thinking he might just have caught it. And still her target goes home pleased with it all. Congratulating himself on having this wonderful life, so well rewarded by the big bosses and the powders-that-be that he is able to give everyone a great night out. Including the girl. He certainly gave her his money's worth. And vice versa. So everyone's happy then.

There are other nights, of course, less perfect, less easy. Nights when Sofia can't quite make it to complete safety in the dance. Where there is no total loss of self and she is always just a little more aware than she would like of exactly what she's doing – if not why she's doing it. But even then, her body is gorgeous, the punters are invariably well pleased, Danny has nothing to complain about, and there is the camaraderie of rubbing naked shoulders alongside good girlfriends. And most evenings there is at least one piece of music that takes her far enough into the dance for it to appease her own desire, satisfy her cravings. It is rare for Sofia to miss out completely. And on the odd occasion that she does, there's always the cash. Which is enough to cushion most blows.

Ten

Sofia arrived home at four fifty-five, thankfully extricating herself from a long conversation with the cab driver about relative theology – and the benefits of a Buddhist homelife. Four nights a week she usually managed to get Matt to take her home, but not tonight. Matt was invariably, blessedly, silent. From pick up to drop off he played loop-recorded Jim Croce and said not a single word. Including the point where most drivers would thank her for the tip – Matt pointed at the meter, held his hand out for the cash and nodded his good morning with an accompanying 'mmm-mmm' which Sofia had eventually decoded as a combination of thanks and piss off. She loved him for it. Tonight though, Matt had finished his night's work before she was done. Sofia had covered the last shift as well, doing a double for one of the other girls who'd called in sick. Glad of the extra cash and relieved to get home even later. Just in case. It would be easier to let herself into the flat in nearly daylight.

The morning was starting to think about getting up – or if it wasn't, then the birds in her tree-lined street were seriously confused. Her evening's extra work had been more than usually successful, Sofia was tired but well rewarded. And she had almost managed to put away her panic of the night before. Until she reached the top of the stairs and held her key out towards the lock. She had promised Beth she'd give the suggested plan a go. And as plans went, it wasn't a bad one. Unlike other therapists, Beth's suggestions were invariably extremely practical. She just hoped she wouldn't need to try it. An empty flat and quiet bed would do just fine instead. No angels, no floor-floating strangers, and definitely no pregnancy.

She walked into the flat, knew something was different the minute she opened the door. Ignored the knowledge. Put it down to paranoia, lack of sleep, too many double vodkas. Put it down to didn't want to know. There was a faint luminosity coming from under the sitting-room door. She dismissed it as streetlight. Pale blue-green streetlight. With the curtains shut and the sun coming up in ninety minutes anyway. Whatever.

The man was waiting for her. Sofia ignored him. He was sitting on the sofa when she let herself in, moved to stand up when he heard her locking her own front door behind her, walking down the short hall to the sitting room. He left no dent in the cushion when he got off the sofa. Even though the old cushion was really a little too thin, the stuffing long knocked out of it, something donated to another home another time by her mother, something she'd meant to get around to replacing for ages, but never yet managed it. That would involve shopping. The thin stuffing of the cushion was not disturbed by his presence. Sofia wished herself implacable as cushion stuffing.

She walked into the sitting room, took in the image of the man standing hesitantly, smiling at her more hesitantly still. Though she didn't want to, tried to cut off, ignore him completely, some part of her still managed to respond to the man in front of her. Good-looking bloke with a goofy, hopeful smile – her barely suppressed fury turning him into an uncomfortable teenager, not knowing if this really was such a good time to ask her out, wondering if there would ever be a right time. She glanced at him and then looked away almost immediately, trying not to actually see him. Eye contact certainly wouldn't help. No connection with the not there. That's what Beth had suggested. Sofia caught herself starting to sigh – a combination of surprise rapidly shut down with irritation – and then checked herself. Because even sighing a little would be acknowledging his presence to some degree. And she had no intention of doing that. Having a conversation was not part of Beth's plan. Not even when the man eventually spoke to her.

'Sofia?'

More angry than surprised, she threw her bag on the armchair to his left and ignored his barely disguised wince when it nearly hit him. She stalked off to the bathroom, grimaced at her tired face in the mirror, opened the cabinet, took out make-up remover, baby oil, cotton wool. Began the ritual cleansing, double speed to get the night over with, make sleeping day begin.

'Sofia? I really do need to talk to you. There must be things you need explained. I mean, not that I know all the answers, but . . . surely you see we need to talk?'

Sofia slammed the cabinet door and went into the toilet. She was good at this. The years with James had made her an expert. She could have consummately ignored the man for hours – figmented imagination or not. She started to close the toilet door as she normally would with a guest in the flat – though not for James, never for James – and then stopped again. Smiled to herself. She pulled down her knickers, sat on the loo and began to wee. Forcefully. Loudly.

The man had followed her down the hallway towards the toilet, but stopped halfway there when he realised what she was doing, 'Oh – sorry. I didn't mean to intrude. I'll wait in the sitting room.'

Sofia bit her tongue to stop herself from shouting it would be a long wait. And for someone who didn't want to intrude he was making a bloody good job of doing the exact opposite. Shut up. Keep silent. Don't talk back. That's what Beth had said. Don't make him real by engaging in conversation with what was, after all, only some projected part of herself anyway. A conjured image. Don't get into it. Which had seemed a good enough scheme at the time, but now she was tired and fed up. What did Beth know? This was her flat. Why should she let the man – the nothing out there – shut her up? Especially if he wasn't real. Don't keep silent. Sing to herself, fart, piss even more noisily, crap like an old man, make surprise phone calls, play loud music, and possibly even disturb deep-sleeping James. Really fuck him off. Except she never did make a noise when she came home from work. She loved the silence of the middle hours. Loved that James slept soundly below her feet, the choice she made to walk barefoot above a man who slept so well anyway. And she wouldn't dream of disturbing people she cared for by phoning them in the middle of the night – she'd lived abroad long enough to know the cold terror of the call that wakes from deep sleep. She could have called people she knew overseas, people from her travelling days who would be wide awake at this hour. But then she'd have to say why she was calling at a time she normally cursed anyone for wanting to converse with her – explain why her brain was racing to find answers that would take her as far as possible away from the weirdness she was determined to ignore. And accounting for that weirdness would be to acknowledge the problem. Sofia chose to stay in denial. It felt far closer to sanity.

The man stood uncomfortably in her bedroom while Sofia took off her clothes. She wanted to tell him to fuck off. At the very least she wanted to charge him a tenner. But she'd promised not to speak to him. She acknowledged the absurdity of the situation – that she was embarrassed to take her clothes off in front of this man, this nobody, when stripping was what she did for a living. Embarrassed to take her clothes off in front of him, when she didn't even believe he was there. He turned his face to the wall and she removed her jeans and jumper as fast as she could, overhead bulb dimmed to almost dark, curtains shut tight against nearly morning.

Sofia turned off the light and climbed naked into bed. Moved the four pillows to either side of her head – two jammed up against her ears, two just covering her eyes, whole body laid out flat the better to care for her exhausted dancer's back. She lay staring at the ceiling, scared to close her eyes, not wanting him to be in her closed-eye sight as well. She heard the floorboards tense as the man came closer to her bed, the old wood sighing beneath the slip of his no-touch glide. She sensed movement rather than physically felt his hand as she knew he'd reached out to touch her foot. And then, to her surprise, it felt good. Safe. Like he was right to be there. Protecting her. Safe enough to go to sleep. Easy now to go to sleep. Sofia closed her eyes, smiled at the thought of him waiting there, too shattered now to argue, couldn't be bothered, didn't really mind, went to sleep, blessed in the bed that she lay on.

He brought her breakfast. At lunch-time. And the papers – the *Guardian, Independent, Daily Mail* – spectrum reading. He held out the tray. Which was real enough. As was the coffee – excessively strong with the merest dash of warm milk, two big sugars – exactly right and better than anything she'd managed to teach James in three years. Or Beth. Or her own mother. And the croissant – no butter, tiny scraping of apricot jam. There didn't seem much point in ignoring him any more, not while his arms were probably aching from offering her this array of delights. And she was hungry. He said he'd baked the croissant himself. The flat smelled of yeast and coffee. It seemed as possible as anything else. Sofia sat up, reached for the T-shirt she kept under the bed, less body-bravado available to her now that she knew they were going to have to speak. She pulled on the old scrap and took the tray, laid it across her legs. The coffee was good, the croissant crumbling and warm.

Sofia finished the coffee, looked up at him, waiting patiently by her bed, 'You can sit down if you want.'

He shook his head, 'Thanks, but I really should be going.'

'Odd time to realise you've outstayed your welcome.'

'I will come back.'

'Of course.'

'I have to make sure you know what's happening.'

'No idea. As I'm sure you know, I've spent the past twenty-four hours convinced I'm going nuts.'

'I didn't know that, I'm sorry.'

'But you know how I like my coffee – I thought you'd know everything?'

He smiled, gently mocking and just slightly pissed off at the same time, 'I'm not the omniscient one.'

Sofia was starting to enjoy herself, 'Leave that to the big guy, do you?'

'It's not really like that. But no, I don't know everything.'

'I see, so you're only following orders?'

The man ran a hand across his face, Sofia almost felt sorry for him.

Almost.

'Look Sofia, as I tried to explain the other night, it's my job to pass on the message. And then to make sure you understand.'

'Fair enough. Except I don't understand. Not at all. Unless – and I have to say this breakfast certainly feels authentic enough – unless you are real and therefore what you told me the other night might also be real.'

'It is.'

'Whatever. The fact is, as my therapist says, I'm an unlikely choice for Virgin Mary. Someone who doesn't believe in the possibility of a Messiah is an unlikely choice for the Madonna, don't you agree?'

'Well . . . your beliefs don't necessarily come into it.'

'So I gathered.'

'And are you sure you really don't believe at all?'

'No, I'm not. I haven't given it all that much thought to be honest. Religion, faith, God, all that stuff doesn't matter much to me.'

'So you're more agnostic than atheist?'

'I'm more fucked off, actually. It's not what I want. I don't want a baby. Don't want to be a mother. Didn't want to be a mother. Yet. Maybe never. I haven't thought about having kids. Not really. Not like I might.' She paused, trying to emphasise her resolve with just a little silence, 'I really mean it. I don't want a baby. Not now. I don't know if I'll ever want one. Let alone a baby which – if you're right – is so special. I'm single, I have no great career prospects, it's not something I was planning on doing any time soon. I'm twenty-eight, not forty-eight. I'm not looking for a miracle.'

The man looked at her for a while, frowning, weighing her up, almost as if the incongruity had only just occurred to him, then he sighed and shrugged, 'As I said—'

'You're only the messenger.'

'Yeah. So look – as long as you and I are talking now – do you have any questions?'

Sofia laughed, 'Loads, but we've already established you don't have all the answers, and you're not prepared to accept my refusal anyway, so what's the point?'

'OK.'

The man turned to leave, Sofia pushed the tray aside and stood up, 'Hey! Where are you going?'

He kept walking out of the room, 'I don't know. I'll be back when you need me.'

Sofia followed him from the room, 'Promise?'

He was at her front door, turned back smiling, 'Cross my heart.'

The man was just closing the door when Sofia called out, 'What's your name?'

He'd already closed the door and was halfway down the stairs but she heard him whisper in her ear anyway.

'Gabriel.'

For the rest of the day Sofia sat alone. Thinking about what the man had told her. Thinking, worrying and, eventually, ignoring. She went to work, earned good money, had a very pleasant night shutting out any thoughts at all, came home to an empty flat, slept alone and well, and then woke up with a clear decision. She would do nothing. Which was something like a choice, if a little less than proactive. She decided to wait. Stop questioning where there could be no answers, give up panicking about the impossible (easier thought than done) and just get on with it. If the man was right, if what he'd told her was true, she'd know soon enough. And if he was right, soon enough was far too soon to think about mothering the Messiah. If, however, she ended up with the far more likely scenario – not pregnant – then it didn't matter, and the more people she told, the more she would convince them and herself that she really was going crazy. There are few uncertainties that time unravels quite as clearly as an unplanned pregnancy.

Sofia had delighted in the classic non-functioning dancer's uterus in her teens – but since a degree of physical and emotional sanity had been hers for the past five years or so, she'd eventually developed her own version of the normal woman's body. Average twenty-eight-day cycle, three days of pain, two more of excessive blood, occasional waves of irritation that Nurofen was neither NHS-free nor tax deductible. In her field of work, pain killers and easily-hidden tampons really were necessary expenses. Because it actually did make some difference to the job, to her body shape, to how eager she felt about spending an evening almost-stripping, Sofia kept a close check on the days of her cycle. Her last period had finished the week before the man first appeared. Which meant she only had another two weeks to wait. As far as she could remember she and James hadn't had sex for well over two months, quite possibly three by now – and she was fairly certain that even in her most advanced states of inebriation she usually remembered a shag. There had been no other possible men for the past three months. So either she'd bleed in about two and half weeks – or she wouldn't. It was simply a matter of spinning out the waiting.

There was the choice of further lining the pockets of the pharmaceutical industry of course, but Sofia had little faith in home pregnancy tests. Her last scare had sent her scuttling off to the chemist at two-daily intervals. Late-night shag, after the last heartbreak and before James, not anyone she cared to remember, too many drugs to count, pill forgotten in the lost long weekend, and then the inevitable, should-have-seen-it-coming of just-in-case condom split in the lure of frantic lust. Girls' angst and Glaxo banks. First test positive, second test negative, third positive, fourth bright blue, fucking scary, really very definitely positive. And then the phone-calls and checking the savings account and making the appointment, the one she'd never yet had to make, the one she'd made so often for other girlfriends, hugely relieved every time that it wasn't she who had to think about it, wasn't her body offered up for examination and excavation, and now just getting on with it, because she had to, doing the necessary. Going through the motions of this isn't the right time. But something wasn't quite right. The nice lady at Marie Stopes did the urine test and then a blood test and no, she wasn't pregnant after all. But maybe her pill was a few dozen hormones too much for her body and perhaps she should think about going back to her GP. She was getting older, she might want to try a different version? Sofia did think about it, and then thought better of it. It was certainly easier than thinking about the nice lady's easy assertion that she was getting older. She read another tabloid scare story, listened to her mother's lecture after another *Woman's Hour* programme about the dangers of prolonged pill use, wondered if every day since fifteen counted as prolonged and then gave up on the pill altogether. She lost half a stone in the first week, another half in the next fortnight and, being everygirl at heart, she had to admit that she was rather more excited about the outcome of unintended weight loss than the initial motive of cancer prevention. Sofia was condom girl these days. James was condom boy. Ever so modern. Usually reliable. And no reason whatsoever to be pregnant right now.

Unless the man was right. Unless the man was real. So she would wait, leave it between her and Beth, not talk about it to anyone else, not allow the spoken word to create an impossible truth. And see what happened.

Eleven

What happened was that James brought home a new girl.

'Sofia, I want you to meet Martha.'

Sofia hated her on sight. Martha wasn't too impressed either. Though she was also far too delighted with James to mention it. As the ex, rather than potential-girlfriend, Sofia had no such must-look-lovely scruples.

'I don't like her.'

'You don't know her.'

'You've never mentioned her before.'

'I have but you weren't listening.'

'You didn't say you were actually seeing someone.'

'Because I knew you'd react like this.'

'How long have you known her?'

'A few months. She's a friend of one of the girls at work, we've met at the pub a couple of times. I've fancied her for a while actually.'

'What's to fancy? She looks like Minnie Mouse.'

'She's quite small and very pretty, yes.'

Sofia made a face, 'My point exactly. You've found some nice sweet girlie to do your every bidding—'

'She's small, Sofia, that doesn't necessarily make her sweet.'

'It does in my experience. Sweet to boys anyway. Terrified of other women, of course, but you wouldn't ever get to see that. What you don't understand, James, is that little girls never have to try. Like natural blondes. The world's been making it easy for them since birth.'

'Yeah, well I'm not getting into your theories of girl unreality. And anyway, Martha's got a masters degree in the history of modern feminism, she's fairly political actually. She wouldn't thank you for calling her a girl.'

Sofia stretched her long legs out across James's lap, 'Christ, that's even better, you will remember to tell her what I do for a living, won't you?'

'I already did.'

'What did she say?'

'That it was a woman's right to choose what she used her body for—'

'But?'

'How do you know there's a but?'

'Isn't there?'

'Well, yes. She agreed with me about the economic realities of your industry.'

'Fantastic, and now you want me to applaud you for having finally found some chick masquerading as a feminist who's going to use her few gems of rote-learned politics to back up your every thought?'

James pushed Sofia's legs off his own and sat up, 'She's not a bimb. She's a social worker.'

'That'll explain the clothes then.'

'What?'

'Nothing. Sorry. Not funny.'

'No. You're right. God, Sofia, I thought you'd be pleased that I've found someone I like. Someone who – maybe, who knows, it's really fucking early yet – but just maybe, I might actually get on with. Have a nice time with.'

Sofia waved away James's suggestion of a happy future. 'You get on with me. You have a nice time with me.'

'Had a nice time with you. You ended it remember?'

'You agreed.'

'Yes, but I didn't promise to stay celibate for ever just because I couldn't have you.'

'So you haven't fucked her yet?'

'None of your business. And even if we had, I wouldn't have fucked her, we would have fucked each other, it would have been a reciprocal, mutual occasion.'

Sofia licked her lips, 'Mmm, reciprocal and mutual. Very passionate.'

'It could be.'

'So you haven't done it. Why not?'

James stood up to leave Sofia's flat, 'I don't want to talk about it.'

'Liar. You always want to talk about it. Talking about sex is your favourite thing. Other than doing it. Of course you want to talk about it. Does she scream when she comes?'

James shook his head, 'Piss off Sofia, I'm not playing. Not with you in this mood. I don't want to hear your jealous observations.'

Sofia coloured bright red, 'James, believe me, I am not jealous. Or not in the way you think. I don't want you. I love you. We know we love each other. We also know it doesn't work. As you so rightly said, I was the one who told you we should break up. What I don't want is for you to waste yourself – a self I happen to find vibrant and exciting and fantastically deviant—'

'Thank you.'

'Shut up and listen. I don't want you to waste your interesting self on some politically correct girl . . . woman, social worker, whatever – who will water you down and shut you up and stop you playing with me and partying and taking too many drugs and having a bloody good time.'

James was silent for a moment and then he looked down at her, 'Sofia, you don't want me to stop playing with you because you don't want to grow up.'

'Neither did you last week.'

James shook his head. 'No. Things change though, don't they?'

Over the next week Sofia did try to get on with Martha. Gave it her best shot. Which was somewhat watered down by her pregnancy-anxieties, but a definite attempt none the less. And less than completely successful. When they were at the pub and James went to get another round in, the two women were forced to discuss their jobs. It was plain each found the other something of an oddity. When they sat in the Scala bar and tried to talk films Sofia was dismissive of Martha's passion for French talkies and Martha was shocked by Sofia's tempting-fate assertion that what she really enjoyed was a good action movie. Sofia didn't think their disparate views were especially shocking, but she did understand Martha's desire to show James just how very different she and Sofia were. Sofia even admitted to herself that she might have done the same thing in Martha's position – though she hoped she wouldn't have done so in a corduroy pinafore dress. Later that night when they discussed politics over a drunken curry, Martha asserted that Sofia knew absolutely nothing. At all. That much, according to the pissed-on-two-glasses-of-wine Martha, was blindingly obvious. For her part, Sofia was incredibly proud that she didn't smack the sweet little thing in the face, and still prouder when she held her tongue and refrained from pointing out that while she might know nothing Martha, for all her theory, had very clearly lived nothing. When their conversation finally ground down to football, Martha stated that she much preferred watching ice-skating. Eventually there was only James to talk about. And even there they had no common ground. Sofia thought James was her playmate and good shag. Martha found him challenging and intellectually stimulating. Which made

Sofia wonder if Martha knew anything about sex at all – and then she promised herself she wouldn't ask. At least not until she was really pushed. No point in using up all her ammunition in one night.

Sofia stomped back upstairs to her own flat and went to bed certain that fourteen feet below Martha was moaning about her to James, ripping apart her messy flat, her messy job, her messy life. Martha – for all her conversational bravado – was jealous and scared of Sofia. Sofia was pissed, definitely paranoid, still more nervous about the baby situation while trying to ignore her terror as much as possible – but she wasn't wrong. Martha was indeed talking about her to James and very little of it was anything Sofia would have wanted to hear. Nor was there a friendly stranger upstairs to distract her. After an hour or so of irritable stirring, Sofia finally fell asleep, tired out with frustration and fear and waiting.

Twelve

Work. A week of work. Ignoring James, ignoring Martha, ignoring her own body except for three-minute bursts of fevered financial activity. Delicious business that used all her energy in body-thrown contortions, ladylike distortions, crawling home too tired to do anything but fall into welcome – empty – bed. Sofia's job was perfect therapy for her ever-increasing panic. She didn't want to be pregnant, she didn't want to be crazy, she didn't want. Turned instead to brain-numbing physical exertion, leaving her so shattered she barely had the energy to take her make-up off at night – though she always did, ritual habitual – certainly not leaving her with enough leftover juice to manufacture angel men in her dreams, God-baby in her body.

Double shifts all round, Sofia became the perfect colleague, filling in for anyone who needed it, anyone who fancied time off, a night out with the girls, an evening in with the boy. Working her little butt off. Working her little tummy off. There was no tummy. Sofia was sure there was no tummy. Except then again, she wasn't. Not completely sure anyway. Girl body paranoia or the real thing? Took another couple of lines of coke, drank the third glass of wine – that was what it was, the tummy trauma, must stop drinking so much. Eventually. But not while all this was going on, Sofia needed her crutches more than she needed a clear head. Clear bed and sleep again. Too tired to dream. Too scared to dream. And three hundred pounds left safe and ready in the bank.

She studied herself in the mirror every morning, every night, every passing shop window, gleaming new car door, shiny spokes of a courier's bike. Held her breasts in the shower and thought about that self-examination thing as she did every six months. Thought about it, got no further, not even this time. Examination, yes. For the cancer concept, no. She held her breasts, squeezed them, weighed them up, perhaps there was a tiny size change, just maybe? Yes, but that could be period, she was pre-menstrual after all. Probably pre-menstrual. Hopefully pre-menstrual. Even prayerfully pre-menstrual on one occasion, where the exhaustion didn't quite manage to outrun her late-night fear. There was no sickness, no tiredness – none other than that engendered by the overwork anyway – there was nothing out of the ordinary and there were no late-night visits and angels in blokes' clothing. Gabriel did not return.

Neither did Sofia's period. The day of expected arrival passed. Blood stayed away. Then another day, and another. Studied her stomach, waited for nausea, couldn't believe it might really be happening. Sofia found herself making eminently reasonable pacts with the body gods. She had been teenage girl, dancer girl, she had crossed the world. Knew that travelling, stress, undereating, even overwork, could fuck things up, a dateline flight might send the moon spiralling out of its gravity spin, skipping her body for one month or two. She knew that worry could do it as well. She stopped worrying. For an hour. Panic returned threefold, magnified in a waning moon. She tried to eat well, to feel normal, to make normality happen by pretending that it might. She drank gin. But she didn't like gin, couldn't finish the glass. Period didn't come.

Sofia stared at her body in the mirror, stared at her career in the mirror. Looked at herself as dispassionately as she could, studied the breasts, the stomach, the long legs, sleekly muscled arms. Took in the picture of herself and then tried to distort it into pregnant Sofia. Distended her stomach, hand placed on lower back, took up the pregnant pose. It didn't look like her. Looked like not-Sofia. Scared her. Sofia as mother-to-be was someone she didn't recognise, the body didn't fit the face, didn't fit her life, was other than the body she wanted. Again. Back again to the terrors of her teenage years as if she'd never overcome her past traumas, as if her semi-agoraphobia hadn't become an almost adequate replacement for body-loathing, as if she were fifteen again, mind and body thrown apart, fingers itching for a blade's pain to bring them together again. She stepped back from the mirror in horror and crawled into her bed. Mothering the Messiah was the least of her problems right then.

Five days late, Sofia had dinner with Beth and Pete and didn't once mention the absent blood. Easy to avoid bringing it up, no reason with the semi-strangers who were also dining, and no reason either in private with Beth, swollen with far more immediate concerns of her own. The talk around the table was of little but Beth's babies – officially they were due in three weeks, but Beth was so classically liner-like, so clearly ready to pop – and dying to do so – it was impossible to talk about anything else. Which was just fine with Sofia. Even home-made ignorance has bliss potential.

There was a stolen moment in the kitchen when Beth grabbed Sofia's nervous hand, thin and worried fingers clattering coffee cups into each other, 'Are you all right, kiddo? You've barely acknowledged me all evening.'

'Not true Beth, we've been talking about you all night.'

'Talking about the babies, not me. Well Pete is, and

everyone else. But you're not. And you certainly aren't talking about yourself either. What's going on? Do you want to tell me about it?'

'What?'

'Oh come on, Sof. What we were discussing the other day?'

But Sofia reached into the cavernous fridge and pulled out another bottle, shaking off both Beth's hand and her concern as she did so, 'Oh good, alcohol.' Then she found a king-size bar of Fruit & Nut, 'Yum. And chocolate, I'll take these both in, shall I?'

'Sofia, you were a bloody mess the last time I saw you and, other than two phone-calls in which you've refused to answer my questions anyway, you've spent the whole of tonight acting as if nothing's happened.'

Sofia stared straight at Beth and shouted through to the others in the living room, 'More alcohol anyone? Everyone?'

A clatter of chinking glasses answered her in the affirmative and she put the coffee back in the cupboard.

'Sofia! Will you answer me? I'm worried about you.'

Sofia held the bottle aloft, 'No more for you of course Beth, God knows what the NCT police would say about the amount you've already consumed tonight.'

'Slag.'

Sofia headed for the door as she spoke, 'Yep. Nasty slag who you don't want to get into any discussion with because I'm so mean. I don't want to talk about it, OK? I don't even want to think about it if I can help it. I want your friendship, not therapy. Tonight anyway. So, I'll just go through and fill all those thirsty glasses, all right?'

The rest of Beth's evening was taken up in discussion about the colour the hall should be, needed to be, had to be – and ideally within the next week. For one who usually expressed a complete lack of interest in home decorating, who thought a thirsty pot-plant from an all-night garage was a perfectly acceptable house warming gift, Sofia was vibrantly involved in the discussion. Like she really, really cared. Pete even commented on her change of heart as he and Beth tidied away the evening's debris.

'She's not interested in paint effect you twat, she's interested in not talking about what's bothering her,' Beth barked back at him, sore back, active babies and irritation at Sofia's attitude all taken out on her unsuspecting husband.

Who was so used to his wife's bad temper he barely noticed the difference, 'Oh, right, and what's bothering her?'

'Nothing I can tell you about,' Beth threw her tea-towel at him and left the room, shouting over her shoulder, 'Blue. I want the hallway blue. Tomorrow, if not sooner.'

Beth went to bed for baby-interrupted sleep and Pete got to work. The undercoat was done by morning.

Sofia was alone in her flat. It was Sunday afternoon. She had the next two nights off work and James had gone away with Martha for a long weekend. Their absence meant Sofia had the whole house to herself. No one to hear her scream. Or cry. Whatever. Now or never. And hopefully never.

Sofia had breathed deeply, taken the plunge, purchased two different pregnancy testing kits from three different chemists – she wouldn't shop in the one closest to home, and the first she tried had far too many people waiting by the counter. So she caught another bus and went pregnancy-test shopping in Muswell Hill. Even in her fear state, she noted that the looks of the sales assistants had changed. Five years ago the man behind the counter would have looked at her with pity or suspicion, the women with fellow-feeling, girl empathy. Now though, they smiled at her. Men, women and children. Though Sofia had a perfect body, great skin, she was clearly in her mid-to late-twenties, she did not look like a foolish teenager caught out unintentionally. She looked like a woman, not a girl. She was expected to whoop with irrepressible mother-joy when the indicator turned blue. Blue. Unlike Beth, she did not want blue. Sofia had not planned for this, believed Gabriel when he said there was nothing she could do about this, couldn't possibly imagine what her role might be if he was right, and yet was still hanging on to a hope of maybe she could be in control.

Sofia had not eaten. She had drunk maybe three litres of water. In two and a half days. She was thin, drawn face, tired eyes, but still looked good. Sofia always looked good, no matter what – even then, wearing heroin-heroine chic. Even in mid-winter with a streaming cold and her annual bronchitis. Sofia had never received enough sympathy for being sick, people didn't notice. She had not intended to fast, but now it seemed to make sense. Lack of hunger because her body knew better than she what was coming. Sofia knew what was coming, but she'd rather not talk about it. Not even to herself. Would not converse with the rumbling stomach. And the thin lines were blue. Like the veins that stood out on her hands, her arms, throbbing in her left temple. Both tests tested blue. Pissed the piss, waited the requisite time, the three minute eternity, and then the lines were gleaming blue. Bright and shiny and staring out at her, waves of blue floating before her swimming eyes, sea blue, sky blue, baby blue. Sofia thought briefly that perhaps she should take one of the sticks to Beth, it was so absolutely the colour she wanted for her hall. And then she threw up and then she cried and then she thought about food, forgot about food, poured herself a glass of wine and cried some more and then she went to bed. At three in the afternoon. It was as good a time as any. It was a better time than ever before. Heavy blue, darker than the pregnancy tests, waiting out of reach to wrap her tight. Smother the night.

Thirteen

When Sofia woke hours later Gabriel was there. She wanted to tell him to piss off, to fuck off out of her flat. But she didn't. Because in the panic and the terror and the frustration and the anger his presence was a strange comfort. Because he knew what was going on. Who else could she tell, who else was going to believe this? And then, just beyond her knowledge that this man knew the truth, there was also a recognition that it wasn't simply the fact that he knew for sure. There was something else as well. It slowly dawned on Sofia that his presence really was a comfort. His being there, sitting on the edge of her bed, soft hand pressure gently stroking her lower leg, did make it feel different. There was a protection with him in the room. There was an ease she had not felt since she was a little girl and used to climb on to her mother's knee to be buttoned back into the pink dressing-gown, and hide there, safe from the world in the cigarette-burned, nylon womb. Right then, Sofia would have taken anything to make it better – even pretend plastic pink.

She slept again and woke angry. She had a lot of questions. Unfortunately Gabriel didn't have quite so many corresponding answers. She slammed around her flat in another fit of uncontrolled tidiness and he followed her, trying his best to make it seem a little bit better. His best was only marginally better than useless.

'So what am I supposed to tell my family?'

Smashing plates into the sink and turning on the water with such force that it sprayed all over both of them.

'I don't know. But you are a grown woman. I mean it's not like you're a teenager, is it?'

Sofia glared at him, 'I don't have a partner. I don't have a lover. I had no intention of becoming a mother, not right now anyway, not alone. It was no part of my thoughts. I repeat, what am I supposed to tell my family?'

Gabriel shrugged his shoulders. Clearly not a trauma he had foreseen. Or if he had, not one he'd worked out a solution for.

Sofia continued, 'How do I explain it to my friends? "Oh, by the way, I'm pregnant – no father necessary."'

'I understand this is going to be a difficult time for you, but—'

'You understand nothing. What am I meant to do for work?' Reaching under the sink for washing-up liquid and knocking over half a dozen old cleaning containers, mostly unused and still unopened, 'How many pregnant lap dancers do you know?'

'None. I don't know any. Didn't. Until you. Now I know you.'

'Don't kid yourself, sweetheart. You know nothing about me.'

'You could always get a different job I suppose.'

'Right, brilliant. Get a new job. That is just so clever of you. I can't actually do anything else, in case you hadn't noticed. It's why I'm a bloody lap dancer in the first place. It's the only thing I'm any good at.'

Gabriel reached his hands out to soothe Sofia's stressed shoulders, 'No, that's just not true, you're wonderful at lots of things, you're a very capable young woman.'

Sofia was not impressed, she twisted away from him, 'Oh please. Believe me, if I want you to start playing therapist – and I find the possibility highly unlikely – then I'll be sure to let you know. Until that happens, don't try telling me what I'm good at. I know what I'm good at. It's what I want to be good at. I've trained to be good at this. I am good at this. I'm good at sex too. I'm fantastic at blow jobs and I'm unbelievably proficient at getting pissed and taking drugs. What I am not good at, what I don't want to be good at, is being the Virgin fucking Mary.'

Gabriel winced but said nothing, Sofia finished washing the dishes and started putting them away, flinging drips of water across the floor as she did so, 'Can't I ask the father to provide? Isn't that what single mothers usually do?'

'Well, you could. Between you and me though, the Father already thinks He is providing.'

Dripping plate in one hand, the other outstretched in furious question, 'And how do you reason that?'

'Didn't you ever do lilies of the field in Sunday school?'

'Yet another example of why I'm not your girl – I didn't do Sunday school. Mine were the hippy parents, remember? I wasn't trained to mother the Messiah.'

'No one was—'

Gabriel tired to interrupt her but Sofia continued, 'Not that I necessarily believe it is anyway. The Messiah, whatever that means. Look, all I ever got was Jesus loves you and so does Buddha and so does Allah and so do we. I was told that Jesus was a nice man who was a good teacher—'

'Well, He was.'

Sofia glared at him and then slammed the plate into a cupboard, the small kitchen echoing with the sound of shattering crockery, 'This is ludicrous. I'm not up for God stories right now, OK? I'm pregnant. Unless, of course, my body has gone crazy along with my brain and I'm suffering from some kind of stupid phantom pregnancy.'

'You're not crazy, you are having a baby.'

'Having a baby that I don't want, haven't planned, don't know how to provide for, can't bear the thought of what this is going to do to my body even before there's a baby to worry about – and on top of all of that, you're telling me this is an immaculate conception—'

'No, I didn't say that.'

'Well what is it then?'

Gabriel put his head in his hands, rubbed his black eyes and sighed, long and exhausted, then he looked up at Sofia, fat frown wrinkling his perfect forehead, 'It's a bit long-winded . . .'

Sofia snarled, 'Do your best.'

'Well, the whole immaculate conception thing is a fairly big theological debate, actually. The one you're referring to was to do with Mary, not her Son.'

'What?'

'*Song of Bernadette*?'

'I preferred *The Nun's Story*.'

'Not *Black Narcissus*?'

'Jean Simmons is a very poor man's Audrey Hepburn.'

'Yeah, but *Black Narcissus* does have Deborah Kerr . . .'

Which was about as far as Sofia was prepared to go in the pleasant chatting stakes, 'I'm sorry, it could have Yul Brynner in it as well for all I care. I'm actually more interested in me at the moment, can we leave the film analysis until I'm a little more sussed about what's going on?'

'Yes, of course, I'm sorry, it's just that it is sort of dealt with in the *Bernadette* film, in a very layman's way of course—'

Sofia frowned her frustration, 'What is?'

'The immaculate conception – Mary, it's not about Him.'

'Him who?'

'It's not about Jesus.' Gabriel said the name almost stuttering, as if it was hard for him to speak. 'Not about Him in the way you mean. She was the immaculate conception. It's to do with original sin. She was preserved immaculate from all stain of original sin.'

Clattering the last of the dishes into the cupboard, chipped cup on top of broken plate, 'Oh wonderful, so now I'm supposed to be sinless? Sin-free? Pure as the driven snow?'

'No. You're not. It would be pushing it a bit much to suggest that.'

'Thanks.'

'Sorry, look, it doesn't matter. Honest. It isn't relevant to you. The whole thing is something of a doctrinal excess anyway. It can be a very interesting discussion, there's a lot of dissent, even in the Orthodox church—'

Sofia interrupted him, 'You know what? I am about as interested in the theoretical applications of all this shite as I am in shaving my eyeballs. Really. I don't care. Whatever you lot have made up to explain all this and con the gullible public is hardly the point is it? Not right now. I'm pregnant after no sex. Whether I want to be or not. And apparently I'm not a nutter and this is real, not some lunatic flight of fancy.' Sofia stared at him for a moment. 'And you – you're real too – aren't you?'

'Yes Sofia. I'm real.'

Sofia went through to the sitting room and threw herself into her old armchair. 'What a fucking mess.'

Gabriel looked as if he might be ready to agree and then stopped himself when he remembered that wasn't his role, 'That's why I'm here to help.'

'You're looking after me?'

'Well, advising, answering questions – the ones I can, that is,' he replied hurriedly, pre-empting another round of abuse.

Sofia reached for her cigarettes on the shelf behind her, she lit one and looked around at the room, the cramped room that barely contained all her rubbish, let alone the collections of a potential child. She looked down at herself and then back to Gabriel, 'OK. So how do I get out of it?'

This was not the question he'd been expecting, 'What?'

'I don't want to go through with it. I don't want this. I don't want to be the next Mary. I don't want to be a mother. I don't want my body to change. How do I get out of it?'

'You can't. You said yes.'

Sofia shook her head, pointing the cigarette at him, 'Not so. I did say yes. But then I said no, and after that I also said whatever. You just pissed off before I'd finished, you should have stayed for the whole sentence, babe. You should have explained yourself better. You should have turned up in the middle of the day. Knocked on the door even. Talked to me when I was sober perhaps. It was hardly informed consent.'

'A whole lot more informed than the last time.'

Sofia shook her head, 'Not much of a feminist, your boss, is He?'

'As far as He's concerned He invented feminist theory. You know, started the ball rolling as it were. Free will and all that.'

Gabriel sat down on the floor beside her, took her cigarette. Sofia grabbed it from him, 'Hey! Don't you dare get all health Nazi on me, I don't even want to be pregnant.'

He took the cigarette, took a long drag on it and passed it back to her, 'I wasn't. I wanted to smoke.'

Sofia threw her packet and lighter at him, smokers' protocol reasserting itself, 'Oh. Right. Help yourself. Sorry. I didn't think you would. Or could, I suppose. It didn't occur to me, I didn't mean to be rude.'

Gabriel lit up and shook his head, laughing at the abrupt switch from abuse to apology, 'No, it's fine. I should get my own really, only I did think I'd given up. I've been finding all this a bit stressful though.'

'You're telling me.'

Sofia and Gabriel finished their cigarettes in uncompaniable silence and then she turned to face him, 'So – free will. That's what I want to talk about.'

'OK.'

'What if I don't want to have the baby?'

'I'm sorry?'

'I think you know what I mean.'

'Ah, no.'

'What if I don't want to keep it?'

'What?'

'Come on, you can't be that stupid. It's not as if this was a planned pregnancy, and it's certainly not as if I've been treating myself with kid gloves since you first turned up. I mean, is this Messiah of yours supposed to ingest a lot of nicotine and coke and alcohol in the first three weeks, or what?'

'That won't matter.'

'Why not?'

'It's protected. You can't hurt it.'

Sofia reached for another cigarette, frowning, 'They hurt the last one.'

That shut him up. Gabriel nodded. Waited. Thought.

'Yes. But he was an adult and it was his choice. Part of the plan.'

'So this one needs to want to be hurt before I can harm it?'

'In theory, yes. But it's a foetus, it doesn't know any of that yet. It doesn't know about choice.'

'How can it not know? Shouldn't it know everything?'

Gabriel ran his wide hands through his curly black hair, 'Yes. No. All that trinity thing . . . honestly Sofia, it's not really that simple. It's not really anything like that actually. I mean it is, but it's just not quite as cut and dried as you might think. I can tell you about it if you want – as much as I understand anyway.'

Sofia sighed, 'Not right now thank you. What if I have an abortion?'

'You can't.'

'Who's going to stop me? You?'

'No. No one would stop you. But it wouldn't work. Or it wouldn't happen. I don't know how, but I do know that it would be impossible. You can't harm it, or remove it, or do anything to it unless it allows you – and it's just a four-week-old foetus. Almost. It can't give that permission.'

'I just have to put up with it then?'

'Um . . . yes.'

Sofia was quiet for a while, then she asked, her hand on her stomach, 'Is it going to have a shit life? Shit death?' Then she corrected herself and added, 'Not that I necessarily believe in the last one, you understand.'

Gabriel shrugged, 'A lot of the stories have been exaggerated anyway. They're hardly what you'd call eye-witness accounts. But no, it doesn't have to do anything. I mean, it's not the Messiah until it chooses to be. Unless it chooses to be. There have been others, they just didn't do anything about it. Didn't want to. And even the one you're talking about wasn't especially keen either, not at first. Didn't do anything about it until He turned thirty.'

'So even the kid has choice and I don't?'

'I'm sorry Sofia, but you did have a choice. You did say yes. That's all it took.'

And then it was too much. Sofia cried. Quietly, softly. Fear and loss and apprehension and uncontrolled lack of understanding. She crawled down from the chair and sobbed her way blindly into his arms. Not because that was where she wanted to be, not because she thought he could change anything, but because it felt like it might be safe. Close to safe. And then she stayed because, despite everything else, it was safe. Nothing was fixed and nothing had changed, but something about being held by Gabriel did make the moment better.

And something about holding her made it better for him too. Another surprise.

Fourteen

His skin smells of jasmine. And a perfume she doesn't know, would not recognise even if she did. And her. His skin smells of her. He does not smell like a man – not any man she has known before. He smells different and Sofia-reflected. She wonders if this is what is meant to happen. She wonders if this is meant. Fate and destiny are not concepts she has previously had much time for, has little time for them even now, when the sense of actual choice is so clearly absent. But she is choosing this anyway. Or believes she is.

Leaning into him, the tears over, dried salt on her face, there is perfume and intention. She does not know whose intention, what intention. She feels driven and at the same time, intensely relaxed, stoned almost, but with a cocaine edge – first cigarette of the morning, slow calm spiced with a very strong coffee on the side. Sofia would rather not smoke too much, limits herself – when she is not crazy. She is not crazy, this is real, she must remind herself, confirming the reality, touching the air close to his skin. But where there are limits there is also the buzz. Limitation is not Sofia's strong point, though it's usually worth the effort. Excess is always too blurred. Sofia would not blur this time if she could help it, the sensations are better with edges. Edge pieces. She is jigsawing, fitting together with the man, she would rather know where his skin stops and hers begins. She would rather know where she is. London, Crouch End, top-floor flat, her sitting room, the creaking loose floorboards, his arms. She is five and would work backwards from the Universe, the Galaxy, the World. Those words are not bigger than she is. Not right now. Beneath this moment there is a flavour of maybe, like whisky in her mouth. Whisky and in that case she is thirteen, sneaking a quick mouthful before school. It is not good whisky, but it is not a good school either. Dance school, not brain school, there is not enough reading, barely learning, never enough concentration on things of the mind. There is just body to be fitted into the perfect shape, perfect place. It is here. Fitted into the perfect shape, perfect place.

There is movement, she does not want him to let her go, would hold on to the cocoon of safety. Then she realises it is her own movement, turning into him, into openness from protection. Turn in to open out. Perfect turn out, ballerina move, perfectly executed. First position, second, possibility of third. She is not sure what is allowed. She feels encouraged, urged on – whose urgency? Gabriel's skin is much darker than hers, but there is a sense of light behind it. She read once – on a bathroom wall perhaps – that angels must not wash too much, their luminosity fades with water. She wants to ask him if that is true, if he rations his ablutions, but it might sound rude, she is not criticising. He does not have the taste of someone who washes rarely. He does not have the taste of anyone she recognises. Except herself. His fingers in her mouth feel like licking herself, a flesh wound, cut finger, scratched arm – primal need to stop the flow of blood, add fresh saliva to the coagulation process. Unthinking, undoing.

They are nearly naked, few remaining clothes slipped off, as if it was perfectly normal. It is perfectly normal. Holding the angel on her sitting-room floor. The songs that have been written about this moment are further from the truth than she could have believed. The man's kiss is fresh water running over her skin, beneath her the crunch of dried lilies turning to soft dust as they lie down to face each other. And yet it is so ordinary as well. She sees herself reflected in his eyes. She looks like Sofia and not. Inside the reflection is the pupil, open to view, wide dilation to the other place. If eyes are the window of the soul, what is she looking at? What is she looking at when she assumes that what she is holding in her arms is all soul, just soul? Sofia looks away because it is too close and too much and understanding right now might include terror. Knowing it all would be excessive, knowing this instant is enlightenment. For now.

In the dance. They hold each other, hold close and then apart. The two actions feel identical. Touch, smell and taste, she begins to listen to him. The sound of his flesh. Her fingernails on his torso are rain dropping measured on to wetter grass. Sunshine falls on their nakedness, fails on their nakedness – the day outside is yellow and blue, washing in through opened windows, but it cannot match the light of this. She sips millimetres from the flesh of his arm and it is cool-juice oranges she tastes, then mango skin ripped through – not cut, not tidy, not polite – to soft liquid dribbling down her chin, his mouth falls to her shoulders, collarbone, breast. It is so slow.

In the dance. There is kiss and fuck and will again one day and maybe did so many times before but she can't remember now. This is not in love and certainly not in lust, there is less desire and more reality, but it is happening. Though she did not expect, would not have wanted, could not have planned, she would not now do other. And then she takes a whole breath moment to think that perhaps she did plan, from the first time he appeared. And maybe he planned too, maybe this present action is also his job. To soothe her, hold her, kiss her, fuck her. Making it all better the old-fashioned way. Certainly Sofia knows there is no space now for thoughts of the future, fear for her body, anger at the unwanted choice. Her skin is taken over by the barely-touch of his, pores filled with the scent of the man that is not him but her, and the her that is not herself. She does not know the other Sofia now. This is new Sofia because she has never been here before, has been many places and many people before but not this one, not this particular Sofia naked on the floor, both surrender and ultimate leap in one. Yield to own, cede to gain. Sofia is giving in and it feels like she's winning.

In the dance. The actual sex. It is no more actual than any other, no less. It is just sex, passion. Lust. He is not her finest, nor she his. This is not about the showing off of 'I can give you the best time ever'. There is no competition with lovers past and present, real and imaginary. There are only the two of them in the empty room, one extra in the womb. Sofia has not let thoughts of the pregnancy run away, it is there between them, solid as the nearly no-flesh on her toned-woman's belly. It is part of them, the reason for this coupling – though not the result. Without the pregnancy she would not be here – with it, she can be nowhere else. Time moves around them while they hold the moment. The sun is thinking about setting, light changing through white to yellow to faded orange. It is hours since they began.

In the dance. There is no orgasm, that would be too easy. That would be release. This is not about the freedom of release, but acquiescence. His goal is to have her agree, late and unready, but anyway. Even now. Even here. She does so, there is no possibility of any other answer, not after this. And maybe she was ready to agree anyway, with no other choice open to her, maybe she was searching for a way to agree anyway. He did not expect it to be so pleasurable. He could not know it would be so good. His recall does not work that way, Gabriel has no sense memory of other skin, another's flesh – though there has been, and often. He has gained her consent. That was the aim. But now Sofia has taken something back for herself. Now she has his consent in return. Which was unexpected.

Not simply fate then, after all.

Fifteen

'I didn't think you were allowed to do that.'

He shook his head and laughed at her. No words, just laughing, body suppressing bigger comedy. Easier now. Almost. Close to easy.

'What? What's funny? I just didn't think it's what you did, you know—'

'Angels and men?'

'Well, yeah. Or women in this case. I didn't think you were allowed.'

'Why not?'

Sofia frowned, unsure if Gabriel meant it or was just taking the piss, 'I don't know. Isn't it what everyone thinks?'

'Is it?'

'I just thought that was how it was.'

'*City of Angels*?'

'*Wings of Desire*, actually.'

Gabriel smiled again, this time more interested, anthropologist angel, 'Ah, a traditionalist. But I thought you didn't like reading movies?'

Sofia didn't like this, didn't want the new lover to have the same knowledge as an old boyfriend, 'You know too much about me.'

'Very likely.'

'Well, however you've got your information, you're right,

I don't like reading films, it irritates me that the translations are usually so bad. But it's not that. Not in this case. It's just that I dislike Meg Ryan even more.'

'You don't like cute?'

'Not when that cute is at least ten years older than me, no.'

'Nasty.'

'Oh yes. Is that something you didn't know about me?'

'They leave us a few things to find out for ourselves.'

'Thank God for that.'

'Maybe.'

A pause and then he leaned up on one elbow, his face close to hers, 'Really? Columbo rather than Nicholas Cage? You'd really choose Columbo over Nicholas Cage?'

She pulled him closer, light kiss to his forehead, 'Bruno Ganz actually, but yeah, maybe Columbo would do. Of course, I'd have to see you in a trench coat.'

The two of them lying on top of her bed, orthopaedic mattress massaging backs surprised by the unexpected bending, unplanned touch. Gabriel tracing her shoulders with lightest fingertips, almost irritating, almost perfect. Sofia's interest in his flesh was self-evident, her interest in his soul was slightly more surprising. To both of them. Another unexpected. Sofia tried again, 'Are you really not going to get into trouble?'

'What?'

'The sex thing. Me and you.'

'It's not disallowed.'

'Not encouraged either?'

'No, not as definite as that,' he frowned, 'Nothing really. Free will. Up to the individual.'

'The individual angel?'

She half-tripped on the word but managed to get it out anyway, only a demi-smirk betraying her awareness of the ludicrousness of the situation.

'That's right.'

Sofia lay on her back and wondered. 'If it's up to the individual, then what about Lucifer?'

Gabriel winced, barely perceptible but for the temperature change on his skin, cool half-a-degree drop. His skin that rubbed smooth and not-touching against Sofia; 'What about him?'

'I thought the fall was about him making a choice to do what he wanted.' Gabriel didn't answer.

Sofia continued, pressing for an answer. 'That's not the case?'

'On this occasion, if you must boil it down to the bare bones, yes. Sort of. Just be aware that what you've always thought—'

'Might well have been a load of shite, yes of course, I'm a dancer, not a fucking idiot. Don't let the great body confuse you.'

She wrapped her legs tighter around his waist. He ran his hand along her thigh.

'OK. I'll try very hard not to be confused. Or distracted.'

He kissed her knee.

Sofia continued, 'So anyway, wasn't Lucifer exercising free will?'

Again the shiver, 'In a way.'

'Then why the fall?'

'All free will doesn't get unrestricted approval, you know. He did what he wanted. And some people think he got what he wanted too.'

'Eternal damnation, never to walk in the light of God again, cast out for all time?'

'For a girl who never went to Sunday school, you know a lot of phrases.'

'For a girl who had an affair with an ex-seminarian I know a lot of phrases.'

'Oh. When?'

'Berlin. It's how I know when the movie translations are rubbish. German ones anyway.'

Gabriel rolled on to his back, pulling Sofia across him, 'OK, well, you could look at it like that, eternally bereft of the love of God, all the usual verdicts. But if you see it from his perspective—'

'Lucifer's?'

'Mmm, him.'

'You don't do names?'

'Not if I can help it.'

'Go on.'

'Well, in the very simplistic terms in which you're viewing it – then it's actually because of the fall that he's got a kingdom of his own, people of his own, only slight losses in the overall battle for souls. Weigh it up like that, I don't imagine he thinks he's doing too badly. You might not want the outcome of his choice, that's not to say he doesn't.'

Sofia laughed, 'Are you meant to be an apologist for the dark side?'

Gabriel shook his head, 'It's not that clear. None of it is. Never has been.'

'So he's real then? The fallen angel?'

Gabriel shrugged, 'Maybe.'

Sofia liked this, it was learning. Learning and fucking. Ideal. They kissed more, easier, calmer, grown adult not virgin teenage.

She pulled back to look at him, 'So what are you?'

'Sorry?'

'You look like a man, walk like a man, talk like a man – but you're not, are you?'

'Not really. But not not either. I'm kind of a go-between.'

'Messenger?'

'Bit more than that.'

'The thing between God and man?'

'Sometimes.'

'Tranny God.'

'What?'

'God dressed as man, man dressed as God.'

'No, definitely not that. Just – different. And same.'

'That helps no end.'

Gabriel kissed her, wide lips open to her mouth, perfect teeth clashing in eagerness, breathing through each other.

She pulled back to look at him, 'Yeah, well, that helps a lot.'

Helping over, she asked again, 'What's your job, then?'

'To be with you.'

'Guide me?'

'Maybe.'

'Take care of me?'

'If necessary.'

'Make sure I go through with it?'

'If necessary.'

Sofia looked at him, tested the dark eyes for meaning, 'So much for free will.'

'This is your free will. So far, you're going along with this.'

'So far, this is fucking me up more than you can imagine. But at the very least, I don't even know if I believe in this.'

'I think you can. I think you can believe in this.'

'Think? Don't you know for definite?'

Gabriel smiled, he had no other answers.

More touch of the no-touch. The act, physical and vocal, completely believable. Tangible lusts, a prototype of perfect desire – two bodies doing the thing and fitting and fucking and making it happen without the words and the thought and the dis-ease of asking. No questions, no answers, no failed comprehension. Misconception. Too late. Already had it on that score. Brief sleep, setting sun.

Tea and toast with lime marmalade and too much butter dripping on to tired fingers.

'Is it . . . alright to keep doing this?'

'The sex?'

Sofia nodded.

'I can't see why not. My choice, your choice, both consenting adults, both ready and willing, I don't think we've done anything wrong, do you?'

'I don't know. I don't know what the rules are.'

Gabriel shrugged, 'Neither do I half the time, I think they wait to see what happens and then make up new rules as we go along.'

'They?'

The man shrugged, 'It's hard to talk about. None of your words works – He, They, It – none of them covers the concept adequately.'

'How about She?'

He smiled, 'Not even that one.'

'OK, you can explain later, but this – well, surely omniscience implies pre-knowledge? I thought he knew everything before it happened.'

'Big words for a dancer.'

'Lap dancer.'

'Stripper.'

'Great shag.'

'Fantastic shag.'

'Thank you, don't distract me. As I said, the seminarian was good. I go back to my original point, I thought he knew everything before it happened?'

'Yeah, well, that is the official line. But that's also a bit dull isn't it? Knowing everything already. I think maybe that there's sometimes no thought about what's going to happen, just so it can seem new.'

'Re-runs of *The X-Files* and kidding yourself you don't know Scully's going to get away from the Fluke Man.'

'Kind of. Like the free will thing – I sometimes think that's why the concept was invented. To make it more interesting – set up the chance of change.'

'And more interesting for us too?'

'Oh yes, definitely more interesting for us.'

Sex. Sleep. Midnight snacks. Bread and olives and Stilton and bitter green apples. Sex. Sleep. Heavy sleep and exhausted body with which to push away the panics and the dark blue and the pre-dawn terrors. No worries and no panic attacks and no dreams. No nothing. Sofia was too tired for fear. And angels can't dream.

Sixteen

Morning comes in across the top of deep sleep night and Sofia awakes, ready to roll into the arms of the warm one. He is not there. She stays in bed, half sleeping, waiting perhaps for the sound of cooking, scent of coffee fresh from the kitchen. Waits twenty minutes and Gabriel does not come in, but worry thoughts do, a slow dawning recognition of alone. The pain fits, jigsaw-puzzle piece she hoped she'd lost for good. Sofia removes herself from the bed with dread heavy legs. Does not bother to call out, does not want silence mocking her too. Checks the flat though. Just in case. Just in case her hormonal condition has affected her better judgement. But he is not in the kitchen, not in the bathroom, and most certainly not in the bed.

Sofia climbs back into her bed and pulls the duvet over her head as if the touch of cotton sheets could make her warm. There is no hot back leaning into the mattress, almost touching with his no-touch skin, no flesh to remind, to reassure her of last night's reality, faded through soft and gentle sleep into rude reawakening. Gabriel – who made it all seem so very possible only four sweet hours ago is not there. And Sofia – and this is not really the point, because she would so have the point be about what it was they did together overnight, undernight, through the night, and the talking and the fucking, and the talking that was like fucking and the fucking that was so much more than only physical – only unfortunately, that is not the case, because he has gone, away, definitely not in the bedroom, kitchen, sitting room, flat – and, though this is not the point, not what really matters this morning, but all the same, and though there is so much more to concern herself with – Sofia is not a well chick.

Sofia is a very poorly girl indeed. Retching from deep stomach, aching, shivering. This is not morning sickness. This is merely the should-have-been-expected unwell of drinking too much on an empty stomach, drinking too much on a full uterus. Sick from alcohol and sick unhappiness. Not morning sickness, though not completely unconnected either. Sofia will be more ill later. Her particular baby sickness will manifest itself in seven thirty evening vomit. Regular as clockwork, three-month contract, and twice as irritating. Planned to start in the middle of next week – hormonal predestination. Only Sofia doesn't know that yet. Wouldn't want to know that yet. Is still dealing with knowing that Gabriel is not there, is no longer in her flat, in her presence, isn't anywhere she can see and hasn't even had the grace to leave a note, and fuck it, but it really hadn't occurred to her that this man, that an angel, could possibly turn out to be just so damn boy.

She walked, tired, bit coked still, bit drunk anyway, bit fucked definitely, from bed to kitchen to toilet to vomit and back to bed again. Walked in disappointed disbelief. Not really, not truly, not with no evidence of his having been there, another morning after, and again nothing to show. She couldn't believe she'd done sex with the stranger at her age, at this adult stage. When she'd decided not to ever again and knew she didn't want to be that girl. Not now. Not now she knew how much it always hurt her later. Except even without the baby idea, the conception concept, even without any of that, it still hadn't felt like just sex. Not in the middle of the night. None of it had seemed the meaningless physical – enjoyable on its own certainly, but not really what she was after right now. All of it, from the very first, had seemed a little more, a lot more. So then that was even worse, because if it hadn't been just stranger-fuck, then maybe she cared, maybe it mattered beyond the weirdness, and maybe she actually wanted him to come back.

Sofia stood at her window for half an hour, looking out beyond the thin curtain just in case Gabriel climbed down from the bus, walked around the corner, shopping bags slamming his thighs. Perhaps he had just popped out to pick up fresh bread and whole-fruit jam and coffee and the morning papers. Sofia stood at her window for another half hour because maybe it was all right, maybe he might be just fine, surprise man again. Maybe, actually, she really wanted this, wanted him. Then she had been standing there an hour, stomach tensed, shoulders arched nervous to her neck and she dropped the muslin curtain and rushed to the toilet, threw up again. Yeah, and maybe not.

She slept for three hours and woke furious. Fighting fit and furious. A far more useful combination than sick and tired. She rose from her bed, speeding Sleeping Beauty. Exercised, ate fruit, juiced fresh carrots and ginger, drank coffee, stripped the undone, done-him sheets and made her bed crisp and clean again, threw open all the windows to the storm-cleared sky and showered, exfoliated, shaved, smoothed, to an own-voice rendition of 'I'm gonna wash that man right out of my hair'. Added out of my skin, out of my blood, out of my sex. There is nothing like a dame scorned. Played neighbour-unfriendly Ella Fitzgerald at heartbreak volume and threw herself around her sitting room in analysis-dance:

I want him here. Because he knows.

He has answers. He knows things I don't. He knows things about me. He knows things about the plans for me.

But he doesn't know why and he doesn't understand any more than I do and it isn't his plan that he is the messenger for.

So really all I want him for is because he knows a bit more than I do. Dashing white charger syndrome. Always crap anyway. Never works. Never met one man who came on as 'let me save you' and didn't end up with 'make it better, mummy' in the middle of the night.

So fuck that.

I want him here. Because he is in charge.

He can tell me what to do. How to cope with this. He can give me the rules, let me know how it works. He can tell me what to do. He can say it's all right if my body changes, when my body changes, he can make me feel that the out-of-control is bearable.

Bollocks. Some stupid little-girl piece of me that wants to be told what to do. Never do it though. Always want someone else to take responsibility for my decisions and inevitably hate it when they do. Never want a boss, never want a parent. Yet want him to take over, take me, make it better, make my choices.

Too late. He already has done. Big Brother syndrome, legal incest. And anyway, he's not the boss, just the boss's lackey. So he can't be in charge, even if I wanted it, even if he could. He isn't the one running things here.

So that one doesn't work either.

I want him because I am scared. Scared to be pregnant, and scared to look different, and scared to be the mother.

But he won't be doing any of those things, I will.

I want him here. Because he is a great fuck.

Because touching him is like all the touching Heaven

myths. Because being with him is being with one who knows me and gets through.

Because I do not want to lose the new-found sex, big passion, and so, like every other time, any other time, I have turned a simple good lover into man-forever, remade him as an eternal possibility in order to have satiated desire on tap. And I do know better than that, and the possibility that angel-want will not wear off, turn tired like the rest, become dull Friday night once-a-week, is an unproved assumption. Looking forward to the improved assumption.

I want him because I want the sex. Fair enough, but hardly heartbreak material.

So the solution then must be to simply not need him, not want him. He can't make it better and he can't take the hurt away and he may be the angel, but he can't fix it. No one else ever can.

In the final analysis, Sofia chooses that she only wants him for the sex. Not that different after all. Tired out from the dancing and the shouting singalong and the theorising, oceans happier now she has dismissed his importance as irrelevant to her situation beyond his sexual prowess, Sofia collapses on to her couch, reminds herself to wake in an hour before she's late for work. Somewhere at the back of her mind, deep in her belly, there is also baby panic, but in this moment, teenage-girl heartbreak is the most she can deal with. Sofia goes to sleep.

Gabriel is in the sleeping. At the back of her eyes. He is holding her in the sleeping and then she is holding him and they are both making it better, better for each other, even with knowledge that neither can fix it, not really. And yet, in truth, it is easier because he is there, because she has made him be there with her, conjured his sleep presence. And even in the dreaming, Sofia is wondering if maybe she is making all this up, figment of mad-bitch, tired-girl imagination. If there is the baby, then she'll have to deal with it, one way or another. But has she created the man from just desire and is that why he can't be there in the morning, when desire has dissipated and he has no more reason to be? And if that was the case, what might make him be there in the morning? Keep him in her bed? Sofia is not sure how much of this she is making up herself, but in her dream he does not go. In her dream she wakes to Gabriel holding her.

He is not all-knowing and he is not Big Brother and this time there has been no sex anyway, and all that is happening is that he is holding her. Which is not a bad thing. Given the state she's in. Given the need she has. Sofia knows she is in the dream and she would have the dream come true when she wakes up.

Seventeen

When she wakes, he is gone again. Sofia went to work. Ignored her situation for five solid hours. Put away anger thoughts of the missing man, terror of potential child, creeping danger of lurking depression, and charged driven through the evening, her twenty-pound dance fevered with classic desire. Sofia danced like she was looking for someone's head to rip off, lion-proud woman in tiger-skin bra. Danny had to have a word with her halfway through the night. She was scaring the punters. Easily scared admittedly, but worrying all the same. Giving her all was just a little more than the revellers were actually after. Something slightly less impressive would do for the next couple of hours if she didn't want to send a room full of semi-pissed men screaming from the building. Danny really didn't want to see them go and he didn't want to see his best dancer chase them off. The buyers wanted pretend sex on a plate delivered to their table by the sweetest of compliant and polite waitresses. They didn't want something so worryingly close to the real thing, served up on a roasting spit, hissing truth and dervishing itself two feet in front of them, a lifetime too close for comfort.

Sofia would have started arguing with Danny, she was the dancer and, while it was his establishment, her boss was not known for his choreographic techniques, until she looked up and she saw both Caroline and Sandra nodding in agreement. Sofia had no interest in Danny's judgement of her abilities, but she knew the other dancers couldn't be wrong. She stepped back, breathed deep, apologised to the boss, smiled at the nice young men in their already-crumpled new suits and took her leave, back in five, ten, fifteen at the most. In the home-base safety of the dressing room she refreshed herself with two showers. One burning hot, one ice cold. Neither helped a great deal, but both reminded her more forcefully of where she was. Girl changing room, girls at work, working girl. Job to do, money to earn, no need for bridges to burn. Not yet anyway, not before she had to. Not before the belly started to show. She'd need the cash then.

Sofia went home, back of Matt's cab, thrilling to the silence of Jim Croce and ignoring the scream of her brain. She showered again, slept surprisingly soundly – grateful that she had so exhausted her body there was no degree of wakefulness left to notice the disturbances of either men or angels. The next morning she woke feeling better and brighter than she had in days and left her flat as quickly as she could, determined getaway halted only briefly by a two sentence roadblock when she met Martha on the front stairs. Martha coming in, picking at spider plant leaves, Sofia going out, ignoring the dry soil and wishing Martha would too. Sofia didn't mind Martha housekeeping James's life, but preferred the brand new girlfriend to leave the communal spaces free of her itching-to-clean hands. For her part, Martha was burning to ask about the fuck-partner whose floor-pounding antics had kept her and James awake the night before, but did not want to evince that much interest in Sofia's life. Not at the expense of needing to seem friendly. As neither woman could force herself to chat beyond weather forecasting, Sofia was into the street before James could open his front door and begin his own neighbourly inquisition. Sofia was thankful for small mercies and counted them as she walked to Beth's. She managed to be grateful for warm sunlight and cold Martha before reigning terrors stopped playtime and fear began to seep back in. The long walk to Beth's house turned into shorter run and panic spate was briefly replaced by sweat state.

Sofia sat on the floor at the feet of the very pregnant one and explained the events of the last couple of days. She bit at the edges of the her fingernails as she did so and it was all Beth could do to listen quietly and not grab Sofia's hands, in an attempt to save her ravaged skin from the vicious teeth. Beth had no problem believing Sofia had spent the other night delirium-fucking a virtual stranger. It was behaviour she expected of Sofia. It was behaviour she had once expected of herself. She had no problem believing the man had left without trace or polite notice the next morning. That, too, was sadly unexceptional. She found it slightly more impossible to accept that Sofia really was pregnant. Unsurprisingly, however, she did have a couple of unused pregnancy tests sitting hopefully at the back of her bathroom cupboard. Three cups of tea, a litre of mineral water, and a running cold water tap later, Sofia emerged from the toilet with two bright blue sticks. Different manufacturers, different sell-by dates, same result.

'Shit, babe.'

'My thoughts exactly.'

'But how could you be pregnant?'

'Magic? Fate? The hand of God?'

'Bollocks of God more like. It must be James's baby.'

'No, I've had at least two periods since James and I last had sex.'

'Yes, but that doesn't necessarily mean anything. What about women who go on bleeding throughout their pregnancies? It's not impossible. Those women who go on chat shows and talk about how they didn't even know they were pregnant until it popped out?' Beth rubbed her own swollen stomach and added with last month irritation, 'Lucky cows.'

'Yeah, could be. Why not? Makes as much sense as the rest of it. Maybe I'll even sell the story to *Chat* magazine.'

'*Guardian* Woman's Page, please.'

'Whatever Beth. The point is, I know about those stories, I've seen as much crap telly as you have.'

'Surely not?'

'More probably, but I'm certain I wasn't pregnant before. Then the man arrived, told me what was going to happen. And now I am. I am with child. Not James's child.'

Beth's protestations made no difference. If Sofia's night with Gabriel had left her hoping for more and disappointed by his disappearance, the almost-met of his angel flesh, touching her as if normal, as if anyman, had also somehow convinced her of his story. For the moment anyway.

As she explained to Beth, 'Look, I don't know what the baby will be. I don't even know if I'll be able carry it for long. Fuck knows it must be full of alcohol and coke and God knows what else – but he said I couldn't harm it. He told me that whatever I'd done wouldn't make any difference. I really don't know if I believe any of this Messiah stuff anyway, though according to him, the career plan is up to the kid not me, anyway. But I am pregnant, and I know I didn't fuck to get it. What has happened is that I have spent a night shagging a bloke who appears in my flat and sometimes behind my eyes. When they're closed. I understand it sounds like crap. But you know what Beth? I don't feel like a loony. It doesn't make any sense, but I don't feel like I've lost it at all. I'm tired and pissed off that he's disappeared and I don't know how to get hold of him – not even if I wanted to, and I'm not sure that I do – but I really and truly don't feel like a nutter.'

Beth forbore to mention that Sofia's sanguine attitude was classic delusional behaviour. Held back the words that might have suggested Sofia could feel as brave and strong as she wanted to right now, but in another day or so, when the exhaustion-euphoria of the unexpected sex had worn off, she might just slip back into teenage boyfriend mourning. Nor did she add that she herself had experienced such major hormonal swings in pregnancy, that the depression dip and the bliss trip might well present themselves just hours or even minutes apart.

She did, though, question what now seemed to be Sofia's acceptance of her pregnancy. 'So you're not even going to enquire about having an abortion?'

'He told me it wouldn't work.'

'And you definitely believe him?'

Sofia groaned, 'I don't know.'

'Do you think you want the baby now?'

'No. Not want it. At least, not like you wanted this pregnancy of yours. But I don't feel like I did before, something's changed. I don't feel in control any more.'

'Of course you don't. You've given all your control over to this bloke, this complete stranger. You know what, Sofia? I still can't tell if you think he's real or not, but he's certainly a good excuse for you to abdicate responsibility.'

'How do you mean?'

'He's said you can't have an abortion, so you're not even finding out about it. He's said you have to go through with this, and it looks like you are. Has it occurred to you that you made him up because actually having this baby is what you really want?'

Sofia bit back, 'Yes it has, and no I didn't. Gabriel is real, when he's with me he is anyway. The baby's real too. And it doesn't have a father that I know of. Nor did I mean to be pregnant. I know all that to be true. But as well as that,

I don't know that there is anything else I can do. I just have to get on with it.'

'Sounds a lot like giving in to me.'

'Yeah, it does to me too. But with no other choice—'

'No other choice you're willing to make,' Beth interrupted her.

'OK then. No other choice I feel capable of making, I don't know what else to do. I'm doing what I can. I'm getting on with it. I don't know how else to be.'

Beth could have gone on with her questioning, but she wasn't sure there was much point. She studied her friend carefully and decided the best course of action was to push nothing yet, just to keep an eye on her. Beth did not believe that Gabriel was an angel and she did not believe Sofia was pregnant with the Messiah – New or Old Testament version. For some reason though, Sofia was not as worried about mothering it as Beth would have believed. No matter what she said about not wanting it, Sofia was doing nothing to get rid of it. Neither her words nor her fear matched her actions. From the therapist's point of view Beth understood this to mean Sofia actually wanted to keep the child. From a friend's point of view it appeared equally possible that Sofia was simply too freaked by what was happening to move on the idea. Either way, she was going to stay pregnant. The child then, may well turn out to be James's. If it was, then they'd simply have to wait for scans and tests to tell them exactly how pregnant she really was. According to Sofia, the last James fuck had been a couple of months ago, if not longer. Foetal age would determine if James was the potential father. If not, then maybe the earlier pregnancy tests Sofia had done herself at home had been a premonition aberration, and these new ones they'd taken today were the truth. In which case, Sofia had fucked Gabriel the disappearing man, and now she was pregnant with his child. Certainly it was a very early reading for ordinary chemist pregnancy tests, but not impossible either. Maybe this angel-man had found a way in and out of Sofia's place and for some fucked up reason of his own had decided to get into her life, into her bed, make his way in just as clearly as he'd found his way into her head. Anyway, the biology of the father wasn't all that important, not just yet. Whoever he was could be proven in time. What really mattered to Beth was her ex-client and friend sitting on the floor in front of her. The fact that Sofia seemed to have gone so far into this new fantasy that, unlike her previous panic just days earlier, she now thought it might make sense that she'd been visited by an angel and deemed the new Mother of God.

At least that was what Beth was concerned with while she made them both lunch, prepared chilli-oil salad dressing, ate anchovy-stuffed baked potatoes. This was what filled her questioning brain while she talked to Sofia about the still-necessary house decoration, sought her advice on stomach exercises she might want to think about doing after the babies were born. Her friend's sanity or otherwise was Beth's prime concern as she and Sofia folded and prepared baby clothes in the corner of Beth and Pete's previously minimalist bedroom. A corner that was rapidly becoming gift-given Baby Gap central. And Sofia's state of mind would have stayed Beth's main concern of the day, had she not felt an odd loosening in her lower belly, a strange slip of the vagina, and then the oddest sensation as her waters broke. A disappointingly small trickle compared to the floodgate-opening her sister had told her to expect, but it did manage to splash Sofia a little. A little baptism. A little early. A little boy and girl born small and healthy thirteen hours later.

Eighteen

Sofia had never been at a birth before. She had not meant to attend this one either, but Pete was as late arriving as the twins were early and by the time he got away from his beyond-the-M25 job and crossed the city in panic traffic, making it for the last two hours, Sofia was enlisted as handmaiden. Beth wasn't letting go of Sofia – or only long enough to shaking-hold and then smack Pete's face for getting her in this position in the first place. And even then the drained fingernail welts in Sofia's arm barely had time to fill with blood before Beth grabbed her again in a push-pull lament. Like any other girl of the TV age, Sofia had seen the gory glory births, both docu-soap and real soap. Nothing quite prepared her for the reality. Neither the excessive sweating nastiness of Beth's wrenching pain – especially laboured as the twins were born over two hours apart and she didn't get to lie back and be bliss-tired mother after the first one – nor the extremity of emotion when first the tiny girl and then her tinier baby brother finally saw the light of day and delivery room. It was awful. And awe-full. And Sofia was scared.

By the time she made it home, work night cancelled, Sofia's passing enthusiasm for the new life brilliance had been completely eclipsed by the lingering image of blood and shit and tears. Unlike Beth and Pete, Sofia did not have newborn life to hang on to, smoothing away the pain vista with squalling breath. What she had was going home alone and no baby to hold to make the pain worthwhile and no partner to assure her it would all be all right in the end. Beth slept fitfully and Pete sat watching over the brand new family. Sofia crouched in the back of a cab watching over the prospect of going through it alone and knowing no one would be able to believe her truth when she did it herself in nine months' time. In less than nine months' time. Three-quarters of a year did not seem long enough to convince herself that it might be possible. And neither the most reassuring of Beth's midwives, nor the gentlest of her doctors or the delighted interest of half a dozen nurses who must have seen newborns thousands of times and yet were still enthused, would make it feel any better when the moment came. Sofia was heading alone towards an event most of humankind approaches in pairs. With overtones of interventionist governments and doom-laden prophecies on the decline of family life spinning through her tired brain, she felt painfully single.

Gabriel was waiting for her when she got in.

'How was it?'

'Fucking exhausting and bloody scary. Exhausting, bloody and scary.'

'Were you there for the whole thing?'

'Other than the five minutes when I dashed out for my usual bout of evening sickness, yes. Where have you been?'

'Wasn't it OK in the end though?'

'I'm sorry?'

'Didn't you feel glorified with the new babies?'

'What?'

'You know – moved, touched.'

'Oh please.' Sofia sneered, 'Beth was amazing really, fine

at first, but then she was screaming in pain for the last hour and a half, begging them to rip the boy out of her when she realised it wasn't over after the first one and she had to keep being in extreme pain despite having gone through all that already, and then when it was done she was stitched up like a roast chicken and sent off to sleep and she looked like shite.'

'But surely Beth and Pete think it was worth it? The new babies? Worth the pain?'

'I have no doubt they think every single second was well worth it and I'm sure they're right. Positively, perfectly, absolutely right. Like every other happy family since time began. But there's two of them. She has Pete to hold her now and play big daddy and take care of the whole new family and I'm sure it will all be deliriously gorgeous when she wakes up – until she tries to walk again, that is – and I expect that just like every other new mother in love with her babies, she'll decide that she remembers nothing of how awful it was because now she has two perfect children. Though actually, I can't quite see Beth turning into some fucking earth mother overnight, but yes, I have no doubt that both she and Pete are completely overjoyed. Still. Will be for days. Years probably. Is that what you wanted to hear?'

Gabriel looked at her, uncertain how to answer, this was not quite the reaction he had been expecting.

Sofia continued, 'You see, whatever you thought I was going to feel about this, you didn't think it through clearly enough, did you?'

He moved towards her, feet not quite on the ground – even in her state of heightened excitement, Sofia could see his feet were not quite on the ground – she held him at bay with an outstretched, trembling hand.

'Leave me alone!' Gabriel stopped. Sofia went on. 'Look, it was amazing. Incredible. It was all that miracle of human life shit, just like every birth anyone's ever told me about, and better for being there, for the warmth of Beth's body and the smell of the blood. And I did cry, God knows I cried the whole time, and I was really moved and impressed and I do think Beth is brave and amazing and all that crap. But Beth wanted this. Planned for this. Spent years trying to make this happen. Beth has Pete. This is exactly what they always wanted.' Sofia started to pace the room, Gabriel backed away. 'This is not – in case you hadn't noticed Gabriel – not exactly what I always wanted. It is nothing like exactly what I always wanted. And while the miracle of human life may indeed be the ultimate blessing to those who get to keep the baby, to have and to hold, to those of us who come home alone in the middle of the night and have to know we're going through that some time in the next year, to those of us completely freaked by what we've just seen, to those of us who have never in our lives even suggested it was what we wanted – to me, stupid – to me, it just looks terrifying. Absolutely terrifying. I'm scared Gabriel.'

Gabriel frowned, 'Scared. Does that mean you've decided to have the baby?'

Sofia looked up at him, 'What do you mean, decided to have it? You told me I didn't have any choice.'

'No, there's always choice, free will.'

'You said I wouldn't be able to have an abortion, you said it wouldn't work. Where's the free will in that?'

Gabriel shrugged his wide shoulders, 'You could try anyway. Choosing not to even try is also making a choice. It is still using your free will.'

Sofia shook her head, tired out with the day and her confusion, 'Yeah? Well that's a pretty loose definition of free will.'

Then Gabriel nodded, 'You're right. It is.'

*   *   *

Sofia cried and Gabriel apologised. He tried to explain the reasoning behind her day's experience. Though he didn't admit to Sofia that he wasn't quite sure of the logic himself. He gave her the party line, hoped it might be more effective for her than it had been for him. Theoretically it had been supposed that the experience would be good for her. It was intended to make having her own baby seem more possible. Remind Sofia that birth and motherhood were really ordinary. Women had been doing it for ever, for centuries without thought, without preparation, without books and videos and classes. Quite often without men. No big deal, just having a baby. But even Gabriel had thought this probably wouldn't work. Of course it was an everyday occurrence, but he knew it was not ordinary for Sofia. It was a millions of times every day experience, somewhere across the world babies were being born, constant churning out of screaming new life to accompany the still more constant snuffing out of the cold old. But not normal for Sofia. Birth and death. The only two completely mundane experiences guaranteed to happen to every human being. And the only real dichotomy events – so ordinary as to happen to everyone, so personally extraordinary as to change each life completely. For ever. Her handmaiden night had not eased Sofia's worries at all. It had just energised the waiting fear, confirmed her solitary sense of powerless inevitability. Gabriel had known this might be the outcome and been incapable of taking better care of her. His job was merely to guard – he was not granted the gift of saving.

Gabriel held her and Sofia felt again that his presence calmed her, even though she didn't want to be calmed, even when she wanted to stay furious with him. For leaving after their night together. For having the presumption to think anyone might know better than her what she needed right now. Sofia had no idea what she needed right now, but she knew that an overload of experiential knowledge, leading to complete terror wasn't likely to be the best option. Most of all, though, she was furious that he made her feel better. That whatever angel thing was going on, whenever Gabriel came closer to her, she did feel better. And Sofia didn't want guardian-calm. She wanted to have a fight. Big, loud, physical if necessary, energy-draining if at all possible, fight. But she was already too tired. And scared. And even in the place of fear she knew she was also, at the same time, delighted to confirm again that she was clearly not crazy. He was standing – hovering nearly – in front of her, radiant skin and seeming perfect calm. Tangible Heaven. Sofia was still pregnant. And Gabriel was still an angel. He was the angel. Her angel. His being there did make her feel better. Just like angels were supposed to. Nothing had changed, none of her fears had gone away, but being close to Gabriel made her feel better. Sofia went to sleep. Gabriel stood at the end of her bed and watched over her. It was his job. It was also his growing desire.

Nineteen

The next morning Gabriel was still there. This time he tried to add education to the breakfast. Toast and enlightenment.

'We need to talk.'

Sofia, bleary-eyed from sleep and confusion wearily raised her head from the pillow, half smile ready for the coffee, full frown showing that the rest of her was clearly uninterested in anything more.

'Why? What do I have to do now?'

'We need to get on, make some decisions.'

Sofia looked at her alarm clock, 'It's ten o'clock in the morning! What decisions can I possibly need to make at ten o'clock in the morning?'

'Pre-natal care.'

'I haven't even definitely decided I'm keeping it yet.'

'But you said—'

'I know. And you said free will. Maybe I will try to get rid of it.'

Gabriel paused and then shook his head, 'I don't think so.'

'Why not?'

'Because this is different.'

'Yes, I had gathered that.'

'Because even if you believe abortion is a woman's choice—'

'Do you?'

'I . . . I don't know. I don't think it's my right to say.'

'Oh, very new man.'

'New angel actually, staying out of the debate is hardly the traditional mode of practice. The point is, though, it isn't just your child you're dealing with.'

'Whose is it then?'

'Well, really, the Messiah belongs to—'

Sofia held out her hand, 'You can stop right there. It's too early for another theological lecture and, as you well know, I'm not at all clear on what I think about this baby being the Messiah. Or not.'

'Yes, but—'

'No buts. I'll make up my own mind about that one. When I'm ready. Meanwhile, I need to work out what the hell I'm going to do next. Because, according to you, there's nothing I can do to get out of this situation.'

'So you understand you have to keep the baby? That's your choice?'

'No Gabriel, I understand that I have no choice. That I'm choosing to put up with what's been forced upon me.'

Gabriel smiled, continued with his original speech, 'A choice by any other name. Good.'

'Yeah, fantastic. Is that it? Can I go back to sleep?'

'No. Now we need to decide what you're going to tell your doctor.'

'I'm pregnant. That's all she needs to know.'

'Your family? Your friends? James? What you're going to do about work?'

Sofia was definitely awake now, 'Oh come on, I hardly think any of that's got much to do with you. Nor do I think that a quiet "By the way Mum, I'm the new Virgin Mary" is going to keep me out of the nut-house for long, so I imagine I'll come up with something slightly less ludicrous. Given time. What I choose to tell people about all this is surely up to me? Unless it's another one of those so-called choices you're planning to take away from me because you can't be bothered listening properly to my answer?'

Gabriel ran a hand through his hair, twisting it out of his eyes, 'Sofia, you have to understand that you were chosen as well as choosing.'

Sofia pulled the duvet tighter around her, it was a cool London morning with sunshine trying desperately to burn off an early summer haze and find a way in, but not yet making much headway. 'Well thanks. You really do make me feel so damn special.'

'All part of the job. But it is all about choices, every moment brings a new determination.'

'I'm sorry?'

'From now on, things have to be thought through very carefully. Even the steps you think you're taking towards a single goal might well end up leading you in the opposite direction.'

'Very cause and effect, Siddartha as the new Messiah?'

Gabriel frowned, 'Cheap consumer Buddhism's got a lot to answer for.'

Sofia sighed, piled her four pillows against the wall and sat up properly, 'You're not a huge fan of predetermination, then?'

'I understand the concept, but it doesn't leave a great deal of room for personal choice.'

'You can talk. It's not as if I had any options about this, I mean, you just came barging in and took over and started telling me—'

Gabriel groaned, 'Enough! You did say yes.' Then he sighed, bit the edge of a piece of toast, put it back down again. 'I don't know, maybe it's about the choices you take on the path, rather than actually attaining the destination. Maybe you're never really meant to get there.'

'Ah well, that'll explain my constant feeling of dissatisfaction.'

Gabriel went for stern look again, it didn't quite work, his face too gentle for proper headmaster, 'Sofia, your constant feeling of dissatisfaction is explained by the fact that nothing you're doing satisfies you. You're not pushing yourself hard enough, you haven't even worked out what it is you want to be.'

'I thought mother of the Messiah was supposed to be my new aim.'

'Haven't you heard of working mothers? Don't you want more from your life?'

'Bloody hell, this is all too fucking difficult. Couldn't I just stay in bed and hide? I thought the Lord was meant to provide?'

'Not food and lodging, no.'

'Brilliant. So I can't set the CSA on him, then?'

Gabriel smiled, set the tray across her legs and handed her the coffee cup. 'Tell me about your first love.'

'Let's not, why don't I explain just a little more about how this whole baby concept has me completely terrified?'

'I know that. Tell me about your first love.'

'I thought you knew everything.'

'Not from your perspective.'

'Is it relevant?'

'Probably.'

'To what?'

'To what we do next. First love affects everything, whether you recognise it or not.'

Sofia reached for her cup, bit into the apricot jam toast, stared at Gabriel for a full minute, weighing up whether to tell him the story or kick him out. Then she remembered her own hand against the curve of his lower back and how highly inappropriate it was to be contemplating another angel fuck without first giving him the low-down on at least one of her other relationships. Regardless of everything else that was going on, any potential lover deserved to hear at least one of her past-shag stories.

'OK, here goes – but get ready to throw up. This is vomit-worthy perfect.'

Sofia was eighteen and working in Lisbon. Back from Japan for a four month contract, waiting tables and dancing with only a feather boa for company five times a shift, every hour on the hour. Split shift days, splitting headache nights. But it was closer to home than Japan and she could hurry back to Mummy and Daddy a couple of times during the contract, reassure them that the ballet school fees had been well spent, she was still a good girl. Was still their good little girl. And she was, just. Sofia had only recently extricated herself from a three month, no-hope relationship with an American English teacher in Kyoto. He'd been in Japan for five years, slowly transforming himself from Midwest redneck to rice queen dream. The man was gay, he just didn't know it yet. Sofia hoped that her leaving the delicious East on a spice route return passage would awaken him to his gender truth. At least that was the only good reason she could find to explain his reluctance to do more than kiss her for hours on end – and accept her blowjob offers. At eighteen, Sofia was starting to think that perhaps it was about time she met up with a bloke who offered a little more than minty-fresh breath and a fine line in foreskin detail.

Sofia was after her first love, first time, first one. She was up for losing it. She had never really been in love before, never known the overwhelming desire that might take her from tongues entwined to genital twist, had felt that, to a degree, she was saving herself. Not necessarily for something better, but certainly from something worse than all the other first time stories she had heard. Sofia had long before decided that any body so carefully honed and cared for as hers deserved slightly more than the back of a car, side of an alley, bridle path grazing, that most of her friends talked about. Sofia wanted satin sheets and real champagne. She wanted it to happen with The One. And she wanted it quite soon.

She met him in her second week in Lisbon. Zack O'Marr. Fourteen years her senior, already once divorced, a trust fund tart swimming in his own small circle. Beautiful, charming, eloquent and elegant. And an incorrigible slut. He was staying in an apartment overlooking the river in a restored Carmelite convent. She was trying to sleep in a two bedroom flat with five other girls from her work. They met when he came into her bar for a drink and stayed for another eight. He asked her out for dinner with him. At two in the morning. And because he looked Californian hunk and because he'd been a generous tipper all night – and because she was starving – Sofia went with him. The logging company heir took her to a tiny house, down forty steep steps, and knocked softly on a door that read Strictly No Admittance After Midnight. In Portuguese. When an old lady pulled back the window shutter of the floor above and started to scream at him, Zack smiled sweetly up at her and spoke softer still. As far as Sofia could work out after only a fortnight in the country, he sounded pretty damn fluent and had certainly perfected the unlikely Slavic-Spanish accent. Whatever he said seemed to please the old lady, because she smiled a toothless beatification and a minute later the front door was flung back on its silent hinges. Sofia followed Zack down a long dark corridor and up into a light and airy room, lined with Moorish tiles and drunken wealth testifying that, for these diners, the Revolution was long over.

That night Zack took Sofia back to his apartment. That night had become this morning. He assumed she was ready to shag and she carefully explained her predicament – 'So you see, I'm happy to give you a blowjob, handjob, or just go right now if this is pissing you off too much. But I do want the first one to be special and I have been waiting quite some time and I do really fancy you and I think you've been delightful all evening. It's just that I have this vision of how it should be. I'd like to know I was going to do it. To prepare myself. Make sure the sheets are clean.' Sofia looked down at her own dress, which she'd now worn to and from work for the past three days, 'To make sure I'm clean.'

If Zack was pissed off he didn't show it. He handed Sofia a couple of towels and a dressing-gown. He showed her to the guest bedroom and private bathroom. He suggested that, if it suited the plan, he'd wake her in time for lunch, she could shop for a new dress in the afternoon, he'd have the cleaner change his sheets, and then he'd pick her up after work that evening. And if she still wanted, they could come back to his apartment then. Sofia ignored the *Pretty Woman* warning signals flashing in her brain, took another look at his all-American beauty and agreed. It was a naff movie and he seemed like a nice enough guy and she did have to do it sometime. This might be the best offer she was going to get.

Best offer, best result. Not great sex, but not bad either. They didn't know each other's bodies, neither was yet in love with the other, it was an unusual arrangement and a steady transaction. And Sofia was only a phallic penetration virgin after all. There wasn't much else she hadn't done. And there wasn't much else Zack was leaving undone. The first night was perfectly adequate. The deed was done. The next night was better. And by their second bottle of champagne on the fifth day they were both getting really good at it. Lots of rolling on the floor, more slamming up against the hall door, plenty of uses for the fizzy liquid. Zack wanted the sex and Sofia wanted the experience. They were both honest with each other and the truth gamble paid off. They got on well and they liked each other and it was all easy and pleasant and summer.

She never forgot him. And she never quite forgave him either. Because though he had been perfectly clear from the very start that he was only in it for the fun and the sex, and though in many ways he had done her a great favour, and though he let her stay in the apartment for another month, rent free and all the grapes she could eat, when Zack climbed back aboard the yacht and sailed off for another season of playing in the Mediterranean with a group of like-financed layabouts, Sofia knew she was in love and he wasn't. Zack had been great first sex, everything she could have teenage-wished for. Everything she had teenage-wished for. For a long time, at least until she'd met James, she'd also thought that maybe he was The One. Then after James she sometimes wondered if she'd passed up her second chance as well. Her fault, her choice, no reason to bother telling Zack about how she'd felt all that time ago. Or about her subsequent depression, when she found herself slammed back alone into dark blue night.

Sofia didn't tell Gabriel this though. She finished the story with herself waving goodbye at the port and Zack throwing kisses and chocolate hearts covered in shiny red foil. All light and frothy and summer loving. Like it really was the perfect first sex she always told as the whole of her story.

'Anyway, that's what happened. The tale of my first love. Why do you want to know?'

'Zack's in London.'

'Oh my God.'

'He wants to stay here.'

'Oh my God!'

'He's in love with an Englishwoman.'

'Oh,' Sofia's just-built myth of delirious-ever-after crumpled with the sheets.

'This woman Katharine is the love of his life. He's finally found her.'

'I'm delighted for him. Why doesn't he just marry her then?'

'He's going to. She has two sons here. They're still at school.'

'Wonderful. And what does any of this have to do with me?'

'He needs a witness.'

'For what?'

'For their wedding.'

'Surely he's made a friend in England in all this time?'

'Several, but it might as well be you.'

'Doesn't she have any friends?'

'None that approve of her marrying Zack.'

'Gabriel, forgive me if I'm a little slow here, but I don't quite have your powers of omniscience—'

'I'm not all-knowing actually—'

'Whatever, why do I need to be his witness?'

'He's only known Katharine for five weeks.'

'Oh.'

'And his friends, like his father, think he's rushing into it. Everyone she knows does too. He needs someone who'll stand up for him and say it's a good idea – at the Registry Office. They both do. Zack also needs someone who's prepared to confirm his story to the immigration authorities in case they question him about the relationship.'

'What's the story that needs confirming?'

'That he's known Katharine for ages and they've been in love for years and her divorce has only just come through so now they can get married. Otherwise it might look as if he's just doing it to stay here.'

'So you'd like the mother of the future Messiah to lie to the country's authorities?'

Gabriel winced, 'No, it's not only that. In fact, that's the least important reason. You also need to get rid of him. And Zack needs to get rid of you. There's a piece of you stuck in each other.'

'That's what happens with first love – well it did to me, I'm delighted to know he remembers me. But that's normal surely? It's hardly a major problem, it was years ago.'

'Yes. And time you both let that bit go. Zack so he can marry without any last lingering looks back, and you so you can get on with this new phase of your life.'

'But he was my first love, first sex. If it wasn't for Zack I might still be a virgin.'

Gabriel didn't say anything, just looked at Sofia.

Sofia stared back, slowly understanding what his look meant. She shook her head, 'Oh come on, I thought you understood I wasn't Virgin material – not even meta-phorically.'

'I do, but it does have a nice resonance doesn't it? You giving Zack away as it were, so you can return to your pre-Zack state?'

'Crazy, self-conscious, poverty-stricken eighteen-year-old?'

'How about a young woman with her whole life still ahead of her?

'Gabriel, I may be somewhat more experienced in the ways of the world than you were hoping, certainly we both know I'm no innocent virgin, but I'm only twenty-eight, I'm hardly the queen of jaded. It's a while before you can write me off as Mrs Robinson.'

'Of course not, but it might be good for you.'

'So might sleeping eight hours a night and fasting five times a year. What's the point?'

'What are you so afraid of?'

'He's my first lover you idiot. Of course I'm scared to see him again.'

'But you'd like to?'

'Maybe.'
'And it might be good to put out the old flame?'
'Possibly.'
'And you'd help him out with the formalities?'
'If necessary.'
'Good. That's settled then.'

Twenty

Sofia wonders about first love. The only one that doesn't die. Can't die because it ended before time and tedium had a chance to play their usual nasty tricks, before reality could sneak in, midnight burglar, killing off passion and replacing it with shared television tastes. Ten passing years have given Sofia a healthy store of boyfriend memories; good, bad and ugly – sometimes all three at once. The same decade had merely left Zack fresh and smiling in her brain. Her first official sex – the memory of sweet sweat summertime had kept him fresh and smiling in her lust. Sofia remembered the clean linen desire outlined in bright white light. She had many times teenage-told the delicious recollection into perfect story and no amount of contact with truth had tainted the tale

Sofia's first sex was all planned and gently prepared for – listening girlfriends swallow an envious mouthful of wine. It was not that special, not her best sex by so very far – strained boyfriends unclench jealous jaws and smile in relaxed bollocks relief. And yet, for once, the best-laid plans resulted in best laid Sofia. Sofia smiles at the thought and jealous world turns on its axis into green-tinted night. The whole event was lovely and it was ordered. Listening men wonder what it might be to have been so together at eighteen. Listening women do not believe her. But Sofia maintains it is truth. To some degree, though officially first time girl, though so much younger than him, so much poorer than him, Sofia maintains she was in charge in a way. Asked, received. Set out her rules, got them back threefold. No surprises and all the more surprising for that.

Fair enough, the audience nods to itself. We should all have done it that way, all have hoped for good first time. Sofia goes on to explain that this experience was back then when she still believed she could get what she wanted simply by asking for it. Let down by her changing body, she had decided that the world really did owe her – having failed to live up to its first promise of perfect career, the universe would then have to give her everything she asked for, any request. Sofia wanted a capable, generous and careful first-time lover. And she got him. She wanted elegant first sex in beautiful surroundings with charming man. And she got it. Ask and she shall receive. The listeners wonder if there was maybe a catch? Please God, can there be a catch – nothing can be that good, not all-good, surely?

And of course they are right. Her story is just that. Every tale needs a moral for coda. It took Sofia another ten years to realise that perhaps there was just the one store of good fortune – and that using it up too fast and too easily might just mean there wasn't all that much luck left over for when she really needed it. There was no audience to witness the sequel to the first love tale, but the fact was, Sofia was starting to realise that right about now was probably when she really needed her good fortune store. Needed it full to overflowing.

Zack had hardly thought about Sofia since he sailed away from Lisbon. Not consciously thought about Sofia for ten years. Perhaps she slid across his memory when he glimpsed a long, smooth arm. Maybe she sauntered into his mind when he watched Hollywood attempting to honour sleazy; some famous starlet blindly failing in grown woman imitations of what the only-just-adult Sofia instinctively understood, long before her first official sex. Fuck-me sensibilities in a just-become woman, overlaid with headmistress attitude. Which translated into permissible Lolita for Zack. Translated into pushing the occasional Sofia memories away for ten more years, in case he had taken advantage, in case it had been wrong. Surely he'd had too much wealth and too many years on her youth and poverty for it to have been a fair transaction? The passing decade had given Zack a degree of boy-feminist sensibility, a succession of relationships had taught him hidden trunkloads of girl secrets. Nothing, though, was ever going to teach him that it had been Sofia who'd really been in charge ten years ago. It just didn't fit the prevailing world view, and Zack's vision wasn't that wide, not even now that he was somewhat older and therefore so much cleverer. Zack preferred to push away his Sofia memories, because nothing had yet persuaded him that the decade-ago month had been an equal exchange. Nothing, that is, other than bumping into Sofia at his local supermarket.

Cat food, cat litter, dog food, inner soles for the boys' trainers, diet Coke for Katharine, real Coke for him, Pepsi Max for still more hyper teenagers, orange juice, cranberry juice, free-range chicken, organic turkey, full fat sausages, old-fashioned non-organic jam, free-range eggs, butter, cheese, three loaves of thick cut white bread, eight salmon steaks, beer, whisky, water, wine, Sofia. Long arms, hair dyed black, cropped, bare at the nape of her neck. Portuguese wine. Feet in thin leather sandals, neon pink toenail polish. Coffee, thick, dark and sweet. Almond-flavoured custard tarts. Tiny pastries. White sheets, crisp beneath his back, soft above his throat, hard beneath her mouth. White shirt, black shorts, no make-up. Cool hands, hot back. Ten years no time and wasn't he supposed to get something else? Wasn't there something else on the shopping list? Sofia.

Sofia stood in front of his trolley. Stood in his way. Sofia stood on tiptoe to reach the top shelf before her. Sofia stood on tiptoe to reach the man before her. Left arm stretched up to grab cans, right arm crooked around half-full basket, bare midriff clear, exposing toned vertical muscles running down in a direct line past wide pointing hip bones and long thighs just wrapped around with loose summer shorts. Sofia was dressed more for work than for shopping. But then she was working at her shopping. Shopping for tins of baked beans and a husband. Sofia did not notice Zack, was ready not to notice Zack. Sofia saw only Gabriel to her right, nodding that contact had been made, that it was time to go to work. Sofia saw only Gabriel disappearing around the corner of the aisle, wondered if anyone else noticed that he didn't actually walk but glide, wondered if anyone else saw him at all. Ten seconds until all she knew was that with Gabriel gone, the usual panic had returned in force, and what had almost made sense first thing this morning, now seemed absolutely ludicrous.

Gabriel had made it sound so simple. 'You bump into Zack, go for coffee, catch up. Be beautiful or be completely ordinary, it won't matter and it won't make any difference. He'll ask you to be his witness.'

'Except you want me to go into a supermarket to make it happen?'

'It looks more real that way.'

'It looks more terrifying that way.'

Anything seemed possible when Gabriel was guardian close, everything seemed too near too insane the minute after she'd agreed to it. She must stop agreeing to these things. She must stop wanting to agree with Gabriel. Certainly until she'd worked out if it was just guardian-angel security she wanted him around for – or more. Probably more, but that could wait. At least until after there had been more lust. At least until she'd seen if he could fuck at night and still be there in the morning. And anyway, she would be doing Zack a favour. Gabriel brushed aside her concerns about meeting up with Zack again and maybe rekindling the flame he was so adamant she needed to douse.

'It wouldn't happen. He's in love with Katharine.'

'Thanks. I thought I had slightly more allure than that.'

'You do. But he's not looking. He's made his mind up.'

'After five weeks?'

'That's how it is sometimes, all he needs to do is get married and his dreams will come true.'

'And what about immigration?'

'What about it?'

'What if there are questions about him and Katharine?'

'You answer them. But you're only there just in case.'

'And there I was thinking I was important to their future.'

'You are. But not as important as getting him out of your head is to your future.'

'Good to know you have so much faith in my sanity. So is he going to be allowed to stay here that easily?'

'He's got money Sofia. Not as much of his father's money as he did when you knew him.'

'Daddy doesn't like Katharine?'

'Daddy doesn't like that it's happened so fast, that she's been married before, or that Zack intends to stay in England now. But Zack does have his own work now and, anyway, it's not as if he's just climbed off a truck in the middle of the night at Dover. He's a fairly wealthy, extremely personable, well-educated American.'

'And men like that don't come to the attention of the tabloids all that much?'

'Don't come to the attention of the tabloids or the immigration authorities. It's an imperfect world. In his own country Zack is one of the people who make the rules –

he looks like them. This is middle England we're talking about, no one's going to look twice at the documentation. Wake up Sofia, it's not as if he's black.'

And for the first time Sofia wondered what colour other angels were.

So Sofia went shopping. That simple. All she needed to do was find her man. All she needed to do was go shopping in the middle of the day and not have a screaming agoraphobic fit. Easy then.

'Oh my God!'

'It isn't?'

'It is.'

'But it must be—'

'Ten years!'

'How are—'

'You?'

'I'm just—' (As happy as can be.)

'Fine.' (Pregnant.) (With the new Messiah.)

They discussed the past ten years with baked beans and irate shoppers for audience. Sofia trying to edge towards the door, Zack too enthused to do anything but follow her movements. He told her most-truths and she told him half-truths. All the truth that kept her story on the sane side of honest. Sofia leaned her basket on the edge of his left-leading trolley and they walked together to the checkout, she relieved, he dazed. They paid for their purchases and paid for the past in credit card complicity. No loyalty cards for either of them.

Zack loaded the shopping in the back of his car, made a quick call to the love of his life. They went for coffee, he ordered tea and she remembered her agenda. Asked about Katharine, tried not to notice it hurt to hear how much he loved this woman. Tried not to notice the stupid girl-emotions that had her minding Zack talking about his brand new love, when she herself had had so many new loves since then, when she was half-infatuated with Gabriel anyway, when she had come out this morning knowing for definite that her job was to get Zack out of the back of her heart as a could-have-been. Sofia knew she didn't want Zack, had no desire for this mid-forties Zack, was not attracted to this man who was more serious, more adult, far less delicious and free than the old Zack. But she didn't want to have to turn the picture of her ten-years-ago party boy into the sweet and sensible man sipping peppermint tea before her. Sofia sighed quietly and told her eighteen-year-old inside to grow up and let her get on with it.

Within an hour Sofia was invited for a meal. Two days later she bravely lunched with strangers – Katharine the Catholic, her lad children, Mike and Sam and their would-be-stepdad Zack. Sofia told Katharine about her pregnancy. Girl talk while the men did the dishes. Barely told the instant-whipped, dream-topping story of a now-departed lover she didn't want further contact with, allowed Katharine to fill in the gaps with her own bad experiences. Katharine sympathised – and, because she wasn't stupid, because she was meant to – she saw what she was meant to do at the same time. Realised that now Sofia had come back into Zack's life, it was her job to keep Sofia in a safe place. Make them be friends. So that friends never mutated back into lovers. Another coffee, another lunch at home. Sofia steeled herself to confide in Katharine. The woman was pleasant enough, but the ten years she had on Sofia, her proper businesswoman job – and the societal status symbols of children and divorce – raised every one of Sofia's insecure fears. Especially as her job that lunchtime was to break the news of her real job to too-Catholic Katharine, sniggering teenage boys overhearing in the kitchen. But good sense overcame shocked sensibilities, as was intended, and within another fortnight Katharine and Zack asked Sofia to be a witness for them. Zack's best woman.

They wedding was booked for five weeks after the supermarket meeting, Sofia would accompany Zack to the Registry Office, Katharine would have her sons with her. Single chick double-drug lap dancer to respectable matron of honour with baby on the way in half a dozen easy steps. It looked like it might all be as simple as Gabriel had predicted.

Just a shame, then, that he hadn't been quite so insightful as far as James was concerned.

Twenty-one

If all Sofia was meant to do was to put out the old flame, remove any lingering yearning from the past, then long afternoons wasted with the would-be-happy extended family were perfectly designed to do it. Little could have assured her how unsuited she and Zack really were more than listening to him simpering about the joys of step-parenthood to two young men who Sofia knew from a sideways glance were rather less the repositories of all their sainted mother's good genes and rather more raging young animals dying to break free and deposit some hormones of their own. But of course nothing was allowed to be that simple. Even with Gabriel guarding and caring, Sofia still had to do the deed, make her own future happen. Having agreed to play her part, she now had to go through with the ceremonial tasks. Outward ease, inner turmoil – she was well practised at this. How could her dancers' toes have perfected the sugar plum pointe without the hidden hard-skin calluses to prance upon? Pretty pink satin is made to hide leather skin and red bleeding blisters. After another five weeks of trying to get on with it, living with the growing baby panic, growing baby, she'd have taken a quiet life any time. Sofia had done prima donna depression to death, she wanted easy, quiet and simple. Wanting too much again.

Sofia turned to James for sympathy and sweet understanding. James already knew the first love story, had
heard the Lisbon lust – and digested it as well as any new
partner could, the tale of perfect first love always hanging in
Sofia's history for unfair comparison. He'd never met Zack.
Never wanted to either. They were laid out in the afternoon
sunshine on Sofia's sitting-room floor, the two of them
finishing a second pot of milky coffee, crumbs of Martha's
date scones scattered across the carpet pile. She whispered
her opening sentence easily enough. Too easily.

'Why?'

'Because he asked me.'

'Doesn't he have any other friends?'

'Yes, but this way if there's any problems with immigration, I can say I've known him for years and vouch for his
honesty and all that.'

'Mmm, the word of a lap dancer – that'll certainly sway
things.'

'Thanks James, I think they're more concerned that
someone can confirm their relationship is real, not just a
way for him to stay in the country.'

'You don't even know the man. You don't know the wife,
he barely knows the wife, maybe they are lying.'

'I don't need to know him. Now. Anyway, I did know
him once.'

'Not well.'

'Well enough thank you. But it's not about that is it?
I'm doing them a favour. Besides that, it will be good
for me.'

'How so?'

'Get him out of my system. You used to say I thought
about him too much.'

'Only when I was pissed.'

'And jealous.'

'Zealous maybe, never jealous.'

'Yeah, but maybe you were right. I should tidy up some of my past. This is a start.'

'And do I count as past that needs tidying up too? Is that why you're steering clear of Martha and me?'

That was the end of the first try. Sofia hadn't told enough of the story for James to understand why she needed to sort out her old emotions, not that she was entirely sure she understood what Gabriel was on about either, though she did realise he maybe had a point. Lying on the floor in the arms of her ex-lover, an ex-lover she still hadn't been able to tell about the baby, probably wasn't the most honest of starts to this new phase in her life. Too much sunshine, too many scones. She left it for a later date. And then was surprised when time passed and the later date became now. Another pre-work afternoon, a week later, cherry muffins this time and warmer sun.

James thought Sofia shouldn't get involved with Zack again, even if the involvement was designed to get him out of her shadows for good. Martha thought Sofia didn't need quite so much assistance from James on this point, preferred James to spend sunny afternoons lying on the floor with her, not his ex-girlfriend. Gabriel counselled persuasion through truth. Sofia resisted, knowing James wouldn't like it. Held out for one week, two. In the end, worn down by James's constant tripping upstairs for early morning repetition of the negatives (and suspicions about her motives), Sofia announced her pregnancy. Nine weeks gone, she'd started to acknowledge the truth herself, and James would have to know eventually. But Sofia had been right to imagine he wouldn't exactly welcome the information.

Smiling, summer-indulgent ex-boyfriend, to angry jilted man in one quick leap. The leftover love they both stored spilled out into the jealousy of real argument. Was it his baby? No. Was it Zack's baby, was that what all this was about? Of course not. Then did she even know who the father was? Sort of. What the fuck did that mean? The quick flight from lack of understanding to intimate profanity told Sofia it was not going to be an easy conversation. Again, did she know who the father was? Sofia went for a yes this time, far easier to lie. Had she told the father? (To be truthful, it was more that the father had told her. Again, this was not the right answer. Not even when James was being a bastard and Sofia really wanted to piss him off.) Yes, the father knew. Why wasn't he around? He was – and he wasn't. James jumped up and paced the carpet, traces of muffin and old tea stains ground into the downtrodden pile. Was she crazy? No. Did she know what she was doing? No. Then why was she keeping it? Damn good question. Too good question. No better way to explain, Sofia went for teenage reasoning. She was keeping it just because. Did she need money for an abortion? No abortion, having the it – still not really baby, not all that real yet, not even now. No point in explaining to James how uncertain she was about keeping the baby, the lack of choice involved, how she found herself powerless to do anything else. Explanations became more stilted, questions more fierce and James's hot anger shone bright in Sofia's unshielded eyes.

There was no justification, no better defence, nothing Sofia could say that would help James make sense of her actions. Her inability to tell the whole truth drove a rift between the two oldest friends and suddenly James didn't understand her any more and didn't get it and wasn't going to be getting it either. Now it had gone beyond simple jealousy that the old lover had returned, now it was Sofia's life taking a whole new move away from what had been their life, and now James would not be able to understand, because it would be a long time before Sofia worked out how to tell him the truth, a long time before she even knew how to tell herself what was really going on.

She tried another tack, not her but him, not her insanity but his transgressions, his lack of faith in their friendship. Defensive girl attacking uncomprehending boy, classic move, classically doomed. Wasn't it true that now James had Martha as his first thought, prime relationship? That James wouldn't understand what was going on even if Sofia hadn't been pregnant? Because now he had Martha, and, automatic relegation, Sofia came second. And if Sofia knew that, then James ought to know it too. He had no right to be so self-righteous about the baby or her new friendship with Zack, her motives, or any of it because, after all, he had a new love, didn't he? Yes he did. Sofia didn't really matter any more, did she? Well, no, now you put it like that, she didn't. James acknowledged out loud – far too loudly for Sofia's ears – that she had slipped into second place. It was not quite the hoped-for answer, slightly more than she needed to know, but truthful, and what did she expect in the heat of the moment, heat of a misunderstood afternoon? Yes, James did have a new love and if Sofia couldn't understand what difference that made, then she was even less sane than he'd overgenerously given her credit for. New love, though, didn't stop James being concerned about her and it didn't stop him wondering what the fuck she was doing having a baby when she couldn't even tell him who the father was. James was concerned about her, James still loved her. Why didn't she trust him enough to tell him what was really going on?

Sofia should have left the conversation there, when there was still a chance they might kiss before she slammed the door in his face. But she was hurt and cornered and more than a little thrown by the situation herself. Sofia was in no position to be careful of James's feelings when all she really wanted was to feel his arm around her shoulders and listen to James promise her that everything would be all right. Knowing he couldn't fix anything, but wanting him to pretend he could. So lost in the fear of her future, she wanted anyone to pretend they could make it better, just as she was learning to do every morning, reassuring mask-face in the mirror. But James couldn't offer solace from his position of ignorance and Sofia had pushed away the chance of reconciliation. Maybe they hadn't seen that much of each other recently, but that was James's fault as much as hers – if he did have to spend so much time with that bloody Martha. James side-swiped back before she'd finished her sentence. In that case she might as well get used to the estrangement, because Martha was going to be moving in. Death knell sounded far distant, but the blood was pounding too hard in Sofia's ears for her to hear it clearly, she was shouting too loud to hear it clearly.

'When?'

'Soon.'

'What's soon?'

'Next week.'

'Why didn't you tell me before now?'

'Why didn't you tell me about the baby?'

'It cuts both ways. You don't tell me and I don't tell you and that's how we know neither of us gives a fuck any more.'

And then they were both all of seven years old and then it was really nasty. Deep breath, lit another cigarette, glaring at each other through self-betrayed eyes. Silence then fast following explosion. James had been meaning to tell Sofia about the new living arrangements for a couple of weeks, but she'd been so fucking preoccupied with all her own shit that, quite obviously, she hadn't even noticed how fantastically happy he'd become. Had she? Sofia hadn't wanted to notice but did at least have the sense not to say so right then. Small piece of sanity, valuably held back. Held back too late, James was on a roll, shouting on, not noticing missed answers, impossible conversation, skipping speech patterns. Maybe they should just give up on all this best friends crap anyway. It was blindingly obvious, despite all their time together and proclaiming themselves now as best buddies, that if Sofia couldn't even be honest about the father of her child – and she really was certain it wasn't James, was she? – well, if Sofia couldn't be honest about that, then perhaps they didn't have such an amazing friendship after all, perhaps it was impossible to be best buddies and ex-lovers. Maybe Martha was right, it was a friendship of convenience and if that was the case, he was better off out of it in the long run, wasn't he? Well fucking well wasn't he?

James stormed out of the house and slammed the door and charged off up the street and Sofia climbed slowly back up to her flat, lay in the hot sun on the sitting-room floor and cried and cried still more and what had he meant 'Martha was right?' Then another cigarette and a too-big whisky and just as the sun was starting to dip below the bus-garage roof, there was Gabriel in her sitting room again, unannounced and barging in on her grief and trying to make her feel better, when better was the exact opposite of what she wanted to feel. Sofia had just been dumped by her best friend and she did want it to hurt.

'Go away Gabriel, I don't want you here.'

'I might be able to help.'

'I don't want you to help, you tosser. I'm not going to let you make it all right this time, I don't want to feel OK about this. Don't you get it? This is a really crap thing. I don't want your angel magic shite making it not hurt. I don't want whatever you do that means I feel better when you're close. I don't want to feel better. Fuck you and fuck the baby. Now piss off.'

He did. Without slamming the door.

Sofia didn't go to work that night, took another whisky and lay on the floor and covered her ears against the rising roar of James and Martha's happiness downstairs.

Not the best of afternoons for the Messiah mother.

Twenty-two

Tears and screaming can only last as long as fury, and even ex-lovers cannot wound beyond exhaustion. Eventually, Sofia pulled herself up from the sitting-room floor and went to bed, arms around herself, holding the tantrum three-year-old, guided back to home base. A quiet care that was shattered the minute she walked stilted into her bedroom and saw Gabriel sitting on the end of her bed. Gentle caressing arms turned rigid with fury, fingernails bit into her own skin in intense irritation and his sympathetic, enquiring look was greeted with an easily translated glare. Gabriel was gone when she came back from the bathroom.

Sofia went to bed with a cold cloth across her forehead and an ache deep in the pit of her stomach. She went to bed hating it all and knowing there was no way out but on. That she was heading further forward and deeper into the necessary lying, the incomprehension of friends and family who might expect much from her but not imminent motherhood, culminating no doubt in the ready accusations of lunacy. She turned her lights out and telephone off and curled up in the cotton-sheet duvet mess, wounded cat woman retiring to the only place of safety. There was no ready ease, but her breathing did still eventually. Night achieved its purpose.

When she woke it was late morning, heavy summer rain, same forecast for the next three days. All of which she greeted with big sleep equanimity. She went from toilet to bathroom to kitchen, television to radio, and then listened to the four messages on her answerphone – all from the working girls, all wishing her love and missing her presence the evening before. Each one was calling to let her know her own version of the new story. They'd had a booking last night from a very occasional visitor, well-known out-of-town big tipper. Sandra knew Sofia would want to be there to take advantage of the sixty-five-year-old juvenile. Helen thought that with a little attention to detail, the four of them might be able to give him an extra show and earn some holiday pocket money. Caroline's call added that pocket money didn't come into it, she'd had an idea that would take them closer to hand-luggage-size tips, if not extra baggage allowance. And, so, how did Sofia feel about meeting up a little early to get in some spontaneous applause rehearsal? The fourth call was Helen ringing back to say she realised Sofia may or may not have been genuinely ill the night before, she'd noticed her looking a bit tired recently, but if at all possible she did recommend giving the coming evening a go. Giving the coming punter a go. Extra-tired meant extra need of a holiday, and the extra cash might help a long way towards a fortnight in Tuscany.

Sofia smiled at the first message and laughed with the last. She pulled back the curtains, and opened wide the windows to allow fat rain to smash-clean her window-sill plants, playing loud-as-possible torch songs as she did so. Nina Simone eternal backdrop to the anygirl blues. As she showered, Sofia easily convinced herself that she did not need James. Of course he was right, it was time for them to acknowledge the long-gone nature of their relationship, to move on to new joys. She would leave him a message, apologise for being quite so extreme the night before – get in before he did and put herself firmly in the place of good girl righteousness. Ideally fucking Martha off in the process. Seeming good girl then. Hot water continued down her stretched back and Sofia exfoliated, aware she did not really need Zack either – though she would do the best woman thing, make her renunciation of old desire official and public. Make Gabriel happy, if nothing else. Besides that, Zack wanted her there, hadn't he said so himself? And, anyway, the good deed of a little deceit to the immigration office might buy her some leeway with the karma police and Sofia had an idea she was going to need to tap into her good fortune store in the near future. Finally, she shaved legs and underarms and cold-water body-rinsed, wholly convinced she did not need Gabriel. Though, pulling a soft bath sheet around her perfect shoulders, she felt the warmth across her lower back and was aware that a quick fuck would not go amiss. She was almost tempted to call out for him, see if genie Gabriel had the bottle to appear when she rubbed herself. But then she remembered she had better things to do. Better cash to earn.

Sad Sofia had died a dream death in the sobbing night and woken to I-Will-Survive-Woman on an in-house brain loop track. She had the perfect antidote to the James argument, the Gabriel desire, the pregnancy angst. Ignore it all. Return phone calls. Invite guests. Make lunch for friends. Eat, drink, take drugs, rehearse. Call it work. Ignore the shit. Have the life. Avoid reality. Party anyway. Denial as the stuff of unbroken dreams.

Sofia hunted out three bottles of fizz. One was non-vintage champagne stolen from an overeager, under-achieving cus-tomer the week before, the other two were bottles of mediocre cava, left-overs from the last house party she and James had attempted. Placed them in the freezer so they would chill to her own specifications – she preferred her bubbles cold enough to make the glass mist. Part of the repast complete. Then she dug out most of a gram of cocaine, unearthed from the special occasion, 'only if I really need it' store – an old earring box, ignored enough for her to actually forget the drugs most of the time. Until she really needed them. Like now. Girl lunch after big tears was clearly the most important event in the past month. Or certainly the most important she was willing to acknowledge on that rainy day. Besides, it wasn't really a drug, for today's purposes, coke was the equivalent of office stationery. The nearly-gram would be just about enough to properly wake four dancers after a boozy late lunch and before their real work started.

She sautéed asparagus in white wine and left it to cool, fat shavings of Parmesan waiting to be thrown over with oil and lemon juice when the other women arrived. She unbottled birthday-gift expensive olives and found an extra-large packet of crisps to lay beside them. Fished out a bowl of dried apples and apricots. One green vegetable with tiny touch of oil, no-fat olives, low-fat crisps and dried fruit. Three bottles of excessively cold wine. Almost one each. Special occasion cocaine. Perfectly adequate diet for four dancing princesses.

Helen arrived with added sustenance for hardworking bodies, three tubs of ice cream, all full fat, all luxury level. Her kids could make do with the Iceland variety. Mum's gone to work and she thinks it's time Dad did the shopping. Sandra made it with another bottle of champagne, vintage this time. The Danish au pair went in to her unofficial night job with a big empty bag and travelled home with a big full bag. Most mornings she hoped to share a little bounty with the official lady boss. Most evenings she was disappointed. Last night was no exception, but today was some degree of compensation. If the Fulham demi-dyke couldn't see the joys of Sandra and champagne, her colleagues certainly could. Caroline arrived with the best goody bag. More coke and a later-in-the-evening supply of fresh clean E's all round from a special tip the week before. Even Helen was impressed, her heroin palate usually too jaded for most surprises. It looked like the dancing queens might be in for a pleasant afternoon.

But first they worked. Moved furniture, rolled up the tea-stained rug, changed the music from girl soul to boy groin. It took them two hours to perfect their routine. First fifteen minutes wasted laughing at Sandra's ludicrous suggestion of extreme number for the rich man, the next hour and a half following her lead and perfecting the performance piece. Minutely choreographed to look spontaneous, easy and charming, with a hidden ease that was difficult to achieve, but well worth attempting. A four-part harmony carefully designed to reach from his groin into his wallet. Then deeper still into both. Fifteen minutes more to make sure it was well and truly ingrained – brain pictures translated into body memory – and then it was time for lunch.

Eat, drink and be Mary. Even while dancing and laughing Sofia had not felt completely free. Starting to become oversensitive to her body, wondering if the pregnancy was obvious to the others, wondering how she would cope when it was. When they sat on the floor to eat there were half-openings for Sofia to tell her colleagues the new story. Sandra's continuing tale of lady of the manor woes, Helen's still-sober account of her second birth baby-blues, Caroline's extended death-and-fuck revelations of the passionate embrace that had sent her spinning from good girl safety to bad girl bliss. In Dalston. And a realisation that new love still seemed to come with old strings attached. Starting with the ice cream – to line their stomachs against the joys to come – each of the other women had her own delicious tale of excess and woe, every story rendered with just enough wide-eyed pathos and stupid-me sensibility to provide a half hour's listening pleasure. With a slightly better fuck-per-minute ratio than *Book at Bedtime*. But Sofia knew they understood about the depressions, had seen her smoothed scars. She did not want to compromise their enjoyment with truth. Particularly a truth that wouldn't be believed. A truth she didn't want to believe herself. She ate comedy phallic asparagus with the others and slow-sipped wine to their fast guzzle rate and snorted just enough coke to look like she was playing, just little enough to beware in case Gabriel wasn't quite right, in case it did matter. Sofia played happy hostess and if none of the other women mentioned her lack of complete abandonment to the occasion, it wasn't because they didn't notice. They could all see the darker lines under her normally clear eyes, had noticed the tense set of her jaw, taut shoulders, as she welcomed them at the door. Had each been pleased to see Sofia calm a little as the afternoon wore on. They knew precisely how much to acknowledge, because it was their job to know where to draw their lines. These women worked at revealing more of themselves nightly than most people physically manage in a month. They knew the only way to retain the sanctuary of the dressing room in the rest of their time together was to treat every revelation like a fairy story and every story as truth. And never to press for more. It kept them friends and it kept them safe. It also kept them laughing. Which, mostly, mattered more than anything else.

Twenty-three

By the time they left for work at six that evening, the four women were shining with personally selected combinations of food, alcohol, drugs and, in Sofia's case, a hugely welcome sense of laughter-induced relief. They maintained their manic pleasure throughout the cab ride, playing along with the father figure driver's sweetly naïve belief that the four of them were simply a prettily packaged hen party. Helen nominated Sofia as shotgun bride. It was too close to kissing reality for Sofia to jump at the chance to practice, but she went along with the game. It was easier than dissent and, five minutes into the journey, she was enjoying her pretend fiancé story enough to almost forget how close it was to her truth. And when the driver decided not to charge them for the ride – 'Nah, it wouldn't be right. Take it as a wedding gift, love' – Sofia was in a good enough mood to think that maybe, just in these five minutes, the driver might actually need more luck than she did. She gave him thirty quid for the unmetered fare and told him to buy the wife an early anniversary present. He drove straight home, thinking what a shame his own don't-call, don't-care daughter couldn't be more like that lovely lot, polite and happy laughing girls without a worry in the world. The four lap-dancing daughters waved him away and then bridesmaid-tripped into their club to get ready for a night of perfectly respectable drinking, drug taking and stripping for cool cash.

Entered the semi-dark from sunlit street, eyes accustomed to change of pace, place, change of clothes. Downstairs into the body of the room, room of their bodies, the bank balance boss clock-watched their arrival, as the perfect foursome paraded their investment figures for his early evening welcome. Each woman greeted Danny in her own particular way. Helen nodded a half smile, her mind now focused on her forthcoming A-class ritual, the perfect timing needed to keep her evening running like clockwork, keep her clockwork body running. Sandra turned Danny's slow hand kiss into a more formal shake, an afternoon with the dancing girls having set her mind firmly back on the would-be-dyke path. For a couple of days minimum. Or at least until a few more rejections twisted her heart from the straight-laced boss lady and turned her wandering desire straight back to Danny. Danny fancies Sandra, Sandra wants her other boss, other boss wants still more Prozac to help her through the tedious hours of a too-rich housewife day. Someone was bound to win in the end. Meanwhile, the private healthcare providers handed out the pills and counted their coins.

Caroline and Sofia planted far less formal, but distinctly different kisses on their employer's full lips. Caroline's kiss was a confirmation – to herself if not the blithely oblivious, though hugely responsive Danny – that yes, she probably did fancy him after all. Sandra's occasional shag notwithstanding. Caroline had recently started to contemplate switching her affections from her Spanish musician to the man with the big chequebook. Love's young dream was all very well, but Mariano had been living off Caroline's hard-won earnings for six months now. He still hadn't found himself a London job and was proving more of a burden than she had imagined. In fact, it was all turning out scarily similar to her mother's dire predictions. Six months away from the St John's Wood prison-palace, Caroline was no closer to acknowledging the truth of her mother's doorstep abuse analysis. She had, however, learnt a singularly valuable lesson – boy travellers with no visible means of support are even less likely to view washing dishes as a valid income supplement once their girlfriends start earning lap-dancer wages. Danny was looking more and more like a far safer bet. No more likely to be invited home to Mummy for supper, but a damn sight more willing to pay for it himself. Caroline could start a financially viable relationship and yet still continue to piss off her mother. It was ideal. She was growing up fast.

Sofia's kiss was less soft with promise, more hard with hope. Hope that Danny would enjoy the coming evening of rehearsed spontaneity. That he wouldn't notice how knackered she looked. That he wouldn't notice she had begun to throw up every evening at seven thirty. That he wouldn't notice the tiny belly she was starting to grow. Or, if he did happen to check out her form more closely than usual, then perhaps he'd just think that her changing shape was charmingly female, a new diversion for the more discerning client, interested in a real woman not a stick figure. Not that Sofia had ever been in the true skinny-girl league anyway, she nevertheless hoped that Danny wouldn't guess she was pregnant for another six to eight weeks, perhaps he'd even put her altered shape down to the far greater sin of simply getting fat. Sofia kissed the boss lip to hip, brazen flush of flesh, bringing on Danny's infamous blush and rushed off while he was still getting over the excess. Too tasked by her audacity to notice the belly potential. Sofia wished his ignorance for herself, walked her changing body to the changing room, nerves close to the surface, itching with uncertainty.

In the door, down the steps, through the heady scented atmosphere of boy pays girl, and into the relative safety of their harem home. Honest pleasure in each other's company magnified still further with a pre-shower vein-flash for Helen and just one more line for Caroline and Sandra's slight-cold noses. Helen's shot was always perfectly measured, just enough to keep her going until home time, not so much that it would mark her out as boring junkie dull. She was too practised with her drug of choice to allow it to waste her evening – at least not until she'd fully utilised the extent of her conspicuous earning abilities. Sofia easily hid her lack of chemical interest from the other women with a later shower and longer making-up, slower dressing down. Then they were four and then they were ready.

The rehearsed scam worked perfectly. Big man arrived, entourage intact, and the six men and their two embarrassed girlfriends were offered a choreographic treat. Apparently random arrangement, impeccable placement in accidental harmony. Each woman turned from her pre-paid table to perform the ultimate money-spinner. Four fine bodies colliding in perfect pitch, spot-lit, stitch-up. The man coughed up, three more requests, three times four mega tips. He couldn't believe his luck, this was a teenage dream come true gift to himself – Pan's People skipped out of the telly and laid out live on the table. His table. Only four of them admittedly – other working women around the room staring open-mouthed and impressed at the audacity – but then he'd never really fancied the little brunette one anyway. Eventually, Danny stepped in to break up the cash fest, there were other punters, he could see what the girls were doing – though he couldn't quite see how. It didn't occur to him the women took their earning seriously enough to plan for it. By then, though, they were each two hundred and fifty quid richer and the partying began in earnest.

Even for Sofia, who had found herself performing the first part of their rehearsed routine acutely aware of her body, her leaning curves, only able to lose herself in the music by the time the third song came on. Which was seven minutes too much self-awareness.

Sofia walked through her own door just after three in the morning. Gabriel was there. She'd known he would be. Felt him near since the moment she climbed into silent Matt's cab. Felt him nearer when she walked up her own stairs. And was pleased. Interested that she was pleased, a little surprised even, but then, on balance, she'd had a good day. She had played with the girls, and eventually managed to subdue her rising body-focus long enough to make the evening's work more than financially viable. She had no intention of allowing the contradictory nature of her own feelings to fuck up the last hour or two. Good days had been rare enough recently, she thought she might as well go along with feeling good. Sofia smiled at Gabriel. Found that she was delighted to see him sitting on her floor. She noted his hesitant uncertainty and was even happier to feel the surge of reversed power dynamic. She dropped her bag, crossed the room and kissed him. Girl lips, angel kisses.

'I'm glad you're here.'

'You are?'

'Yeah. Didn't you know?'

'Should I have?'

'I thought you were supposed to be here whenever I need you.'

'Want isn't the same as need.'

'Not necessarily. But it is tonight.' Sofia leaned back, looked closely at his perfect unlined face, 'Are you all right?'

'I'm supposed to ask you that.'

'But you didn't. And I did.'

He hesitant, she remarkably sure of herself.

'Nothing. I'm fine. I think. But I was worried about you. It's why I waited.'

'No need.'

'No need to wait or no need to worry?'

'No need for either.'

'No need, just want?'

'That's right. I'm glad you waited.'

'So you're not upset any more?'

Sofia laughed, took off her shoes, 'Of course I'm upset, nothing's changed, I still have no idea what's happening with my life – if it even is my life. I've still got to work out what to tell my parents, what to do for work once the bump really starts to show. And now I find I'm paranoid about how I look and terrified I'll turn into the body-neurotic I was as a teenager. In fact, none of my problems have gone anywhere, I'm just having a pretty good day, very good night. Right now, I almost feel like I may well be able to cope. And if I were you, young man, I'd make the most of it.'

'How do you mean?'

'I mean, I know it won't last. It's probably just some hormone surge, a pregnancy thing. But right now I don't feel like crap. At the moment, even with all my fears, it actually feels possible, like I might just get through all this shit with some measure of sanity to hold on to.'

Gabriel nodded, still unsure.

Sofia continued, 'The point being, if I were you, angel in my house, in the middle of the night, with God fast asleep or watching over afternoon Australians or whatever it is he likes to do before dawn . . . well, I'd take advantage of the offered hospitality.'

Gabriel rose to his feet, came to standing with no discernible effort. Other than the strain of understanding written all over his uncomprehending face.

Sofia held out her hand, 'Come on angel, let's fuck.'

*　　*　　*

In the semi-dark of the unlit bedroom. With morning beginning outside. Her clothes half on and his barely off. The sex is fast and urgent. They have been waiting to do this since the first time, since the slow gentleness, which was merely an introduction, where both noted and confirmed a future possibility. This is neither slow nor gentle. But it is different all the same, not as might have been expected. Not as Sofia had expected. Now there is time and with time she takes a moment to analyse what she feels. Work out what is happening when she touches-can't touch him. She feels unusual. He feels unusual. Where Gabriel is not dressed, exposes new freed flesh, his skin should touch hers, but it just misses, is not quite there. Their clothes catch on each other and in the place of no cloth, she finds that he glides over her. A silk stretch of agitated air smoothes itself between their outer layers. Reversing the usual aim of feeling all, this sex becomes about the point of no contact, centres itself on the sensation of almost untouched body. Where they do not meet, there is created a greater warmth, closer contact in barely missed skin. The ultimate don't-touch fuck. Getting in deeper because of it. The base is there of course, everyday physiology still eager to play, boy ready, open girl. It is the rest of the movement that has changed. Furious like first-time fifteen, but because the skin remains detached, the mind rests clear. Clean and sober now. It looks like light. No touch for greater feeling.

Sofia would take a moment out to wonder what he thinks of all this, but she is doing, not thinking. Gabriel might like to imagine that this time and place could be always, her happy and he not to blame, but the man-angel knows better than that. When he is thinking. Which is not right now. Now they are fucking and it's so easy. Backs arch, head bends to head, toes point at other options, ignored possibilities. He is laughing out loud and that's partly because right now, she isn't crying. Because she is smiling too. Sun pulls itself up through heavy cloud, summer rain humidifies, sleep comes. There will be stewed apples for breakfast.

Smiling beatific Madonna rests flesh-exhausted in angel arms.

Twenty-four

The morning after the wanting the night before, Sofia woke knowing that Gabriel was gone. He'd left coffee ready to be heated and bread sitting in the toaster, new jar of lime marmalade and just-soft butter. And orange juice and vitamins. It wasn't a love note, but Sofia took it to mean he wasn't leaving a Dear Joan letter either. Either that or angels didn't do reading and writing.

Sofia knew it was time she began the practical arrangements for the baby. Past time. Time to do it. Pregnancy. Birth. Doctors and nurses, mothers and babies. The initial medical consultation proved remarkably easy. Sofia booked an ordinary appointment with her doctor and informed the innocuous locum GP that she was pregnant. The woman with scarily too-young-to-be-a-doctor clothes, took a few notes, shrugged unconcerned when Sofia told her there was no father available. Blood pressure was checked, a couple more questions and then the overworked young woman passed over a handful of leaflets about maternity benefits, private midwife care and the dangers of drug and alcohol use in pregnancy. She advised a good balanced diet, putting on as little weight as possible initially, and told Sofia to come back in two months' time. No fuss, no concern, practically no interest, in and out in fourteen minutes.

While she hadn't wanted a major interrogation, Sofia had expected something more in the way of societal concern.

As she remarked to Beth, 'I don't know, I just would have thought they might want to know more.'

'Why?'

'All the fuss about the family. As in "the most appropriate social unit in which to bring up a child".'

'I hardly think your GP is the best person to be an apologist for the norm.'

'Why not?'

'She probably sees more of the damage done in the name of happy families than anyone else. The GP is the one who has to patch them up.'

'She didn't bat an eyelid when I told her what I did for my living.'

'Trained to keep those eyebrows under control sweetie. Hang on—' Then Beth kept silent until she'd completed the tricky manoeuvre of shifting boy child and girl child from one breast to the other, 'She pulls more on my tit than he does, I have to switch them over or I end up lop-sided at the least and bloody sore otherwise.' Babies resettled, Beth looked at Sofia, 'So you're hanging on to this no-father idea, then?'

'It's the truth.'

Beth frowned, unsure which part of herself – therapist or friend – was required. As the new mother of six-week-old twins, she really didn't have time to indulge any of her friend's lunatic whims, on the other hand, as the ex-therapist of a now friend, she knew Sofia needed her. And she knew part of her needed Sofia. Even after only six weeks, and as tired as she was, Beth already wanted slightly more stimulating conversation in addition to the feeding talk and newest show-off possibilities of baby clothes sent all the way from Australia. She only required this stimulation in short and occasional bursts. But she did want it. Probably therapist-head then.

As an older mother and, more particularly, one whose career involved helping other people prioritise their traumas, it had taken Beth just over the first fortnight to get her attitude sorted. Friends who phoned first and then came over with cakes, casseroles and/or champagne – which only they could drink, but even the most sensible hadn't seemed to notice that – were welcome to settle in for an hour or two as long as they fed and watered Beth as well. Pete didn't have two feeding machines latched to his tits, he could look after himself. The other category of friends though – which, to Beth's surprise included an astonishing number who were already parents themselves – were the ones who came for a hold or a cuddle and then expected to put the babies down and to continue the uninterrupted conversations they'd been having with Beth prior to double motherhood. Beth reasoned that they were welcome to stay a good twenty minutes before she either handed them a shitty baby – or two – or pointed out that she'd managed six hours' sleep in the past forty-eight hours and perhaps it was time they caught the bus, went shopping, or – if their stories really were that tedious – fucked off until they became a tad more sensitive and the twins needed a little less of her unadulterated attention. In about twenty-five years maybe.

Sofia was being extra-sensitive friend. Called first to make sure she was welcome. Went shopping to bring new provisions – and probably only Beth knew exactly how much that shopping cost Sofia – came over with good bread, exceptional cheeses, four different fruit juices, and a big bag of chocolate and cream doughnuts because Beth loved them and had told her that breastfeeding mothers needed to eat at least an extra five hundred calories a day. Which Sofia interpreted as a good call to eat sanctioned rubbish. Or, at least, to enjoy watching Beth doing so, her concerns about her changing shape meaning that pregnancy was not likely to turn into an opportunity to enjoy the things she normally rationed for herself.

Sofia was being perfect good friend, not talking about her new problem, not mentioning her pregnancy at all, in fact. She asked about the babies, Beth's stitches, the lack of sleep, Pete's coping abilities, and then offered to do the dishes. She also hung out the washing and changed Beth and Pete's sheets. Around about the time Beth mentioned she could have had a home help for a week if she'd really wanted one, but had turned down the offer because her Orthodox immigrant work ethic made her even more stupid than the lack of sleep and mother-head, Sofia semi-whispered, in passing, that she was definitely going to keep the baby. It was the first time Sofia had mentioned her pregnancy to Beth since their pre-birth argument about it. It came out half-heartedly and extremely defensively. It came out about an hour later than Beth would have expected. But she jumped at the chance to go back into career-mode anyway.

'How pregnant are you now?'

'Ten weeks.'

'What made you decide to keep it?'

Sofia hesitated, tried to form a coherent answer, 'Well it wasn't as clear as that, isn't clear at all . . . I don't think I can have an abortion. Really can't, I mean not as an emotional choice, but really . . . see, he said, I mean . . . oh fuck it, let's just say I don't feel like I've got much choice.'

'You always have choices Sofia.'

Sofia sighed, shook her head, didn't look up. Beth continued, 'What does James think?'

'I don't know. Not really. I think he maybe thinks it's his kid, I'm sure Martha does.'

'But you know it's not?'

Sofia sighed, 'Yeah, Beth. I know it's not. I believe what I've been told. Well, most of it anyway.'

Beth unlatched her nipples from the fed-up babies, handed her daughter to Sofia, lifted her son to her own shoulder, 'Believe who? This bloke who's been coming over to yours? What's his name?'

Sofia took the little girl, appreciated Beth's gesture – clearly her friend thought she was a nutter, but not quite crazy enough to have to protect her daughter from her, she smiled at the baby, 'His name's Gabriel, Beth.' Beth looked at Sofia. Stroked her son's back gently and rhythmically.

'The Angel Gabriel came over in the middle of the night, announced that you were pregnant?'

'That's right.'

'OK. Well, we'll look out for a big star around Christmas time, shall we?'

'Maybe. I don't know. I don't get it any more than you do. But it is what's happening.'

'And this wedding? It's not the best of times for you to get involved in other people's legal problems.'

'I'm just doing Zack a favour, I said I'd vouch for them if there are any questions.'

'That's what I mean. What if there are problems from immigration? What if you have to lie for them?'

'I doubt anything will happen, really. Some of the girls at work told me they know some people who've done it. Nothing ever happened to one couple, the other pair even got called all the way out to Heathrow – passports in hand, but it was all just very much formalities in the end. If Katharine was after a green card it might be harder, but they're doing it here, Zack's middle class and comparatively wealthy.'

'Welcome to England, then.'

'Exactly,' Sofia giggled – 'I hope.'

'What about James?'

'Other than the fact that he hates me right now?'

'Hates or disapproves?'

'Oh disapproves. Loudly. I know he'll come round, he always does in the end. And I expect that Martha and I will find a way of being friends, eventually. Perhaps once she starts thinking of me as a mother and not a terrifying sexual predator, she'll stop being so jealous of me.'

'Will you stop being jealous of her?'

Sofia snarled, 'Don't know me so well. Yes, of course I'm jealous of her. I don't want James for myself, but I don't want him loving anyone else instead. I want him on tap for whenever I need him. It's not pretty, but it is human, isn't it?'

'Very. Extremely normal. And you're going to deal with it?'

'It'll work out. It has to. James is pissed off with me right now, I'm not happy with him either, but it will pass. Anyway, I really do have more important things to worry about than minding that James is in love with a boring social worker who probably still has half a dozen batik skirts hiding in her wardrobe.'

'Glad to see you haven't lost any of your old generosity of spirit. Things to worry about like what?'

'Like telling my Mum and Dad.'

'Are you worried about their reaction?'

Sofia winced, 'Maybe. Or not. I really don't know how they'll take it. I'm going down next weekend. They'll probably be fine about the baby, underneath all that Eighties achievement shit they got into for a bit, they still say I'm the most exciting thing they ever made—'

'So what's the problem?'

'I don't know, telling my parents kind of makes it all—'

'Real?'

'Yeah. Really real.'

Beth laid her son out across her lap, indicated Sofia should do the same with the baby girl, 'And are you going to tell them about Gabriel?'

'Don't be stupid. No one's that much of an old hippy. Not even my Mum and Dad. No, I think they'll be pleased I'm procreating. My mother will have some bollocks about me finally activating my feminine side and I think my Dad will just be delighted that it means I'll have to stop working at the club for a while. They may be fairly liberal, but they're not honest enough to actually have meant it when they told me it was my body to use as I chose.'

'So what will you do?'

'No idea. It's terrifying. Become a choreographer. Give in to the teacher shit. Get a job as a bloody waitress, God knows. Except I'd be crap at all of it. I think I'm going to have to find some place where they think pregnant lap dancers are sexy.'

'Really?'

'No. Yes. Maybe. Probably not. I don't know Beth. Honest, I really don't. This was so incredibly unplanned – as in not merely not wanted, but not even contemplated. And I'm really paranoid about what I'm going to look like and if I'll cope looking different, terrified it'll send me off the deep end again.'

'Not likely.'

'I hope you're right. But, you know, I also figure that other women cope, don't they? So probably I will too. I'll have to, won't I?'

'Yeah. You will.'

There was a lull in the conversation, both women sleepy, Beth thinking about what she'd just heard, Sofia waiting for a verdict, diagnosis, answer. Ideally all three with glowing approval thrown in.

'Well, doctor, am I nuts or what?'

Beth frowned, sighed, remembered to add a half smile to soften her own confusion, 'Fuck knows, Sofia. I mean, I don't think you're crazy. But then I never did. Prone to bad times, possibly chemically based, with a bunch of solutions for that. And you've used them, you've sorted yourself in the past, even if you are a bit loopy now – and I'm not saying that you are – I'm sure you'd be able sort yourself again. If that was what you really wanted.'

'But you don't believe me about Gabriel?'

'I honestly don't know, kiddo. As I say, you're very plausible. Maybe I should meet your angel bloke for myself?'

There was silence while Sofia wondered about the idea of Gabriel and other people. It hadn't even occurred to her a meeting might be possible. While the sex had convinced her that at least some of Gabriel was physical and real, she knew that all of him was not. That he rested behind her eyes. That his presence was emotional as much as physical. And she knew if she couldn't produce him – or if Beth couldn't see him – then that inability might well confirm an insanity Beth was so far very generously refusing to commit her to. Sofia hesitated to answer, scared to offer an invitation to meet in case it proved impossible, wanting Gabriel there with her to answer Beth's questions, but aware that even he was not always genie-available. This was clearly a case of want not need, and she suspected he wouldn't feel proving his own reality was quite as necessary as she might. Then again, a good part of Sofia didn't know if she did want to share Gabriel with anyone else. Yes, he might confirm Sofia's truth to Beth, but then he wouldn't be only hers any more. Beth was still looking at her, waiting for an answer, the comfortable quiet was turning into a difficult silence and then, just when it became close to impossible, Sofia was saved by an earshattering yell from both babies. Hard to tell which one started the screaming first, but easy to see that neither planned on stopping soon. Saved by the squall.

After three-quarters of an hour in which Beth and Sofia did everything they could to calm the twins and not a single thing worked, Beth eventually asked Sofia to take them to bed with her.

'I don't know if it'll help, but when Pete and I lie down, both of us curled up around them, it seems to do it. Sometimes. Can we give it a go? Please?'

Sofia was so grateful to the red, harassed, screaming things for saving her from the increasingly difficult moment, that she would have been willing to put up with another forty-five minutes of wailing as avoidance, but she could see Beth had switched completely from therapist to mother-mode and figured the sanity questions were probably over anyway, at least for the next day or so. They went upstairs and held the babies between them. A combination of afternoon warmth, intense discussion and the slow peace of the tiny babies eventually covered all four of them.

Just as Beth felt herself drifting towards sleep, she remembered there was something else she'd meant to ask Sofia, she muttered it through sticky sleeping lips, 'This bloke, your angel – have you done it again?'

Sofia whispered back a dozy, 'Ah-ha.'

'And is he good at it?'

Eyes closed, Sofia smiled and nodded. 'Beth – he's brilliant.'

Beth laughed, 'Would you go so far as heavenly?'

'Hell yeah, miraculous in fact.'

The two women giggled and slipped into sleep as Beth added, 'Oh well, as long as he's a good shag . . . if he is a figment of your lunacy, then I guess you might as well enjoy the physical manifestation. It's probably a damn sight closer to reality than most people get.'

When Pete came in an hour later, he found both Beth and Sofia asleep, stretched out on the bed, the two babies sleeping between them. What he didn't see was Gabriel, resting his cool hands on the twins' troubled heads, holding them still and calm.

Twenty-five

Sofia made the trek to the west, planned each revealing word on the journey down, ate a nasty train burger and then followed it up with too much chocolate, contemplated vomiting at the station, but held on until she made it to her parents' house. Her mother opened the door, arms out to welcome-hug the apple of her eye, fruit of her womb, and Sofia pushed past her up the stairs and into the toilet. Had it been a soap opera, Sofia's mother would have guessed then and there that she was in the process of becoming a grandmother. Instead, Sue assumed that her only child was suffering from the after-effects of the night before, and the indulgent father whipped up a quick Bloody Mary to get his darling daughter back on her perfect pointed feet before she even made it down to the kitchen. Only once she'd downed the proffered drink did Sofia tell them about the baby. Sue and Geoff were, predictably, overjoyed, excited and thrilled. All of which masked an understandable parental concern, darted worried looks when Sofia's back was turned, and joyous smiles when she turned to face them – muted concern which slipped slowly into an alcohol-haze panic as the day wore on.

Sofia was sitting in the garden which had grown increasingly wild as her parents had mellowed; money, and more time to play, had slowly pulled Geoff and Sue from the easy-care traditions of their olde English country hollyhocks and foxgloves to a far more vibrant, free-roaming mess. With wild herbs throughout, self-seeding flowers wherever possible, Spanish succulents for the driest corner, and New Zealand ferns for the damp one opposite, the garden was green and lush and delicious. Sofia stretched out on the old striped deckchair, memory of childhood holidays beneath her back, ostensibly enjoying the afternoon sunshine, but actually hiding from her parents' shock. This way she could delicately give them time to adjust to the news, to work out what their next concerted action would be. She had long ago learned that her mother and father worked best in tandem, and leaving them to sort each other out meant she then had a damn sight less work to do herself.

Sue and Geoff were hiding in their kitchen. The old tie-dyed scraps of material had long gone, giving way to a more modern Ikea tradition – Che though, still gazed defiantly into the garden from his wall-mounted position above Sue's mother's old sideboard. These days he glared at the failed future from a new frame, his Blu-tack frayed corners clipped off for more stylish presentation. Neither Sue nor Geoff had used the intervening twenty years to acquaint themselves any further with his politics and, for his part, Che had endeavoured to remain the ideal kitchen revolutionary, no matter how many Channel Four documentaries came along to assassinate his once glorious character.

More champagne for the two grandparents-to-be, another glass of elderflower cordial for Sofia. She hadn't yet broached the conception story – doubted she ever would – so there was no point explaining that Gabriel had told her she could drink as much as she wanted and the baby would still be fine. Angel intelligence was probably a little more information than her parents needed right now. Sofia took her father's lecture on the foolishness of downing a Bloody Mary – without bothering to ask how much her own mother might have drunk while pregnant with her – and then gave in to drinking as much as she wanted for the rest of the day. As much as she wanted was nothing. While her parents got steadily, and then more rapidly, pissed themselves. Offspring sobriety had always been the safest option in darkest Glastonbury.

In the kitchen Geoff refilled Sue's half-empty glass, 'Has she mentioned the father to you?'

'No. Not at all. You?'

'I hardly think she'd tell me.'

'Why not?'

'Isn't that the kind of thing girls talk to their mothers about?'

Sue shook her head and looked out at her beautiful daughter, long limbs dangling from the deckchair frame. She could see Sofia lying asleep in the same chair twenty-five years earlier, nun-draped towels protecting her delicate little girl from the North Devon summer holiday sun. 'I don't know Geoff. I don't know what mothers and daughters talk about. I certainly never managed to have any revealing conversations with my own mother. I've talked to Sofia about where she's travelled.'

'So have I.'

'I know. So that's not a specifically mother-daughter conversation, is it? She's told me how much money she makes dancing – I have nothing to say in response. And I doubt you do either?'

Geoff shook his head, Sue continued, 'I thought not. She knows we don't want to talk about it, so that's hardly conversation material either.'

'But last time she was down here you and her were chatting in here for ages.'

'She asked me why we gave up smoking dope when she was three.'

'What did you tell her?'

'That you finally had a proper job and it was making you too tired to get up at seven in the morning.'

'True.'

'I know. But I got the impression she was hoping for something more.'

'Like what?'

'I have no idea. I honestly have no idea what mothers and daughters talk about. It's not part of my experience. I only know what Sofia and I don't talk about.'

Geoff finished his drink, poured the dregs into his glass, reached into the fridge for another bottle. 'Which is what?'

'The scars on her wrists and legs. Why she and James broke up. Any of the men she went out with before him. Why she left home so young. Why she still has panic attacks every time she goes shopping—'

'She does what? How do you know?'

'Her friend Beth told me when we met her last Christmas, at their party? The Australian woman, Greek girl, you remember? She wondered if I knew when it started.'

'And do you?'

Sue shook her head, 'I didn't even know she'd ever had them. She's never mentioned anything about panic attacks to me. I just knew she didn't like shopping. And then, of course, there's the question of why Sofia hates us for pushing her to be a dancer.'

Geoff slammed the fridge door more in fear than protest, 'Oh come on! She doesn't hate us!'

Sue sighed, shook her head, held her glass out for more, 'I think, if you scratched the surface just a little bit, you might find that she does. Not always, not totally. But of course she hates us a bit. We're her parents. That's normal. And it's not as if I could give her a satisfactory answer.'

'To what?'

'Why she had always to be the best.'

'No! We didn't push her. We encouraged her. We gave

her everything we never had. And, if I remember rightly, we were a damn sight more generous – with our time and not just money – than most of her friends' parents.'

'I know Geoff. You're right, we were. We tried really hard. All the time. All the bloody time.' Sofia's mother smiled into her empty glass and held it out to her husband for a refill, 'We tried so hard. And I think that's probably why she only comes home twice a year.'

Geoff waited for his wife to explain, hoping for a women's intuition, girl-talk elucidation, mother-love reasoning. There was none to be had.

'That doesn't make any sense at all!'

'No Geoff, I know. But it probably does to her.'

Sofia let herself fall to half sleep in the deckchair and her father carefully put up an outside umbrella to protect her from sunburn. Sofia heard him despite his best attempts to be quiet, but she carried on with the charade of sleeping. She told herself it was so Geoff wouldn't have to be uncomfortable, talking to her about the baby, without Sue to help him through the tact minefield. As she sank back into real sleep she could see Gabriel behind her eyes, shaking his head at her. He was right, she was probably just as scared of the honesty as Geoff. But she didn't pull herself back from sleep into disclosure either. Gabriel could frown all he wanted, she was home, she was playing their little girl, she might as well make the most of it.

Two hours later there was bread, wine, sparkling water, Geoff's homemade pasta, lemon meringue pie with real lemons from the real garden.

Whole food, half-baked conversations:

'And you're sure this is what you want? To keep the baby?'

'No. Not really. Not sure. But then I don't know how I could be sure – by myself, doing this alone. But it's what I've got to deal with. And anyway, how does anyone else make these decisions? Do you really think every woman who has a baby knows for definite it's exactly what she wants?'

'I did.'

'That's different. You intended to have me. Most people don't plan their babies. Even these days, most of the women I know who've had kids have done so by accident. Happy accident loads of them, but unintentional all the same.'

'Well then, look, Sofia, who is—'

'I'm sorry, Mum. I'm not going to talk about the father.'

'But he must be made to take some responsibility!'

'He will.' Sofia lied, her words so much more certain than her access to fact.

'You have told him, haven't you dear?'

'Of course I have!'

Outright lie as mother-succour. Sofia ignored Gabriel behind her exasperated-shut eyelids, his nodding head urging her on to greater truth. Personal adviser to the best-known single mother in the world was all very well, but Gabriel clearly knew nothing about the day-to-day difficulties of dealing with flesh and blood-alcohol levelled parents.

By the time Sofia called a cab to take her to the station, Geoff and Sue knew when the baby was due, said they believed it wasn't James's child, and had readily agreed to Sofia's suggestion that she'd probably find teaching work soon enough. Sofia herself didn't know this to be true, but she did know it was true that her parents wanted her to say it. Had been wanting her to say it any time within the past five years. They both promised an open house should she ever need them. Geoff gave her fifty pounds when Sue went out to throw breadcrumbs for the birds and Sue shoved a crisp twenty at her as they kissed goodbye. Sofia had long ago stopped telling her parents that they should keep their cash, she could usually make the same in tips in half an hour, every half an hour. She knew they didn't want juicy snippets from her night job and this time she took their money anyway. For all she knew, maybe there wasn't that much tip-earning time left. She didn't mention Zack's wedding, he was another piece of her past she kept closed to them. For the parent-edited version of her life story, Sofia had been happy to allow her mother and father to believe she'd come through her big travels completely unscathed. For their part, Sue and Geoff figured that something truly awful must have once happened to Sofia, and that was the reason for her reticence to divulge many details. Not enough truth from her and too vivid imaginations from them – Sofia was scared to be honest with her mother and father and they were terrified to expose their fearful worrying to her. She went home alone on the train, Gabriel watching over as she dozed towards London.

Three fully grown adults went to bed that night, each one wondering how they could connect so little and still love each other anyway. And not one of them daring to say so out loud. Perfectly ordinary almost happy family.

Twenty-six

Sofia sat in the train thinking over her day. She had rejected her mother's offer of honesty as she had so many times in the past. Not that she'd actively lied to Sue, but she had chosen, yet again, to tell half-truths. It had always been easier to assume that Sue and Geoff would not understand how she felt, than to attempt the painfully revealing task of actually being completely open with them. She couldn't talk to them about breaking up with James because she would have had to talk about having sex with James. She couldn't talk to them about working at the club, because she would have had to explain how she felt about her body, the one they'd made, the one she had recreated. Sofia had always been glad when listening to her gay friends that, being straight, she'd never had a reason to be out to her parents about anything deeper than her current bank balance and would her Dad help her hang new shelves in the hallway. Her self-enforced lack of candour meant that she couldn't now claim their total support. Even the most adoring of parents, as Sue and Geoff were, could not be expected to offer unreserved aid when only half the reason was given. And then, while thinking about the half-conversation with her mother, Sofia had another realisation. At the time it felt like she had been trying to persuade Sue that it was right to keep the baby. Now she felt like maybe she'd been persuading herself. Like maybe she'd finally been persuaded.

Another cab ride, another driver disappointed by her refusal to discuss the relative merits of air conditioning or back-seat heating, another cabbie losing out on her always promised (but unvoiced) ten-pound-for-silence tip. Sofia let herself into the downstairs hallway, unlocking and relocking the door as quietly as she could, she didn't want to face a James-and-Martha inquisition on the state of her family health. As she climbed the stairs to her own flat, carefully avoiding the third from the top that creaked right above James's bedroom, she felt Gabriel close. And though tired, she was still alert enough to her own senses to note that she also hoped Gabriel was close. She was right. His pale blue luminosity just lighting the room, Gabriel was back in his tentative place, his no-dent weight marking his place on the sofa opposite her door, nervous kitten man – ready to hold or hide depending on Sofia's mood.

The woman who opened the door to Gabriel's smile was tired and not a little fraught after her long day, parental revelation bravely delivered and, disappointingly for all that courage, still without any firm conclusions. Gabriel's welcome home hug turned into a there-there hold, come-here kiss, and thence to a comfort fuck. Comfortable for both. Eventually, her body rocked into an almost soothed silence, they fell into bed.

Gabriel asked about the day with her parents.

Sofia skidded back from post-sex ease to her current, ever-present confusion, 'I thought you were there. I felt you there, you were nodding at me, pushing me on. Weren't you?'

'Only in part, and anyway, no amount of observation can tell me how it was for you to be with them.'

Sofia shifted herself closer to the heat of his body, 'Just as expected, I suppose. Same old irritating, unsatisfactory, want it all, can't have it. You'd have thought I'd have learned by now, wouldn't you? I always hope for so much more from my parents, but I honestly think they just don't have it to give.'

'More what?'

'More understanding. More complicity in my life. And I know that it's really my fault.'

'Why?'

'I'm sure it's the same for everyone, that half-relationship thing you have with your parents—'

'What do you mean?'

'You know, where you tell them stuff, what you're doing, what's happening in your life, but you never tell them all of it. Just in case.'

Clearly, Gabriel had no idea what she meant. 'In case of what?'

'I don't know – in case they don't get it. Can't get it. I mean, of course I want them to be the perfect parents, to love all of me, to approve of every single thing I do – and yet I know they don't. They can't. At the very least, our lives have been too different, I've lived apart from them for too long. So, even when they make the effort to ask about what I'm doing and how I feel, and they try to be involved, I end up only telling them half of it and then I get pissed off that they don't really understand what's going on,' then Sofia sighed heavily, almost laughing.

'What?'

'I can't bear it. I must be a grown-up.'

'Why?'

'I just acknowledged that I'm as crap as my Mum and Dad.' Sofia shook her head in her hands, 'Oh God.'

'That's good though isn't it? Being a grown-up? Taking responsibility?'

'Piss off, I don't need that much self-awareness at this time of night. Get me a drink, will you?'

*   *   *

A glass and a half of wine later, Sofia was slightly more sanguine about her new-found maturity. They were quiet for a
while, Sofia processing the awareness her tired mouth had
just surprised her with, Gabriel listening for her answers.
And the questions inside them. Sofia put her glass down
and stretched, her back smooth against Gabriel's body, she
pulled him closer around her, his wide hand on her nearly
noticeable belly.

'Do you have parents, Gabriel?'

This was not the question he'd been expecting, his
shoulders stiffened, he was uncomfortable, pulled away
from Sofia's body.

'What's wrong?'

'Nothing. I'm sorry. Really. It's nothing.'

He was laid out along the bed beside her, an inch gap
between the two of them at the most, Sofia felt the space
growing exponentially as he continued—

'Look, it doesn't work that way. I'm not like that.'

'Not like what?'

Gabriel frowned, 'This is hard to explain. Hard to understand. I don't have parents. Never have.'

'You were born like this? Already adult?'

'No. Or yes. Sort of.'

'What?'

'Well, I wasn't born, not in the way you mean.'

'You've always been? Like God?'

Gabriel shook his head, the idea worried him, 'No. Not
God. Never God.'

'What then?'

'Different. My happening was – is – like a thought you
only just had. You know, how it's probably always been true
that the problems in your relationship with your parents is
as much your fault as theirs, but it's also a truth that you
only just realised today.'

'You were realised?'

'In a way, yes. Being with you, I'm being realised. As we speak.'

'I'm making you because I'm thinking about you?'

Gabriel groaned, 'Again, it's not that simple. I'm here for you. Because I'm your messenger.'

'And guardian.'

'Yes. Definitely. But also because you think about me, think of me, and each time you do so, you remake me. For you.'

'So I am making you up?'

'No, definitely not. But you are part of the reason for my being.' Sofia was looking confused and Gabriel continued, 'Anyway, what that means is parents are just not necessary.'

'Not necessary to angels?'

'That's right.'

Sofia shook her head, 'Not necessary to angels, but necessary for the Messiah. Weird.' Then she half-laughed, 'Still, I guess it saves on unnecessary immaculate conceptions, yeah?'

Gabriel didn't laugh back.

'Oh I'm sorry. I forgot you take your job too seriously to have a sense of humour about it.' She turned her head to kiss him, 'Of course, I mostly forget your job entirely when we've just spent an hour or so fucking like the world's about to end.'

Gabriel kissed her back, 'Sofia, one thing I can promise you is that the world is not about to end.'

'And you know that for a fact do you?'

Gabriel shrugged, smiled, said nothing.

Sofia returned to his family history, 'So you really didn't get born? What does that mean? You've been around for ever? Not born, not dying – not growing?'

'It's more complex than that.'

'Yes, but if you're not born and you're not going to

die – what are you going to do? Don't you change at all?'

Gabriel rubbed his hands across his face, 'Oh yeah, I'm changing all right. I've definitely changed since I met you, since being here. This has made a huge difference to me.'

'Like how?'

Gabriel remained silent.

Sofia carried on, 'Like you want me? You're happy to be with me? You've changed enough to know that maybe you might even want to be in love? Come on, Gabriel, answer me – you're not some ordinary bloke who doesn't know how to say what the truth is. Bloody hell, surely you know how to be honest?'

Sofia leaned over her own private angel and glared at him. Holding his gaze, demanding an answer. Knowing she was pushing it, but well aware that with everything else that was going on in her life, she might as well demand answers. At least if she heard from Gabriel what he was feeling about her, she might acknowledge her own feelings for him.

Gabriel groaned again. Then sighed. Covered his face with his broad hands, rubbed his eyes. Looked at Sofia again. Frowned. Closed his eyes. Opened his mouth to speak and stopped himself. He turned on to his side, his back to Sofia, then turned over again. Gabriel was clearly very uncomfortable having this discussion, Sofia had never seen him so edgy, not even the first time they'd met, the first time she'd screamed at him, the first time they made love.

He tried again, 'Sorry. I'm sorry. Of course I'm feeling things. Probably love. Certainly lust. Passion. Excitement. Of course I am. We both are. It's obvious.' He hesitated for a moment and then asked her, 'You are aren't you?'

Sofia grimaced, 'Yeah, I am. I mean, I think I am. It's scary.'

Gabriel nodded in agreement and Sofia took that as a sign

to continue, 'Good, you're freaked too. Now we're getting somewhere.'

Gabriel frowned, 'No we're not. It doesn't get us anywhere because we're talking from such incredibly different places. The problem is, you and I are so different, at base, underneath, that I don't even know if I have the words to explain it. We might think we love each other, are in love with each other even, but then again, maybe we're just talking about completely different things.'

'But that's true of anybody, any relationship.'

Gabriel ignored her, continued with his stilted explanation, as much to himself as to Sofia, 'It's like the whole birth and death idea, I can't even begin to explain what it's really like, because it simply doesn't exist for me. I don't know how to tell my truths so they make sense to you.' He paused, groping for a way forward, 'You know that Mars and Venus stuff? About men and women?'

'What the heal-yourself bollocks about people coming from different planets?'

'Yes. That. Well for us, for me . . . it's even more different . . . more than just planets, like we're from different galaxies probably.'

Sofia laughed, the suggestion too preposterous to take seriously. Not with him beside her, not with his naked flesh beside her, half an hour after another very real, extremely tangible, fuck. Not with Gabriel's lips breath-close against hers. 'You're telling me the nutters are right? Angels are aliens? Oh, come on Gabriel, I may have accepted this pregnancy shite – and only because I have the physical evidence of my own, very real, growing stomach, only because I absolutely have to – but that's a little far-fetched even for me!'

Gabriel shook his head, 'No, no. None of that rubbish. Far less clumsy than that, it's actually much finer, much more elegant. A minuscule difference between you and me, incredibly delicate, it's barely there. Except that this differentiation is all that's needed to make you and me so separate it's hard to even begin to comprehend the distance between us. Not another galaxy, nothing as crude as an actual physical place – more like a completely different space, but at the same time and in the same physical plane.'

Sofia lay back on her pillows, 'You're right. It is getting a bit bloody complicated, sounds too much like physics for me.'

Gabriel lit up, 'Exactly! Angels are physics. There is maths for it. There is maths for me.'

'A formula for grace?'

'Of course. There's a mathematical formula for everything. Angels to rainbows.'

Sofia screwed up her face, 'Mmm. Very hippy-pretty. How about something slightly less naff New Age? Angels to earthquakes? Dangerous ones, destructive ones? Is there a formula for that?'

'That too.'

'Yeah, well, somehow I don't think that trying to understand the algebraic gibberish for what you really are is going to help. And anyway, if that's the case, if it's all just some big maths-fest, why do you need to use me?'

Gabriel didn't follow the leap in her argument, 'For what?'

'To mother this baby. If there's a mathematical formula for the whole thing, and it's all been arranged so bloody perfectly, and everything is so complex and – what did you call it – elegant? If that's the case, then why go to all the trouble of making me pregnant? Putting me through all this shit, making such a fuss, the whole no-sex-conception thing. Just to make a baby? Which, I might point out, any old slapper can do, has done, billions of times. You need mathematical formulas for angels and yet making a baby is so pathetically simple?'

Gabriel looked at her and then nodded. 'Yes Sofia, I think that's the point.'

Much later, when there had been more sex and more of her skin not against his, weirdly absent, strangely comforting, when she was close to falling asleep, Sofia's thoughts returned to her own parents. 'They're not bad people you know, my Mum and Dad.'

'I know.'

'And they did try to do the best job they could with me.'

'Of course they did.'

'They're probably OK as parents go.'

'They probably are.'

Sofia agreed with herself, 'Yeah. I think they are.'

Gabriel held her in the dark, his own light outlining her shadow on his body. He whispered, 'it's OK Sofia. You don't have to be the perfect mother either. You just have to be the mother.'

The Wedding. Sunshine morning with dark clouds sitting heavily on the edge of the flat city horizon, hot weather storms looming from beyond the M25, threatening the afternoon peace. Sofia woke up and dressed to blue skies, loud Dusty Springfield, and half a bottle of champagne, vodka topped. Gabriel, as she now expected in the morning, was elsewhere, neither missing nor, on this occasion, especially missed. Sofia figured being the best woman was one thing she could probably manage without a guardian angel. It wasn't as if there was an aisle to walk down. Or a best man to make a fool of herself with.

The Registry Office. Tight-gathered pockets of smiling people, only just become the two made one, or waiting to be, wanting to be, terrified to be. An ankle-high flutter of confetti picked up with each sullen breeze despite the staunchly defensive notices: No Confetti. By Order. Clearly the anti-naff police had long since given up enforcing the rule and certainly the just-made newlyweds had no intention of obeying, beaming photo-opportunity grins from the steps, basmati rice and hole-punch leavings stuck to their big day coiffures. The official celebrant smiled, polite but completely uninterested. She was matronly and just about pleasant enough. Conducted the entire ceremony by careful rote, her expressions changing automatically from welcome to serious to smile and quick-smart back to stern, as if each particular look and gesture had been pencilled in the margin of her word-book. Conducted Katharine and Zack's wedding ceremony like it didn't matter. To the two of them, of course, but not to her. Because it didn't. Because this busy woman had another six weddings today. Because it was just what she did for a living. Four years ago her profession had been to register births and deaths, then there was a change of personnel, a new boss who decided to shake things up a bit, a couple of intensive courses in being nice lady with important job – and now she married people. James gave people alcohol, Beth played with their heads, Sofia took off her clothes. Just a job.

The happy event took place in a square room that could be generously described as almost passable, considering. No expense had been spared to emphasise the extreme functionality of the space. But not even the council-issue chairs pushed up against the firmly security-latched windows could hold back the heady patch of overgrowth outside, pink-fluttering lavatera overgrowing its corner plot and wild irises holding up proud purple heads in defiance of the borough-sanctioned gravel that tried to hold the green within delineated boundaries. On the official table inside there was a single colour splash of five yellow roses in a blue glass vase, a lone concession to the romantic state – generous gesture from an official state employee, the underpaid cleaner who nevertheless brought in fresh flowers for the room she dusted and polished every single morning. She'd had a huge Russian Orthodox ceremony herself thirty-five years ago, and while the marriage hadn't lasted, the memories of her one perfect day certainly had. And so had her wedding flowers, forty yellow roses now turned to fine dust, preserved in a glass box on her dressing table. Her husband might have left her for a thin and pale English girl – she had never left him. And her wedding ring cut tight into her now fat hand as she scrubbed new boot marks from the vinyl tiled floor.

Despite Sofia's desire to see Katharine and Zack in red taffeta, silver sequins, top hat and tails, the happy couple opted for inconspicuous and safe. The bride wore dark ivory, so did the groom. Hers silk, his linen. Both flowing lines, cool clothes, summer light. Sofia herself stuck to barely-excessive baby pink. Sheer georgette baby pink, but subdued all the same. Sofia had roped in her own friends and acquaintances to make the wedding party look more traditionally full. Beth and Pete stood behind, approving parental figures holding the sleeping twins. Mike waited awkwardly by the getaway car outside, parked on a double yellow line for the duration of the ceremony while Sam smoked an illicit fag on the steps. In a finely measured time slot totalling forty-two minutes, Zack obtained initial rights for legal residence in Britain, Sofia witnessed Katharine marrying herself to Sofia's first-fuck true-love, and the nearly three-month-old foetus gained a ringside seat to one of the oldest human traditions. The old tradition of the bride getting married having known the groom for all of twelve weeks. No glasses were smashed. At least not until James got completely slaughtered much later in the day.

The extended non-family tubed, cabbed, and drove back to Sofia's flat for the reception in James and Martha's back garden, with Sofia as perfect hostess. Her ex and his new love were out of town for the day and Sofia had begged the use of the back garden from James. A garden party was her wedding gift to the happy couple. James had agreed provided everything was clean and perfect by the time Martha woke the next morning. Sofia spent five hundred pounds she could ill afford on champagne and designer nibbles mostly, as it turned out, to entertain her own friends, Zack and Katharine having none of their own to contribute. No yellow page was left unturned in her attempt to provide at least twenty different bite-sized delights for each person – delivered to the door rather than bought in person. Plenty left for the late arriving Sandra, Caroline and Helen – all dressed down for work, already un-sober, each woman individually and knowingly tantalising Katharine's slobbering sons from the moment her manicured toenails touched the fine cut lawn.

The rest of the day was play time. Playing pretty bridesmaid, playing happy extended families, playing that Sofia was every bit as smiling and at ease as she tried to show the guests. It was early season hot and the threatening clouds stayed at bay, glowering from the cut off horizon of London postmarks. There was plenty of sparkling, both pink and white, and a couple of bottles of vintage champagne which Sandra had brought with her, saved from work the night before. Stolen from work the night before. It's amazing what a lap dancer can fit into her laundry bag under the guise of a few grubby G-strings.

But the sunshine-alcohol glow couldn't last for ever. Helen, Sandra and Caroline left late afternoon to go back to Helen's and prepare themselves for an evening's work – Sofia wasn't going in that evening. Katharine's sons left not long after Sofia's colleagues. The alcohol was nearly gone, their mother didn't approve of them smoking, and without the lap dancers, there was rather less temptation with which to feast their dream-on-lads imaginations. Besides that, James, home early with Martha from their day out, had slipped them a couple of joints each – which went rather well with the wrap of leftover coke Mike had pinched from Caroline's bag – and Katharine and Zack were spending their wedding night at the Savoy. A single note of luxury which wasn't intended to set the tone for the rest of their marriage, but which would no doubt become a yardstick against which to measure how far they settled into ordinary domesticity. Which left Mike and Sam free to spend their evening watching MTV and fantasising Sofia's workmates into their boy-brain videos. By the time Mike had opened his first can of beer at home, Sam had already put the deep-frozen pizza in the microwave and out the thin shining lines and lit the first spliff. It looked like being a great night.

For everyone except Sofia. As the afternoon progressed she became more and more aware of the spirit of easy coupledom settling over the garden. Katharine and Zack in coupled kiss, Beth and Pete with a screaming baby each and delighted smile to match each ear-splitting wail, even James and Martha smiling benignly and seemingly happy to join the party. Sofia had drunk too much too soon, not eaten enough because she was worrying about her size, been over-excited for no good reason and now found herself dumped in the well of depression just as the evening sky began its turn from baby blue to pretty pink and the kissing couples noticed how perfect their partners looked in the glow of summer night. Sofia noticed that the wine had run out. Martha offered to go to the off-licence, James volunteered to go with her, Zack and Katharine suggested they take a gentle stroll, their arms and hearts entwined, Beth and Pete thought it might be just the thing to settle the still-screaming babes. Sofia was having none of it.

'No. Look. I'll go. It is my job, after all. You lot just keep on with your bloody kissing and carrying on and believe me, you won't even notice I'm gone.'

And after the first raised eyebrow and the second 'ouch', and the third 'do you think I should? . . . No, OK . . .' they didn't.

Sofia ran upstairs and slammed her own front door behind her.

'Fuck shit cunt fuck shit fuck!'

'Anything I can help you with?'

Gabriel was waiting on the sofa as usual. So usual that

Sofia didn't question his presence, just launched into her tirade.

'Yeah, come downstairs and be my boyfriend. Cuddle me, kiss me, let me hold you, talk to me and no one else, ignore other people, make me the centre of your attention, forget that there are other people in the world and pretend that nothing matters but being in a fucking couple.'

'Nice day?'

'Shite day.'

'Surely you didn't think it would be easy helping your teenage sweetheart get married?'

'Of course I didn't.' Sofia lied.

'I just feel really left out.' Sofia told the truth.

'Fair enough. You are being left out. That's the best woman's job isn't it?'

'Unless she's shagging the best man.'

'And you're leaving yourself out too. You're not talking to them, you're just sitting there feeling sorry for yourself and being pissed off.'

Sofia glared at him as she pulled her shoes on, 'I don't need a lecture, I need a lover. I don't need understanding, I need explanations, and right at this moment, I don't need an angel either, I need wine.' She stood by the door, 'Coming?'

'Where?'

'Off licence. I might need your protective presence to get me through the major panic attack that's on its way.' Gabriel didn't move, smiled at her, Sofia didn't get the joke, 'Look, I mean it. I really could do with you coming with me. I don't want to go into this shop, into any shop at the best of times, but I feel especially crap right now and I have to go.'

'No you don't.'

'The wine's run out.'

'I know. And Sofia, you don't have to go and buy the wine.' Gabriel looked at her, stood up, held out his hand, 'Now do you?'

Truth and miracle dawned at the same time. Sofia looked at the half empty bottle of Evian on the floor by Gabriel's feet. The one she'd left there after her exercise session first thing that morning. Now it was red. And heavier than water. And, given that it was only just made, had a remarkable depth of age to it.

'Did you do that?'

'No.'

'Fuck! Did I do it?'

Gabriel laughed, 'Hell, no.'

'So . . . what . . . ?'

Gabriel shook his head, 'Don't ask. The physics would be beyond Stephen Hawking, the proof's in the bottle. There's not a lot of point in trying to understand and sadly for you, Livingstone's Dance and Performance Academy wasn't exactly a Jesuit education.'

Sofia held the bottle in one hand, held the other over her stomach, 'So you think I should just go with the flow then?'

'Well, you could just count your blessings. At least you don't have to go shopping now, do you?'

Sofia and the wedding guests drank on for a couple more hours. Sipped the champagne that she and Gabriel hastily transferred to what had been empty bottles, guzzled the generous red that James and Zack spent a good half hour trying to place by grape and year. By the end of the evening Zack and Katharine had presented Sofia with a two-foot-long fine silver chain as an expression of their everlasting thanks for her fantastic generosity all day, Beth had handed her babies over to the clucking Katharine, James and Pete were getting steadily more stoned, and Sofia was over her single-chick trauma. For the time being. She was happily the centre of everyone's gratitude for the wine, and she also had their undivided attention as she performed a special Malaysian – fully clothed – wedding dance for her happy couple. And then taught the group steps to everyone else. They were all, tiny twins included, dancing in the candle-lit garden at eleven that night, Gabriel watching Sofia from her bedroom window. Sofia looked up at him and offered an otherwise unnoticed hand. Then there was Gabriel giving in to Sofia's desire, dancing behind her in the dark.

Twenty-eight

The morning after the wedding party, Sofia woke bright and shiny, her irritations of the previous afternoon gone in five hours deep, easy sleep. Gabriel was already gone. Clearly he had angelic duties to perform elsewhere that meant she couldn't hold on to him for more than twenty-four hours at a time. Maybe there were half a dozen other virgin births he had to take care of. Either that or he just didn't need much sleep. Or any. Then again there was always the chance that, despite his pale blue light and the soft no-touch of his perfect skin, maybe Gabriel was just being any other bloke and rushing off first thing before Sofia's insecurities dragged them back into another difficult conversation about the current condition of their love/lust state. A conversation in which neither knew what was expected or what was taboo. Not enough practice across the angel-human divide. And then Sofia's final, disturbing thought – maybe Gabriel wasn't there at all, had not been there last night and perhaps she was only truly sane when she woke in the morning and found him gone. And in that case, it was definitely time to get out of bed, before the curtains became too weighty to pull back and she found herself falling into the heavy blue. Sofia believed she had given in to being the mother because she had no option. She hoped, if at all possible, that she might still have a choice regarding the quicksand depression. She was doing what had been asked of her after all, keeping the baby. Sofia found herself bargaining with God without even knowing if she believed in Him. Not insane then, just ordinary.

She got out of bed, made her way to the bathroom, peered at herself in the mirror, and was pleasantly surprised to note that she had woken with remarkably healthy looks given her alcohol intake of the day before, though no doubt the late-night dancing and angel-sex had been exercise enough to dissipate some of the excess. She contemplated showering to top-volume Martha Reeves but remembered just in time that while James might sleep through anything at all, she didn't yet know that to be true of Martha, and she didn't want to upset the façade of neighbourly friendliness they'd maintained throughout the previous day. At least not now that they had finally managed to reach an impasse which they were almost able to disguise as might-be friendship. In public. When absolutely necessary. And when Martha had done such a great job of putting up with the wedding party. Sofia didn't feel the need to piss off her new-found friend just yet. Maybe once the weekend was over. Or after she'd had a coffee.

She sloughed off the last vestiges of could-be depression with a fast hot – and then very cold – shower, extra-vigorous exfoliating scrub, and then pulled back her bedroom curtains to reveal the traditional London blue sky hiding itself behind a fine summer haze of lightest grey. A bright shock of diffused light that perfectly illuminated the downstairs garden in need of serious repair. The shrubs and flowers were mostly OK – though the lavender could have done with rather fewer drunken tussles with its delicate blooms and the rhododendron had not been particularly well placed for circle dancing, the lawn however would need a month's fine care to recover. The usually neat, paved section by the kitchen door was littered with empty bottles and cans, paper plates and glasses collapsed on to their sides – pretty much exactly as their owners had done themselves at about one that morning when the party was deemed to be well and truly over. Sofia knew Martha would hate to wake to the imperfect vision and, suddenly filled with a spirit of neighbourly gratitude, she grabbed a couple of bin bags and sent herself off to make Martha smile.

There had been no sounds of life from downstairs and so, rather than go through James's flat to the garden, Sofia pulled on an old pair of painting shorts and an exceedingly skimpy T-shirt, and took the upstairs route. Out of her own bedroom window, across the six foot corrugated iron extension that was the downstairs kitchen roof, past the rickety guttering in dire need of replacement, and over the edge on to the roof of the outside loo – unnecessary old amenity now recycled as garden shed – she then laddered her way down the fence to the ground. The three-minute reversal of burglar entry and not a single scraped shin or broken fingernail in sight. It was only when she reached the ground that Sofia remembered her pregnancy, touched her stomach in surprise and, more surprising still, concern. A beginning-to-grow concern for the baby. She looked up at the shed roof and figured she would go back to her own flat the long way round.

Three-quarters of an hour later, while there wasn't much Sofia could do for the lawn or the rhododendron, everything else had either been neatly rubbish-bagged or piled to be washed up. Sofia had lived in the downstairs flat for three years, she knew how to get in the back door without a key, had done so many times in the past, usually half pissed. Pull the door towards yourself, turn the handle once to the left, lift the door slightly, turn the handle again, push the door away and inwards, wiggle the handle fiercely, push the door in again once and then pull back hard and fast. The lock clicked open and Sofia let herself into James's kitchen. Despite the lengthy celebrations of the day and night before, the room was still decidedly tidier than it had ever been in Sofia's day. Tidier and, at base, far cleaner. For while James might have been prepared to tidy away Sofia's mess at regular intervals, neither of them had ever bothered with anything more than a perfunctory sweep of the floor. The most they managed was to put things away out of sight, which was not quite the same as clean. Actually scrubbing the kitchen floor was something neither had contemplated. Clearly Martha thought about nothing else. Sofia had never before noticed the little mauve and yellow squiggle patterns on the old lino. An unexpected blessing of her squalid nature for which she was now profoundly grateful.

She was just running hot water into the sink when Martha pushed open the door. Martha was naked. Which Sofia wouldn't have expected – had she thought about it at all, she might have assumed Martha slept in a pretty flannelette nightie. With pyjama bottoms for added safety. So the sheer sight of skin was the first shock. Martha's nakedness also revealed that she had a fantastic body. Which led Sofia to wonder why the fuck she chose to hide it in boring Seventies social worker clothes. Coming sharp in on top of the naked surprise, Sofia's alcohol-addled brain struggled to comprehend the vision her eyes presented her with – Martha also had a massive tattoo. A line of several Chinese symbols, no pictures, wound its elegant way down from immediately below her left breast almost into the low line of her pubes. Martha had clearly not been expecting to find the tidy fairy in her hangover kitchen.

'Oh! Sofia! What the hell are you . . . oh! Yes, right . . . I see. Well, thanks, but . . . oh, I'm . . . right, hang on. I'll be right back. I'll help. I mean, sorry . . . shit . . .'

Martha was surprised, half asleep, stunned that Sofia – of all people – had made the effort to clean up, annoyed that she'd missed out on a chance to further advance her perfect housewife role, hugely embarrassed at her own nakedness, delighted that she wouldn't have to clean up herself, and mostly shocked. One emotion slamming into her after the other and then pretty much the whole lot echoing shock at the same time.

She backed out of the door, shouting after herself, 'I won't be a minute. Just get dressed. I mean, me . . . I will. I'll help.'

Sofia raised an eyebrow in pleasant anticipation of the tattoo conversation she would later have with James, turned off the hot tap and reached for the coffee pot. That particular vision had been well worth the effort of removing her ex-boyfriend's soggy cigarette butts from Martha's prized window boxes.

When Martha returned – sensibly attired in clean jeans and ironed T-shirt – Sofia handed her a cup of coffee. Martha smiled awkwardly and accepted graciously – despite the fact that she hadn't drunk coffee in the morning for three years. The two women worked together in near silence for ten minutes, then Sofia asked if James intended to get up to help, Martha told her he had a headache and couldn't bear to be disturbed. At which point they both reached for the volume switch on the CD player and cranked Ry Cooder up more than a few notches. James had hoped his ex and his current lovers might find a way of getting on, what he hadn't counted on was the two of them using him as a punching bag to smooth over a sticky start to their own relationship. Very silly man. By the time he finally got out of bed an hour and a half later, Martha and Sofia were laughing and joking like old friends. That Sofia was being so nice to Martha because she wickedly thought telling Martha old truths about James might help break them up a little sooner than would otherwise be the case, and that Martha was being so pleasant in return because she saw ingratiating herself with Sofia as a way to get on better with James, was irrelevant. It was classic ex and current behaviour, each one trying her damnedest to manipulate the other in order to maintain their status with the lover in the middle, and only James the real loser. Not that both the women weren't aware of this as well – they just saw it as his due. If he would stay in bed on such a delicious morning, then it served him right if they fell into girlie-bitch patterns in his absence.

Sofia put the last cup away and turned to leave, 'This has been really good. James is such a bloody idiot at times. I would never leave an ex and my new lover alone for more than five seconds without checking on what they were up to. And thanks for everything yesterday, I do appreciate it. I'd better get on and tidy up my own pit upstairs.'

Martha held out a hand to stop her, 'No, thank you Sofia, listen . . . I've been hoping to get a moment with you alone. There's something I wanted to speak to you about. I mean, if you don't . . .'

Sofia's heart sank, it had all been going so well. As long as they stuck to mocking James she'd hoped they might get away with veneer-friendliness. But now Martha had turned into lady do-good again. Serious social worker expression, deep frown tram lines in the middle of her forehead, cool soothing hand on Sofia's arm. Too bloody understanding face.

Sofia removed the interfering hand from her arm. 'Look Martha, this has been fine, this morning, tidying up and all that. But you know, you and I, we don't really know each other that well – perhaps we should just leave it like that? Taking the piss is all very well, but I don't think either of us really wants to keep up the boy bitching thing for too long, do we?'

'No, I don't want to talk to you about James, Sofia—'

Sofia shook her head, 'That's not what I was scared of. I know you want to talk about me, it's written all over your professionally concerned face. And I don't want to talk about myself or the baby, OK? It really isn't any of your business Martha. And it isn't James's business either, it's got nothing to do with him, and you're just going to have to believe me, it never has done. His sperm did not do this.'

'No. I do know it's not James's baby. At least I believe that now. It's not about him, or your baby – or maybe indirectly, I don't know – I just wanted to ask you, last night . . .'

Sofia had had enough of playing best buddies, 'For God's sake, Martha, what do you want?' Martha took a deep breath, put down her tea-towel, looked up at Sofia, 'I don't really know how to say this . . .'

Sofia wanted to slap her, 'Yes?'

Martha nodded, as if encouraging herself to speak, 'OK. That bloke you were dancing with last night—'

'What?'

'That man. The man who's usually with you, standing behind you. Who is he?' Martha looked down at her twisting hands, then brought her frowning question back to Sofia's eyes. 'I mean, what is he?'

Twenty-nine

Martha sees things. She has seen things since she was a child. The tones of people. The moods of strangers neon-lit in the dark. Martha would far rather not see things. Martha keeps herself busy so she doesn't have to see things, cleans, tidies, cooks and bothers far too much so she does not have to listen to the noises or see the shapes. She cannot bear to simply sit still and listen because it's all too loud. Martha runs miles from people like Sofia, specifically women like Sofia because Martha does not want to be perceived as the same sort of flaky girl. Martha hates the idea of herself as a girl loony, although much of the time it is what she thinks she really is. Hence, she hates the appearance of other women who enjoy the notoriety, disguises her fear as big politics and bigger words. Not that she doesn't believe her own politically correct fervour, but Martha didn't become a vegetarian because she knew that the exploitation of animal welfare for the feeding of the few Western rich was an aberration of true societal values, she became a vegetarian because she really did feel sorry for the little lambs. No political values there, at least not at thirteen, Martha honestly felt the pain of the little lambs. With every melting mint-drenched mouthful. Far more sensible then to dress her oversensitive soul in political colours than openly announce her true weirdo status. To be do-good girl and try to make it better, even in the tiniest way. Far more sensible to stick to work within a system of rules and pre-ordained plans. No blame, no responsibility, blinding her own searing vision with triplicate photocopied layers of sense-dulling system.

Martha does not enjoy notoriety. Martha revels in the complete absence of attention. Because she sees so much and her mind is too distracted and all she really wants is to be able to close her eyes and find it quiet inside like anybody else. All Martha wants from life is that people should find her ordinary. All she has ever wanted is to be normal. But Martha is not normal, far from it, though God knows she tries hard enough. Tries harder than anyone else she knows. Does not dress to draw attention to herself, does not behave in any way that might draw attention to herself. The tattoo is a different matter, private, a body-marking to ward off the knowledge of too much. The nasty things that might get in, her tattoo is a personal evil eye worn on the skin to keep her safe. Martha would rather look at the floor, scrub the old lino raw than look up and see what she sees. She does what she can, personally and politically, acknowledges it is pitifully little, and then turns off whenever possible.

Until now, Martha has simply seen emotion, been too close to certain people and felt too much of their feelings, usually their hurt that gets through and never enough of their pleasure. James is therefore the ideal lover for her, ordinary man with normal desires, but his head mercifully cloaked in a cloud of dope and alcohol half the time so that there is often very little to get through to her. Martha likes that. It gives her a chance to be almost herself with James, just her own suffering, own happiness, none of his feelings leaking into hers. Martha cannot read minds or see the future, she simply sees a little more of what there really is. Which is usually too much.

When she first moved in with James, almost a month ago,

Martha realised she needed to keep herself clear of Sofia as much as possible and, as Sofia seemed to have the same idea, things looked like they might just work out this time. But for over a week now, Martha has seen Gabriel. Martha is shit scared. She has seen Sofia's concerns, understood Sofia was worried that she was mad herself. But Martha has seen Gabriel as well. She knows neither of them is crazy. Which means Gabriel must be real. And Martha finds this very scary indeed. It would be so much easier just to stay hidden on her hands and knees, scrubbing the floor.

They went upstairs to Sofia's flat, Martha had her second cup of coffee that morning, hands shaking as much from the caffeine as from the strain of revelation. She told Sofia some of the truth, long stories of her fear of what she sees and Sofia told her very little in return. She figured that if Martha was as prescient as she believed herself to be, the rest would come out in time, meanwhile Sofia's new-found protection passion leapt into play. She knew enough about the current state of mental health care to guess it probably wasn't ideal to reveal herself as the mother of the new Messiah to a social worker for the local borough. A childcare worker for the local borough. Particularly not when she didn't even know what being the Messiah meant, when the idea of giving birth to something – anything – that important terrified her, when the idea of giving birth to someone that was part of a greater plan, someone meant to be and more than human, was a concept she found herself running away from ever faster as the day of truth approached. Certainly she wasn't about to let on to someone who had worked in the system for the past fifteen years.

Someone who, according to Martha herself, had chosen to give herself over to the system rather than make her own decisions, because the responsibility of seeing too much terrified her. Even if Martha could see Gabriel, even if she did seem to know that he was, as she put it to Sofia –

'a guardian of some sort' – even with all of that, Sofia couldn't bring herself to trust Martha completely. Or even partially. She just couldn't quite see Martha turning up at the birth, single bright star overhead, agreeing that this child was indeed the son of God, and then not whipping the baby away from Sofia's lunatic clutches the minute her aching back was turned. In fact, Sofia knew she would have probably thought about doing exactly that if one of her own friends had tried to tell her the same story any time before the past few months, knew that Beth was still very concerned. It wasn't that she was judging Martha's presumed course of action especially harshly, she just didn't see much point in setting up difficulties for herself. She had a feeling there would be plenty of inevitable trouble coming of its own accord.

In a way, of course, it was delightful that someone else could see Gabriel, acknowledged his presence, verified the fact of his existence. To some degree this was a relief for Sofia. It was just that she hadn't counted on having Martha as her birth plan confidante. Or as any kind of friend at all. It wasn't that she didn't believe Martha and it wasn't that she wouldn't have appreciated the opportunity to talk to someone else about Gabriel – it was just that Martha kept inviting her to 'share'. And then she offered to 'take on board' some of Sofia's concerns. Eventually Martha nodded and added profoundly 'I hear what you're saying' – and by then Sofia's main concern was that she had ever become soft enough to engage in a conversation with someone who used so much jargon.

Then again, she was also disinclined to have any conversation about Gabriel. Part of her enjoyed thinking that Gabriel was hers, only hers. Sofia liked having her own private angel. She didn't want to share him – literally or metaphorically. And certainly not with the woman downstairs who'd turned out to be a semi-clairvoyant social worker. Who wanted to talk about him. Because talking about Gabriel made him more real on the outside too – on the outside of her life. Which in turn made the pregnancy more real and the fear still more solid. Sofia finally got rid of Martha after another coffee and promised absolutely to 'take some time out together' later in the week. Girl kiss, air kiss, at the door and fingers firmly crossed behind her back.

Gabriel was waiting for her when she went into her sitting room.

'I'm so sorry.'

'What for?'

'I didn't know she could see me.'

'Is it a problem?'

Gabriel frowned, ran his hands through his thick dark hair, shook his head, 'Not necessarily, I mean she could be some help to you if you get her on side, getting benefits when the baby's born, things like that.'

'But?'

'But I didn't know she could see me and if I had, I would have been a whole lot more careful.'

'How could you not know that when you know so much else?'

Gabriel shrugged, 'Too close to me, I guess. Or I'm too close to you and therefore not being careful enough.' Then he sighed, 'Unfortunately, I think that's more likely to be the truth.'

Sofia didn't think Gabriel feeling close to her was such a bad thing, but she let it go for the moment, 'Should I have told her I didn't know what she was talking about?'

Gabriel shook his head, 'I don't think so. I think you did the right thing. You're right to be worried about telling her everything, she wouldn't understand, not the whole truth.'

'I don't understand the whole truth.'

'Well exactly. And she wouldn't get it at all, wouldn't want to. She's freaked by what she already knows, let alone anything bigger. No, I think it's sensible to keep her on your side, just don't let her get too close. She doesn't need to know any more.'

Sofia frowned, screwed up her face, 'Believe me, I have no intention of letting her get any closer than necessary.' Then she laughed, 'I don't know – call me a nasty, cynical old bitch, but I far prefer to know secrets about my ex-lover's new lovers when my exes tell me the secrets themselves. I certainly don't want to hear them from the new lovers, and I definitely know I don't want to be best buddies with them.'

'You were getting on OK when you did the dishes this morning.'

'Nah, I was just being friendly. Trying to be friendly. Pretending to be friendly because it's easier than not. As much as anything else, I was trying to get back in with James. I miss him. He's my mate. And if I have to play girlfriends with Martha to get him to be best friends with me again, I will. Besides that, it makes for far more harmonious living arrangements to get on with both of the neighbours.'

Gabriel shook his head, 'You nasty, cynical old bitch.'

Sofia smiled, took his hand, pulled him in closer to her, 'Angels with dirty mouths. Certainly beats Hail Holy Queen.'

They fell into sex again then. Slipped into the safety of sex because it was easier than talking about it, any of it. Martha's knowing, Sofia's feelings for the baby, her future, his role. What they might be together. What was going to happen. Easier for Sofia to feel Gabriel's no-touch, than to ask him what he thought the touch really meant. Impossible for Sofia to open her mouth and risk the chance of declaring her desire for Gabriel, her feelings for him, risk the chance of rebuttal – or worse, incomprehension. Far easier to simply open her mouth to his kiss, to respond and then take control in the small part of her life that was left controllable.

And easier for Gabriel too, not knowing how to feel, merely beginning to understand that he did.

Thirty

Sofia worked solidly for the next three weeks, avoiding both Martha and James as much as possible. Which, given that she worked nights, Martha kept office hours, and James was currently working day shifts at his bar, meant almost all of the time. The one occasion that Martha did manage to catch her on the front doorstep, Sofia fobbed her off with a stream of stuttered questions about Martha's work – the first time she'd ever shown any interest in the subject. Then she attacked with a comedy aside regarding James's penchant for naked sunbathing – while the neighbours' teenage children were watching from their bedroom window, her apparently innocent utterance guaranteed to divert Martha's attention. Finally compromising with an eventual promise to absolutely, definitely, really, go with Martha for a coffee some time soon. Not this weekend though, or next, Sofia was working double shifts and needed to rest whenever possible – she was sure Martha would understand, what with the baby and everything – but yes, they really did have a lot to talk about and she was dying to get Martha's opinion on all the exciting things that were currently taking place in her life. Really. For his part, Gabriel took rather more care about his appearances, waiting for Sofia in her flat, passing up on the dancing opportunities.

Sofia was now just over four months pregnant. And suddenly, at week eighteen, she realised that she looked it. Her own mother had described herself as a 'five-monther', one of those women who presented no outwards signs of pregnancy until five months when it looked like maternity had arrived overnight. Sofia had been hoping for the same for herself, but found herself cheated by a fortnight. She got up late after her night at work, walked past the full-length mirror in the hall on her way to the loo and stopped with the sudden shock of seeing herself side-on. It was as if she'd suddenly emerged from the pages of a Mothercare catalogue. As long as her body still looked pretty much the same, despite her occasional panics, Sofia had been able to convince herself that she, too, was pretty much the same. So much so that she really hadn't thought about taking more care until she'd climbed all the way down across the roof the day after the wedding. Because she had always used her own body for her work, it was not until the physical changes became pronounced that Sofia realised that the pregnancy she'd been nodding an uncertain head to, was now an actual belly-touching fact. As long as she hadn't thought it was obvious to anyone else, Sofia had simply looked like an ordinary girl with a fantastic body in every other respect and a slightly rounded tummy. To many eyes, still more fantastic because of the tummy. But now she knew the truth to have solid proof, it seemed that suddenly the whole world knew as well. Mothers with screaming babies in the street smiled at her encouragingly. Three different old men nodded pleasantly enough – and with not a hint of lust in their eyes. And when she walked past a building site, not one wolf-whistle flew down to bless her straining, terrified ears. No doubt it was simply chance, but Sofia felt as if a neon sign reading MAMA had suddenly lit up above her head. And try as she would, there was no turning it off. The fear she'd been hoping to avoid for the past weeks came flooding back – an overflow from the terror she had dammed up and tried to ignore.

As if to prove the point, Danny asked her to come and have a word with him the minute she arrived at work that night. Sofia dropped her bag in the changing room and Helen nodded a sympathetic, be-brave smile. Unfortunately, Sofia knew it wasn't bravery she was going to need. It was a new job. She stopped at the door to his office, steeled herself and then pushed the door open, head high, shoulders back, tummy in. As much as possible. Danny was not in his office, Caroline was. Sitting on the edge of his desk in floods of tears. She looked up and saw that Sofia had come in, for some reason this only intensified her grief and set her off again, rocking backwards and forwards and wailing noisily into her dribble-covered arms clasped tight around her heaving chest.

'Caroline, what's happened, what is it?'

Sofia had made her way down the long and narrow room as quickly as possible, a journey hindered even more than usual – Danny's office doubled, and sometimes tripled as a storage room for costumes, tables and chairs that needed mending, alcohol deliveries yet to be removed to the bar and, on this occasion, five bunches of white roses for Helen in varying stages of drying-out, sent by an admirer every day since he'd first been taken by her extraordinary beauty last Wednesday night. Helen didn't want the flowers, dismissed roses as naff and unoriginal anyway, but was also unnerved by the idea of an over-ardent admirer and didn't intend to give him the pleasure of seeing her leave in the middle of the night with the flowers in her arms. None of the other women was interested either – though any one of them would have happily pocketed their value in cash. Danny, however, thought it would be insensitive to leave them out in the street, in case the punter walked by and saw his love tokens callously discarded. Insensitive and not a great way to build good customer relations. Which left the dry and dying roses stockpiling in the boss's office until they could be whisked out the back door for Wednesday's rubbish collection.

'What is it Caroline, has Mariano come back?'

Following the last bust-up with Mariano – and a by no means unofficial flirtation with the boss – Caroline had made no secret of her desire to move the guitarist out, thereby freeing her up to make a stronger play for Danny. Both things had been accomplished within the space of a weekend just after the wedding party. Faced with the option of either starting to pay his way in her life, or getting out of it altogether, Mariano chose the latter. Moving in with a young Argentinian woman. And her trust fund. Caroline turned her attentions to Danny – with Sandra's blessing. The man of the house was away for a month on business and Sandra's employer was once again laying down her copy of the *Lady* in favour of laying down the au pair. In fact, everything seemed to be working out exceedingly well, although Helen had voiced the occasional misgiving about what might happen if it didn't all work out so well with the Argentinian – or when Sandra's boss's husband came home. For a few weeks, though, nobody was stepping on anyone else's romantic toes and things had seemed summer-smooth for all concerned.

Caroline's wail had turned into a whimper, Sofia had just made it across the room, and she tried again.

'Babe what is it? Is it Mariano?'

The younger woman shook her head furiously, tears beating the centrifugal force to splatter on Sofia's feet anyway.

'Is it Sandra? Are her and Danny at it again?'

This time Caroline's grief turned into words. A wail first and then words.

'No. Not him. Not Mariano. Not Sandra. It's Danny.'

'Oh. Shit.'

Sofia and Helen had only been discussing this possibility last week. Of course Caroline was bright and happy now, the crap boyfriend was gone, the good boyfriend was in position, but how long could it possibly last? Especially as the good boyfriend was also the boss. And amenable though he was, all the women who worked for him knew how seriously Danny took his business. If he and Caroline had fallen out, it was a foregone conclusion that Caroline's job would be the first casualty. Followed pretty swiftly by the rest of her life – Mummy and Daddy's little angel may well have escaped the clutches of St John's Wood, but she hadn't given up on the lifestyle. Caroline became a lap dancer because it was the only way she could provide for herself in the style to which she had been accustomed from birth. Without this job, the chances were Caroline would find herself back home within the week – and no one wanted that for her when she was doing so well at looking after herself.

Sofia had her arms around Caroline now, 'Hey honey, come on. What's happened? Isn't it working out? Danny can't sack you, you know. Not legally. I mean, if you want to we could stop him. Find a union or something – Equity could probably do something. He can't really get rid of you – and you know, there are other clubs, this isn't the only one, there's loads of others you could try . . .'

Sofia let her mouth run off with soothing sounds. Soothing sounds she'd been prepared to make to herself if Danny had tried to sack her. Soothing sounds she so wanted to believe that it took her a little while to notice that Caroline was still shaking her head, was in fact, starting to sob in the negative.

'No . . . not sacked. Not broken up. Not that . . .'

Eventually the sound of Caroline's denial broke through

Sofia's own statement of personal intent. She held off her new deal diatribe long enough to hear Caroline stutter out the real problem.

'No, not that . . . not Danny. It's me. I told him.'

'Told him what?'

'About the baby.'

'What baby? You're not pregnant? Is it Mariano's? No? You mean it's Danny's?'

In her concern for her distraught friend, Sofia was unfortunately missing the blindingly obvious. Caroline's grief wasn't for her own situation but for Sofia's. In fact, Caroline's grief wasn't grief at all. It was guilt.

At which point the boss himself pushed open his office door.

'Safe to come in now, girls?'

Danny crossed the desiccated bouquets and three champagne cases in a single – ungainly – protective bound, to wrap his eager arms around the still shaking Caroline, who managed to sob out another apology though her sorry tears. Sofia took one look at Danny's face and understood what Caroline had been trying to say.

She groaned, rubbed her stomach and looked up at Danny, 'Oh. Right. I figured that was why you wanted to talk to me anyway, I was going to tell you . . . there just didn't seem to be a right time, and . . . well, I do need to keep working.' This time she stared at Caroline who at least had the grace to shut up and not attempt another feeble apology. Sofia sighed at Caroline's pathetic face and added, 'What with being on my own and everything.'

Danny nodded, 'Yes. I know. And that's what I wanted to talk to you about. I'm not blind. I've known for ages. Well, a few weeks anyway.'

'And you want me to leave?'

'No. I don't, not at all. Not if we can help it. But I do

think we need to talk about what's going on and now that Caroline's brought it up . . . well, it's always better to get things out in the open, isn't it?'

With that he hugged Caroline again, patted her head, stage-whispered a sweet nothing and shooed her out of the room. She left with yet another sorry glance to Sofia who wasn't in the mood for forgiving smiles. Nor was the sight of Caroline walking off with the blessing of yet another rich Daddy to cocoon her likely to prompt her into ready forgiveness.

Once Caroline had closed the door behind her, Sofia sank back on to Danny's desk, curled her arms protectively around herself and looked up at her boss. 'Danny, I don't want to stop work, I can't afford to, let alone that it's the only thing I have right now that feels like it's really mine, but what else can I do?'

Danny half-smiled, a grin that quickly eased into a grimace. 'Look Sofia, I don't know how to say this, because it might make you feel even worse . . . but, well, you're becoming an attraction.'

'What?'

'Some of the punters, they like that you're not skinny, not just boobs and bones like Helen and Sandra. I don't know if they realise it's because you're pregnant, but they like you. More than before. I mean, not that they didn't like you before . . .'

Sofia shook her head, 'Danny, I'm not here for the flattery, I know what I'm worth to you. What are you talking about?'

Danny rolled his shoulders, bit his lip. 'Well, I understand you could think of it as a bit tacky . . .'

'It isn't already?'

At this he bristled, 'I like to think not.'

Sofia backed down, 'Sorry, go on.'

'Yes, good, OK, and maybe you wouldn't want to do it

for that long. I don't know how you feel about keeping working, getting tired—'

'A lot better than I feel about not working and getting evicted.'

'That's what I thought. So, as a special number maybe, just for another couple of months . . . you'll probably make in a week what you'd normally make in a month . . . I mean, I don't know what you'd want to do, maybe get one of the other girls to help you out with the choreography or something, Helen perhaps, she's usually got some good ideas . . .'

Sofia interrupted, still not certain she could be correctly understanding what her boss was trying to say, 'Danny, what the hell are you talking about?'

'Something new, create a number that doesn't hide it.'

'You want me to make a feature of the pregnancy?'

'Yes. That's it, exactly right. We'll call you a double act. Two for the price of one. Get it?'

Sofia got it. And didn't know what to say.

Thirty-one

She didn't know what to say, but she did know who to ask.

Helen thought it was fantastic that Sofia would be able to stay in employment, 'Christ babe, if it's all right for those Hollywood chicks to show off naked and pregnant on all those magazine covers, then it's got to be OK for you, hasn't it?'

'I suppose so. But I have this idea that Demi Moore and Sharon Stone get a whole lot more cash than I do when they get their kit off. And anyway, it's the movies, not reality.'

'If you're getting your kit off darling, it's still stripping, no matter who pays the bill. Besides that, you've far better legs than either of them.' It did occur to Helen to mention that Sofia might not feel quite as ready to expose her body post-pregnancy as she seemed to believe pre-birth, but then she figured she'd had completely different experiences with each of her own two children, so who was she to pre-empt Sofia's decision? Besides that, Sofia would discover the joys of stitches and stretch marks for herself soon enough. Helen silently reiterated her vow of silence from the conspiracy of motherhood, knowing she only had a few months more to wait until Sofia knew exactly what she wasn't talking about.

Caroline, in the throes of tearful shock, new love, and

timidly hopeful of a friendship reprieve now that Danny had attempted to salvage her from the implications of her big mouth, simply stuttered what a brilliant solution it was to everyone's problems and then fell gratefully into the arms of her knight in shining armour. She allowed herself to be bundled into a taxi and sent back to Danny's house, there to order takeaway Thai food, watch videos and pamper herself silly after crying herself sick. Helen watched Caroline drape herself around Danny for a goodnight kiss and whispered to Sofia, 'You can show a rich girl how to look after herself, but there's always going to be some part of her that really just wants Daddy to make it all better.'

Sofia felt equally put out by Caroline's sudden turn around on the self-sufficiency front, though she knew there were times when she would have given anything for someone else to come along and simply make it all better. Being a strong single girl with her own guardian angel was fine, but she figured there were occasions when anyone could do with a Sugar Daddy. Mummy. Generous retainer bearing sweet gifts. No point in mentioning that to Helen, though, who had long ago given up on girlie addiction to love. After three major relationships and one failed marriage, and with two children to support half the time, Helen was sticking to the Class A as her drug of choice. At least with heroin, she knew what she was buying.

Sofia spent that night at work acutely self-conscious, dancing like a first-timer, paranoid about the size of her tummy. But Danny was right, far from seeing her as less than perfect, the punters seemed to delight in her thickening waistline. Not that any of them openly mentioned the pregnancy as such, but now that she'd acknowledged what they were seeing, she was able honestly to assess their appreciation from the level of tips she was getting. Whether the paying customers got off on the idea of a pregnant lap dancer, or maybe they just appreciated the image of a slightly more normal-shaped woman performing for them, Sofia's tips were a good ten per cent up on the usual. Then again, her patterns were changing with her increased body-consciousness, the dance had changed. Sofia found it harder to lose herself in the music. The wider curves, the change in power she felt with her broader axis – these were less to do with the pregnancy itself, more that there was simply more of Sofia. She was growing and there wasn't quite so much that she wanted to lose.

That night she went home late and did her best to fall asleep as soon as possible, a perfunctory almost-kiss to Gabriel the most she offered by way of conversation. In the morning she was glad that he'd already left when she woke up. While she had no doubt he knew exactly what she was contemplating, she wasn't yet ready to speak aloud and prompt his advice on the subject. A Sugar Daddy might have had his uses, patriarchal disapproval wasn't one of them. Sofia was sticking to the kind of unquestioning girlfriend support that greeted any new move as perfectly acceptable simply because she chose to make it.

Sofia had discovered very early on that almost everyone she knew felt perfectly justified in dispensing uninvited opinions on the contentious matter of her work. More recently she had discovered that pretty much everyone from the old man at the bus stop to her never-been-pregnant friends believed they also had a perfect right to offer advice on her health, her pregnancy and what they absolutely knew would be her future now that she was going to be a mother. Put the two things together and the result was a deluge of firmly held, highly principled, totally diverse opinions. After opinions. With a few more opinions to follow.

'What do you think I should do, Beth?'

Juggling one baby on her lap and the other at the breast, wiping yet another mouthful of milky vomit from her shirt, Beth sighed. 'Do whatever you want to Sof. That's what you're going to do anyway. And I reckon the fact that you're even considering keeping working means that maybe carrying on is what you really want to do. But I do have to warn you—'

'Yes?'

'You're talking about lights and costumes and make-up and turning the whole thing into a big show number, right?'

'Well, in a very small space.'

'Right. Then my main reservation would be that within a couple of months you might find that your image of yourself as the Amazing Bareback Rider comes down with a bump and turns into the Freaky Fat Lady instead.'

'Great, thanks Beth.'

'Very welcome, now grab one of these kids, will you? I'm fucking knackered.'

Job or no job. New plan or old pain. It was a difficult one. She could, of course, leave work, sign on, gratefully receive whatever meagre benefits the state provided. She could try setting herself up in business, as a teacher or choreographer – but with no backing and no current customers, Sofia knew it would take longer than the few months she had until the birth to make a going concern of a business, and she hardly pictured herself running five classes a day with a screaming newborn. Or she could take Danny up on his offer. At least dancing openly pregnant might give her back a degree of power. Dancing as a shy-to-be-showing pregnant lady may have led to better tipping, but it also left Sofia with a nasty taste in her mouth. Even when she felt incredibly strong while raking in the cash, there were times when Sofia understood many of James's anti-lap dancing arguments, an understanding born of her own experience. But at least while she made herself out to be the strong and powerful Amazon dancer, she didn't have to show those feelings to the punters. She could keep up the charade of being in charge herself, whistling a happy tune of girl-defiance to convince herself that 'they' weren't getting in. Feeling self-conscious, though, feeling on show as the real Sofia, that was different. Then they did get through and then she really didn't like it. Which meant that performing as officially-pregnant Sofia instead of hiding-pregnant ought to do away with that problem. Her body would be even further enhanced as a performance tool. Probably. Maybe. Or maybe not. But she wouldn't know unless she tried and she didn't know if she even wanted to try, but then again she didn't know if she could dance a single night more while pretending to be other than she was – and there was still the rent and her bills to pay. And a future baby to provide for. And a decision to be made soon. Time to turn to still more other people.

Sandra drew her personal line at the idea of flaunting swollen flesh at the clientèle.

'I don't know Sofia, it just seems so – exposed. I don't think I could do it.'

Given that Sandra nightly flaunted more of her multi-pierced and brightly tattooed body than almost any of the other women, Sofia was a little surprised not to get a more positive response. Then again, Helen had heard things weren't quite so rosy on the au pair's home front, so perhaps the further-cemented liaison between Danny and Caroline was also part of Sandra's problem with the whole idea.

Caroline herself was both impressed with Sofia's potential audacity, though part of her was still as shocked by the whole idea as she had been when Danny first brought it up.

'So you're really going to do it? Like a whole number?'

'Several probably.'

'God, that's amazing. Really brave of you Sofia.'

'I don't feel brave Caroline, I feel forced. I don't see I have any other choice.'

'No, sure, but bloody hell, it's so—'

'What?'

'Well, open! So showing yourself. Just really . . . I mean . . . bloody hell . . .'

'Yeah, thanks Caroline. Useful advice.'

Caroline continued to be stunned and amazed for a good two hours more. Until Helen pointed out it was her fault that Danny knew this early anyway, and Sandra snarled that she'd never told Danny any dressing-room secrets when she was fucking him, and Caroline eventually realised that silent acquiescence was quite likely the better part of a guilty conscience.

Despite the lack of overt encouragement from her colleagues, Sofia found herself taken by the idea, it certainly solved several of her more immediate problems. By the end of her next shift she had almost talked herself into it. Yes it felt odd, and yes, now that she knew the punters could tell she was pregnant, she felt far more exposed dancing for them. In which case, the sooner she worked on a new routine, the better. Of course she was going to feel exposed, but she'd been feeling that for years. This was just another version. Only now she had a baby on the way to care for. Dancing as an actual show might feel different, but she wasn't sure that her concerns were justified. After all, unless she was prepared to accept James's theory that her work was already exploitative – which she clearly wasn't – then why should she feel obliged to stop now? Besides that, the most disconcerting objection to the new routine idea had come from one of the bouncers. Not asked for, but voicing his opinion as Sofia left the club anyway.

'I don't think you should keep working Sofia.'

Sofia stepped back into the entrance, 'I'm sorry?'

'This new dancing idea. I think it's wrong.'

'Thanks for your input Joseph. I personally think that slinging drunken punters out into the street at two in the morning but stopping first to grab whatever spare cash is in their wallet isn't especially commendable either, but I've never bothered to tell you that before, now have I?'

'This is different.'

'Why?'

'You're going to be a mother. That's special. Motherhood is special.'

Sofia could see Matt's cab waiting outside, hear Helen and Caroline coming up the stairs, all she wanted to do was rush for the cab before they got there and joined in, but Joseph clearly needed to get this off his chest, he'd hardly been able to look at her for the past two nights. She sighed, 'How so?'

'Well, see, what I think is that having a baby is special. You should be being looked after.'

'There's no one to look after me Joe.'

'No I know, and I'm sorry about that, but you should be taking more care. You should be resting.'

'I'm not sick!'

'Yeah, but you're flaunting yourself around here—'

'Flaunting myself? What the fuck does that mean?'

'Now calm down, all I'm saying—'

'Bollocks Joseph. You're not concerned about my health at all, or the baby's. You're only bloody worried about what I'm doing, aren't you?'

Joseph gave in, 'All right. Maybe I am. I do think it's wrong. You're defiling your state. Motherhood should be sacred.'

Sofia shook her head, 'Joe, you have no idea how right you are. I'm going. Thanks for your input. Believe me, you really didn't have to. Good night.' Sofia waved Matt over and climbed into the cab, ignoring Joseph's protestations. She sank back into the seat, delighted to get away into the dawn. She knew Joseph wouldn't be alone in his feelings either – for every punter who wanted her to dance, there would no doubt be another who thought she was wicked, firmly believing all pregnant women should be locked up at home knitting pale pink bootees. While he tucked twenty-pound notes into the G-strings of the non-pregnant ones. Sofia understood it was a fine line, but the bouncer's ill-timed opinions helped to push her over it. Joseph clearly still believed that the female world could be divided up into virgins and whores. Sofia knew that within four months she would have proved the exact opposite. She was the fusion girl. Even more than for most women, the idealised mother as pregnant virgin was a little much for Sofia to stomach.

Thirty-two

Sofia talked to Danny about what she wanted – a way to keep working, and about what he wanted – another way to keep the punters happy. Danny had been meaning for some time to diversify beyond the ordinary confines of his late-night licence, this seemed like the perfect opportunity, and it would give Sofia a chance to broaden her skills too. Then maybe, if the mini-show idea worked out, she could look at choreographing for the other girls too. That would keep Sofia in work for the last couple of months of her pregnancy – without a great deal of extras from tipping, but better by far than the dole – then once she'd had the baby she could come back to work first as a choreographer if it turned out there was a need, then as a full-time dancer as soon as she was fit enough to do so.

It all seemed more than possible. It also terrified Sofia. This would mean taking control of what she was doing. More then simply making scary decisions, she would have to offer up her work for judgement, not just from a sole punter, but for the other dancers and Danny. Teetering on the edge of a depression cavern, but knowing she really had no option, Sofia wrenched herself sideways and made yet another leap into the unknown. She dragged Caroline in as a co-dancer – it was the least she could do after getting Sofia into this mess in the first place – and went to work. They rehearsed during the day while working at night – Caroline complained about the workload, but once Sofia pointed out she was still fending for herself even if Caroline now had Danny's vast resources to fall back on, the complaints subsided to an occasional muttered moan. After trawling all the music the club possessed, Sofia came up with a medley of mother and baby songs, and then turned them into a comedic parody of everything else the women had in their repertoire. Caroline's usual mode of performance was sweet baby doll – which certainly worked for the punters, but was limited as a means of self-expression – and Sofia pushed her far beyond it. Then pushed herself further. Exhausted herself because it was one way of ignoring the mother and baby fears growing at the edge of her mind, concentrating all her efforts on the dance and the music, hiding from both her uncertain future and Gabriel in hard work and shattered sleep.

Concentrating on the new dance meant Sofia was forced to concentrate on her developing body. There was now more actual Sofia-body than there had been for years and Sofia liked it. Though she had early on chosen to reject the anorexic dancer tradition, she had nevertheless been living inside that culture, was still tainted by it to some degree. For almost fifteen years Sofia had believed herself to be strong because of the power she had over her own body. Power to keep it in shape, to subdue the flesh. Now, for the first time in her life, she was starting to feel strong because of the power within her body. Not the baby, the whole idea of what was to come still terrified her, the idea that it might be a Messiah, the Messiah, too much for her to contemplate. But now she was exploring the power she gained from using her new size, instead of fighting it. Sofia had forced herself into pared-down Amazon for more than half her life, it now seemed that full-on Amazon might well be just as strong. If not more so.

Sofia did not explain her career expansion to Martha and James, having neither the energy nor the political vocabulary to engage in a debate, she chose not to risk it. They knew she was choreographing for the club and both of them secretly congratulated themselves for, as they believed, having planted the seeds of escape in her mind. Sofia would have loved to have explained that actually it was Danny – the evil exploitative boss man – who'd suggested her way through the current impasse, but that would have meant telling them the whole truth of her change in direction. Their gentle smile of neighbourly smugness was a trade-off she was prepared to put up with. Just.

Gabriel, though, did know what was going on. While she had plenty of unpleasant scenarios as possibilities, Sofia couldn't imagine what his reaction was going to be. She didn't know how to broach the subject so she stayed in hiding. Barely spoke to him for three nights, falling exhausted into bed, waking relieved that he was gone. Then, on the morning that the new routine was to be shown to Danny and the other dancers before work that evening, at precisely the point Sofia was feeling most vulnerable about her change of direction, Gabriel asked about the new workload. He was an angel, but it didn't stop him being a touch insensitive at times as well.

They were lying in bed, the whisper of his no-touch skin soft against her back, close to falling asleep, Sofia's ideal time to drop into unconsciousness, just before morning hit her curtains with too much bright, and while Gabriel was still there to warm and guard her back. Gabriel spoke into her hair, two months' growth of dark roots bleeding into the blonde, Debbie Harry memories for the punters, easier care for Sofia.

'I watched you rehearse last night.'

Quick back from nearly sleep. Lower gut fear pushing on baby. Nerves at his attitude to the idea of her performing, performer's nerves at his judgement of her attitude.

'Oh. Where?'

'At the club. Before your shift started.'

More fear, always waiting since Martha's revelation.

'Did anyone else see you?'

His body rocked gently against her with his shaking head, 'No. No, of course not. I sat in the back. In the dark. Anyway, they're hardly the most aware people, that lot at your work. Too many drug and alcohol combinations muddying their intuitive waters.'

'Right.'

Silence. Held too long. She wanted him to like what she did and hated herself for needing his approval. For needing any approval, but especially his. Really didn't want to need Gabriel to think she was a good girl. Wanted it anyway. Still more waiting. Fat silence screaming loud, tension beating around their bodies with heavy moth wings. Finally she gave in.

'Well?'

'Well what?'

'What did you think?'

The whisper of air between them had turned into a defrost chasm. He hated it. She knew he hated it. Hated the idea of it and hated what she did in it. Didn't like the performance and didn't like her performance either. He was going to come out with all those tedious old clichés and she couldn't bear it if he did, probably couldn't expect anything else from an angel, for God's sake, but she so didn't want him to give her all of Joseph's virgin-mother rubbish. Major defensiveness setting in, an ice-cold steel door slammed shut between them. Shutters closed, big fear. Bigger angry before he'd even said a single word.

'Oh for fuck's sake Gabriel, what did you think?'

'Well . . . there's certainly historical precedent for what you're doing.'

'What?'

'Pregnant women, dancing. Very healthy. It's quite a recent thing for women to be shut away from view when they get bigger.'

'Oh.'

'Victorian really. In many cultures it used to be very important for the whole society to get a good look at a pregnant woman, see how well the community was doing at keeping itself going. In some places it still is, though of course the Western world's far too prudish for that sort of thing these days.'

'Other than on magazine covers.'

'Yes, other than that.'

'So what I'm doing is anthropologically correct?'

'I suppose so. Why? What did you think I'd say?'

Sofia turned on to her back, wriggled into the mattress and Gabriel to make herself and the bump more comfortable, 'I don't know. That I was exploiting my pregnancy? Using the unborn baby to make money?'

Gabriel, resting on one elbow, smiled smugly down at her, fingers entwined in the two-tone strands of her longer hair, 'Why would I bother? You've just said it for me.'

'So you do think it's wrong?'

Gabriel sighed, 'Sofia, what do you think?'

Sofia frowned, 'I don't know. I think I like it. I like the dancing. Mostly. I do like the choreography, I'm enjoying that part of it. I think the punters will like it. I know Danny will. And I think I've done a good job.'

'You have.'

Sofia stopped, performer's fears briefly relieved. 'Yes?'

'Well, I'm no judge, but yeah, it looks good, you and Caroline look good together.'

Sofia was appeased only momentarily, returned to her

defensive stance. 'Of course we do, we've been working bloody hard enough. And anyway, this is still the only way I know how to make money and, I'd like you to remember please, you already knew I was a lap dancer when you came to tell me.'

'To ask you, but yes, you're right, I did know what you did for a living . . .'

'And anyway, what right do you, of all people, doing your job—'

'It's not a job Sofia, it's what I am.'

'You know what I mean, what right do you have to talk to me about the representation of women in society, about objectification, about using women?'

Gabriel shook his head, 'None. No right at all. That's why I'm not.'

Sofia was silent, waiting to hear if she had just been tricked. She hadn't.

Gabriel continued, 'I'm not arguing with you, Sofia. I don't have any right to. I'm not telling you off. That's not what I'm here for.'

'Oh.'

'I'm not commenting on your job. You're right. You were chosen. It is meant to be you who is the mother. As yourself, doing what you do. That's what was deemed necessary. Perhaps it was already known that this was what you'd start doing when you were pregnant. I really don't know.'

Sofia shook her head, 'You're only the messenger, right?'

'That's not fair. I'm the messenger and the carer. I take care, but I can't do and I can't fix.'

'Not in the job description?'

'Not in the abilities I'm afraid.'

'So you can't make it better?'

'No one can.'

There was silence for a moment. Then Sofia answered,

'But Gabriel, you do make me feel better. When you're close I feel better, easier, safer.'

Gabriel sighed. 'I know that's how you feel. I know that's what I do. But it's not real. It's just an angel thing. It's not a solution.'

'Oh, Pity.'

Out of the quiet Sofia asked her next question, 'Gabriel, I thought that was the point of the baby?'

'What?'

'To be the one who would make it better?' Gabriel was silent, Sofia went on, 'Well? Isn't that the point of me having this baby? Giving birth to the Messiah?'

'Do you believe it is the Messiah?'

'I don't know. Sometimes I do. I start to think about it, about the circumstances of me being pregnant, about you, and it seems the only logical explanation is that it must be. But then it scares me. I don't understand how it can be. Even now, it's hard enough to believe this has happened to me, let alone what's going to come next, when the baby's born, when it's real.'

'I suppose it must be.'

'And so I just don't think about it if I can help it. I figure what's the point of the Messiah if the Messiah doesn't make it better?'

Gabriel put his arm around her in the not quite dark and held her tight, 'I don't know Sofia.'

Sofia lay there in the relative safety of Gabriel's almost-touch, trying to understand what she wasn't being told, wondering at herself for mentioning the Messiah idea aloud, wondering if she did believe that it was the baby's future. She believed in the pregnancy, knew the child was coming, anything beyond that, though, seemed still more impossible. More impossible than Gabriel. And if he really didn't have the answers then she wasn't likely to get them for herself, exhausted and confused at five in the morning. Eventually, hard work and pregnancy taking over her body, she gave up on the not understanding and started to fall asleep, grateful as always that summer's passing meant later mornings, easier to doze in the nearly light than really light.

Just as her body finally stopped agitating for answers and started to succumb to the mattress, the last question finally formed itself and spilled out of her mouth, 'Gabriel?'

'Yes?'

He answered immediately even though Sofia was certain he'd been asleep.

'Gabriel, is this baby going to be safe? I mean, not like before?'

There was a pause as he moved himself closer to her body, tighter around her flesh. She held his hand.

'Is my baby going to be all right?'

'Sofia, I really don't know.'

It was the first time Sofia had named the baby as her own. Gabriel had no more to say. She hoped he was telling the truth. She hoped he knew what the truth was. And in another half hour, with real morning, sleep came anyway.

Thirty-three

In the new dance. Sofia as teacher, mama-choreographer. Caroline for once uncomplaining, hard-working and impressed. Sofia was surprised by Caroline, the combination of big-mouth guilt and willing appeasement made her an excellent student and co-worker. But Sofia was surprised still more by her own work. She quickly discovered that she liked what she was doing, enjoyed the making, found satisfaction in the leap from invention to practice, practice to effect. Thinking about the choreography was different from simply making the dance in the moment with the music, or even from the few occasions when the women had pre-planned the dance – and the cash – for themselves. This new routine was a thought-out show. Five numbers, each one designed to segue smoothly from first to last, to create an impression that grew through the performance; beginning, middle and climatic end. Sofia was used to sustaining a short sharp impact across a three-minute soundscape. Here she was aiming for something rather more daring. Here she was trying to tell her story.

It didn't happen all at once, this was no damascene conversion from slap-happy lap dancer to Martha Graham acolyte. She didn't arrive at the first rehearsal fired up and raring to go with ideas that were spilling out of her on to the dance floor and ready to be interpreted by Caroline's willing limbs. But she did come fresh from a helpful telephone conversation with Beth determined that both she and Caroline might remember why they'd started dancing in the first place. Wondering what it was about the ballet show she'd seen at four, the dancers who were merely background to the musicals she'd attended with her parents that had moved her to want to join them in the first place. And for Sofia it wasn't the pretty dresses that had attracted her, nor the shining princess ladies with their big eyes and pointed toes. It was Coppelia coming to life, Giselle dancing herself to death, both of them as valid as Pan's People acting out word for word the Top Ten lyrics. When Beth asked what had made her want to become one of those women, Sofia's answer was that she liked the stories. Then she knew she did have something they could work on. A five song story to tell a six bar tale. From 'Papa Don't Preach' through 'Mama Mia' down to 'Mother and Child Reunion', Sofia found a way to make herself reverse-Salome, replacing a veil for each month she would work pregnant, beginning semi-naked and ending, Caroline as maternity-dresser, fully clothed. Sofia took her ability to move with and in the moment, and retraced the steps to the origins of her dance. Making it up before she went along. Creating the new dance prior to the moment of performance, so that with glitter and lights to hide the sweat, the recreation would seem sparkling as new thought.

Sofia was working fast, they only had a few days, which wasn't especially unusual. But the planning, thinking about the words, using her music-moved body to inform her thought rather than merely her bank balance, that was new. She was taking the chance of the choreography to leap from creation in the moment to invention of a piece. Not that she hadn't studied her own work before and not that she hadn't tried every time she danced to improve on the last. She had, but not always with awareness. In the four days of rehearsal, though, Sofia took a conscious look at what she was making and realised she liked it. Then, after half a week of sixteen-hour days, she took a deep breath, grabbed Caroline's nervous hand, and they presented themselves to the most critical of audiences. Their co-workers.

In the new dance. This time Sofia is not hiding inside her body, behind her flesh. Sofia is her body, the skin no longer masking truth, but naming it. Sofia has taken music and touch and Caroline as dancing companion and blended them together in an acknowledgement of her pregnant state. In warehouse theatre or minimalist gallery, and dressed in still less, this would be art. Here in the club, with glitter-ball lighting and pounding music and sequinned backdrop, it is an immediate show-stopper. It is as fast-paced and sex-driven as a teenage Friday night. On a tiny stage, bed-sized four foot by six, Sofia and Caroline carry their critical audience beyond the noise of late-afternoon traffic, past the acrid scent of last night's spilt drinks and desire, into something both theatrical and personal. The girls are still only a stretched arm's distance away, but the action of story-telling takes them beyond physical reach into a place of pure spectacle. Sofia holds centre-stage and her rounded body is hard. This is not mother as sweet Madonna, nor handmaid offering attentive but gentle girl-caress. This is far more brutal, and open, and revealing. And funnier. Much funnier than anything the club has seen in a very long time. Sofia and Caroline offer flesh and honesty, comedy and skin.

First they showed the new piece to the other women and to the boss. Danny loved it, the routine was everything he'd hoped for. Everything he'd hoped for and would be even more just as soon as they perfected this one and then took the time to come up with another two or three. He liked what he was seeing, believed his punters would too, but he wanted choice. Variety is the spice of night life. He'd take this offering for now, but Sofia and Caroline needed to get on with another two of the same as soon as possible. Helen thought they were brilliant and wanted to be part of it, volunteered herself as another dancer to flesh out the next piece Sofia came up with. The other women applauded too and only Sandra and Joseph continued to disapprove officially, though even they were eventually forced to admit that with lights, music and costume – Laura Ashley mama frills giving way to dancer skills – the routine may well have been unusual, but it certainly wasn't anywhere near as tacky as either of them had been afraid of. Or Sofia for that matter.

In the new dance Sofia created an intimacy that had previously been denied in the building. Where before it had been about show and don't touch, now it was show-and-tell with no need to touch. Everything was there to look at, no hide and seek, no peep-show suggestion. Incredibly daring for a room full of dark corners, bright-light exposing for two dancers used to hiding beneath a sheen of pretend-desire. They danced together, turning their bodies out not in, opening themselves instead of flaunting to hide. Sofia and Caroline moved within the music like it was a real dance, not a porn copy. Moved as if they wanted to dance, wanted to be there, as if they were doing it for the dance not just the money. The dance was better because of it, more interesting because of it, more real because of it. And, inevitably, in the way that not aiming to please always pleasures greatest, the dance was also far more lucrative because of it. Just as Sofia had expected – the new work certainly pleased her, but nothing was so pleasurable that it negated the financial reasons she was there in the first place.

As the next few weeks passed, Sofia discovered that she did enjoy the choreography, looked forward to creating new routines, teaching them first to Caroline and then using Helen's expertise to flesh out more of their work.

As the next month wore on, the requests to be part of the mini-show began to come from the other shifts as well, when the other dancers began to recognise Sofia and Caroline seemed to be having a damn sight more fun on stage than they were on the shop floor. For the first time since she was six years old Sofia actually began to think that just maybe she might be able to do something other than be a dancer. Admittedly, she would have preferred to gain this knowledge in a less forced way and, had she been offered the choice, she might have chosen to be well over thirty before such adult awareness came her way, but growing daily as she was, it was a valuable insight none the less.

Thirty-four

It went well for three weeks. Really well. Three weeks of good work and good money and enjoying herself, not worrying about the future, planning as far as the next routine and no further. Going to work and liking it and being applauded and then coming home tired but satisfied. Home where she was playing with Gabriel, not quite saying the words, not quite revealing the extent of her desire, but playing anyway, and whispering close to the truth often enough for it to feel still more real, more relationship. Going early to the club to work on new routines with Helen and Caroline and several of the women from other shifts, sitting backstage between performances planning new ideas to try the next day, doing just the four shows a night week nights, five sometimes six on Friday or Saturday, taking home with her both the cash and the accolades. Sleeping the tired sleep of one hard-worked and well-loved. Successfully avoiding facing what was coming, successfully avoiding contact with Martha and James, sneaking past their door out to work and then late at night home again to the angel upstairs.

Three whole weeks where nothing seemed to distract from the possible, no new blows struck fear into her getting-on-with-it head. And then came a Thursday night, a new routine Sofia was particularly happy with, she and Caroline and Helen as three graces, three muses, three mamas supreme. Danny and even Sandra had laughed out loud when they showed it off an hour before opening, she fully expected the punters to do the same. Laugh out loud and then reach deep into their gently tickled pockets. And they did, without fail, just as predicted. Except for one man. The young man who'd been pretty much a regular for the past couple of months. Paid for Sofia several times when she was still dancing alone, when the bump was just beginning to show, but only if you knew what you were looking for. And now he'd become a regular, sitting up to three nights a week at the small table to their left, just below the two-foot stage. Sofia had realised he was there for her, all the women had a few men who came back regularly specifically for them, it wasn't unusual and, as long as the guy behaved himself, it was a welcome source of regular income. On a wet and quiet night, knowing you'd have at least one punter turn up especially for you was what made it worth leaving the comfort of home and telly. This bloke was probably in his mid-to late-twenties, usually came in alone, though once or twice he'd been in with a bunch of like-minded, like-dressed lads. They were harmless drinkers who spent enough on their alcohol to spend enough on the girls. Not City boys with too much money and therefore a propensity to assume paying twenty quid for a dance was the same as offering fifty quid for a fuck, and not the just-in-town-tonight boy racers who were in for a stag night or twenty-first or football match and whose every drunken hiccup turned into a fumbled lurch. The same guys who would have no idea where their five hundred quid had gone the morning after. This man was not any of them. He was an ordinary regular punter. Didn't chat much – or at all really – but was pleasant, smiled, polite, drank a little, enjoyed the show, paid well and then left. A perfect regular really.

Until he started to look too closely. Until he noticed Sofia was changing; the dance, her body, her self. His smile turned to a hard stare, a look of disbelief. Then when the songs confirmed that the belly he was looking at was pregnant stomach his look hardened even further. He continued to turn up two or three nights a week, still sat and watched – though now he stared – at Sofia. Paid his money like the other men, wasn't loud or too drunk or rude in any way. Other than the way he looked at her, the way he looked through her. There was nothing she could actually complain about, certainly no reason to ask him to leave the club, but he made her feel uncomfortable. Sofia was used to this, all the women were, used to the odd bloke brought along by his mates who didn't really like the club, didn't approve, secretly loathed the women for what they did. For what they did to him. Knew how to handle it, how to ignore it. But with this punter she couldn't. He wouldn't let her ignore him, placed himself carefully at the side of the stage when he came in, made eye contact whenever he could, made sure she knew he was watching. Made sure she knew he didn't like what he saw.

And then, that Thursday night, he insisted she heard what he had to say as well. He was waiting outside when she left. Sofia finished work earlier now, the other women performed with her and then stayed on to work the floor for a while as well, she did her five shows and then headed home. She was usually tucked up warm in bed beside Gabriel by two thirty. She climbed the stairs, said goodnight to Joseph and then headed out, down the short alley and into the cold street. Now that she was finishing earlier she was less likely to get a ride home with Matt, but then again, it was also easier to find a cab, she rarely had to wait longer than five minutes.

The punter had been waiting for an hour. Watched the last run of the routine then left while Sofia was getting changed. Waited in the street while she chatted to Helen, picked up her money from Danny, listened in on the latest unsatisfactory instalment in Sandra's love life. He held out his arm to her, dark jacket bled to brown in orange streetlight. 'Can I have a word?'

Sofia jumped, the baby jumped with her. 'What?'

'I just wanted to talk to you. About your work.'

Sofia had no intention of encouraging a crazy punter on the street. 'I've finished work now, sweetheart. I'm going home. Maybe you should too, yeah?'

He stood in front of her, 'I've been watching you.'

'I'm sure you have.'

She tried to walk past him but he stood his ground.

'No, I've really been watching you.'

'I know. I've seen you.'

'I've been studying you.'

'Of course you have. That's what you pay for. To look. As closely as you want. Now you can either go back and get a look at the other girls, there's plenty downstairs still working, any one of them happy to take your cash, or you can watch me get in a cab and go home. Either way, you can piss off, because I've finished now. I don't have to be nice to you.'

'I don't think you should be working. Not now. Not with the baby.'

'Oh for God's sake, like I give a flying fuck what you think. Go home, will you?'

Sofia shook her head, took a tighter grip on her big black bag and tried to side-step past him, but he grabbed her free arm and twisted her back, belly unprotected, to face him.

'Hey! Fuck off!'

'You shouldn't be doing this. Not now. It's wrong.'

Sofia wrenched her arm from his grip, stabbing at him hard with a handful of sharp fingernails as she did so. 'Listen darling, you're the one who's wrong. So far, this only amounts to harassment and basic assault. I'd leave it there if I were you. There's a bouncer on the door within shouting distance, there's half a dozen blokes sleeping in three or four doorways all along this street – guys I give money to every second night. They like me, they won't fucking like you touching me. I don't fucking like you touching me. Now piss off!'

With that she pushed him backwards off the kerb, ran past him into the path of an oncoming cab, waved it down and jumped inside in the same moment, leaving her would-be attacker grovelling in the detritus of a Soho night. The cab drove off and she turned in the seat to see him still staring after her.

By the time she got home, the bravery of the encounter was over and she was shaking. Gabriel was waiting for her. And she was waiting for him. 'Where the fuck were you?'

'I was here.'

'Don't you know what happened?'

'Yes.'

'Well why weren't you there? I needed you.'

'No you didn't. What you told that bloke was right. There were plenty of people who could have looked after you, but you didn't need them either. You took care of him yourself.'

'I could have done with your support.'

'Sofia, you had my support.'

'Yeah metaphorically. That's really bloody useful. Christ! He really fucking scared me.'

Sofia threw her bag down on the floor and collapsed on the sofa, waited for Gabriel's reply. None came. 'So, despite all this guardian angel bullshit, I can't always count on your being there, is that it? Is that what I'm supposed to learn from tonight's delightful encounter?'

Gabriel didn't answer.

'Well?'

Gabriel sighed, 'Sofia, you always have my strength with you. Sometimes it's just not as obvious as others.'

'Yeah well, you'll forgive me if I say that's not quite the reassurance I was after. Bloody hell Gabriel – and just as things were looking OK. Fuck this, I'm going to bed. Goodnight.'

Sofia slept alone and angry, Gabriel waited for her to wake.

The next morning he brought her breakfast.

'What are you doing here?'

'Waiting to talk to you.'

'Don't you have to be somewhere else?'

'Where?'

'I don't know, wherever you go in the morning.'

'I only have to be where I'm needed. I'm sorry you didn't feel I helped you last night.'

Sofia shrugged, but into her toast, 'Doesn't matter, you were right. I did take care of him myself. I've always taken care of myself. God forbid I should end up relying on you, right?'

Gabriel smiled, 'I don't think it would be all that bad.'

He moved the breakfast tray to the floor, took the toast from her hand to kiss her fingers instead.

'Do you mind? I'm hungry! And I'm still pissed off with you.'

'I know. That's why I'm here to make it up to you.'

Sofia shook her head, attempting to keep a snarl on her face, 'Angel delight for breakfast? Bit sickly isn't it?'

'I don't know, worth a try.'

Later she ate cold toast and told him about the man.

'He's been watching me for a while now, I've been more aware of him since we started the new routines. I don't like him.'

'I know.'

'No, I mean I really don't like him. He looks bad, his eyes. He's got evil eyes.'

'Evil's a little excessive Sofia.'

'He didn't grab you on the street in the middle of the night.'

'Yes, but that's not the same as evil. You people use that word very lightly.'

'You people? You mean people people?'

Gabriel smiled, 'Yeah, people people.'

'All right then, what do you think's evil?'

Gabriel shivered a little then, Sofia pulled her arm tighter around him. 'Well, it's not like that. Not something you can see in someone's eyes anyway. Evil's more like a black hole.'

'Science or Calcutta?'

'Science. Black holes pull everything in, endless vacuum. It just goes on being nothing.'

'So evil's nothing?'

'If God is everything, yes.'

'And is God everything?'

Gabriel smiled, 'Oh no, you don't get the secrets of eternity out of me that easily.'

'OK then, what about eternal damnation and wickedness and sinners and all that hellfire and brimstone stuff – what about all the stories?'

'That's the point. They are stories. Ways of making sense of the nonsense, unsense. But we need the differences. We need dark to know light, chaos to know order. Neither one is better than the other, we need both light and dark, chaos and order to create, to live.'

'OK I understand that, we need the opposites.'

'But they're not really opposite.'

'Good and evil aren't opposites? That'll be news to the Sunday school teachers.'

'Not if they're good teachers. Good and evil – as concepts, they're less tangible than simply being opposites. They're far more intertwined. Like black holes, no one knows all of what they do yet, the physicists are starting to think that maybe we need them, maybe they're part of the essential creative factors for our universe too.'

Sofia shook her head, pushed scattered crumbs off the sheet, 'So good and evil aren't really opposites, order and chaos are both necessary, therefore my bloke last night wasn't a bastard and black holes are really lovely?'

'Yeah, could be.'

'Bet it doesn't feel so lovely when you're getting sucked into one.'

'Bloke or black hole?'

'Both. But I meant black hole, when you're falling into a black hole I bet it doesn't feel intangible.'

Gabriel closed his eyes, 'Any fall is a loss of control. That's always difficult.'

'Unless you give in to it.'

He smiled, eyes still shut, 'Oh yes, there's always submission.'

They fell asleep then, in the late morning sunlight, thoughts of the stranger held at bay by their body warmth.

Held at bay, but not entirely forgotten.

Thirty-five

Early autumn bloom time. No sign of the man again, he hadn't returned since the altercation in the street, no doubt aware that Sofia would have told the other women and the bouncers about what had happened. The fresh approach to the dance continued to go well, Sofia enjoyed her new-found freedom in stagebound limitations – the daily challenge of creation for the tiny stage behind a fourth wall of lighting and cigarette smoke dividing her from the punters. By the sixth month her hair was thick and glossy, shiny girl-mane like in the French ads and American sitcoms. Three weeks later the Blondie catcalls had switched in tone and intent to Jane Russell whistles. Though only among the older punters. Gentlemen may well prefer blondes, ordinary blokes will take what they can get. And those old enough to remember Little Rock before it was merely a Clinton reference would willingly take anything they could get their arthritic paws on. Happily take it from Sofia's hand anyway. Long, fine hands, now with fantastic nails – doubled calcium intake paying off, and great skin just as predicted too, utterly and positively glowing. A latest edition Sofia bigger and stronger in her body. Sofia filling out to fill in her own new lines. Just as in all the mothering books, the academic texts, the old wives' tales, she was coming into her own – and Sofia still the only old wife that she knew. Summer turning into early autumn, then later still.

Pre-dawn Sofia fallen in love with Gabriel, and surprising herself by saying it. Shocked into spoken-aloud honesty by another early morning of his not-quite skin.

'I love you Gabriel.'

Gabriel smiling back at her.

'I mean it. I do love you. Are you laughing at me? What are you smiling at? What's funny?'

Sofia wanted to stuff her hand in her mouth, shut herself up, eat the spoken words out of the air and hide them inside again. Too late.

'You love me Sofia. That's good. I love you too. But I love you before you say it.'

'What does that mean?'

'It means I don't need to add "too" at the end of the sentence. It means I can say so independently of you.'

Sofia telling Gabriel the truth and he knowing her truth even before she made it so by announcing the words, knowing because he was reflective angel, reflexive angel, and he had the same knowledge anyway because he felt it first, knew it, had it all along.

Gabriel could not have been Sofia's messenger without a degree of love, the descent of love, without consciousness of his own ability to fall – for someone, for her. Falling in love, falling into other arms, learning how to be with the just-touch, no-touch skin. Sofia was leaning inwards and forgetting to look out.

Then the season turned to fallen leaves. Soft harvest growing and growing soft with it, easy time, all just too calm, Sofia was lulled into the danger of lullaby sleep. Resting in reciprocated love with Gabriel, playing with him in her lust, in her bed, in her head. Loving the playing at being together, even while she knew they weren't really together, never could be a true coupling. Even while the growing baby fed her growing fears, she still wanted to hide in the safe place that their joined hands created. She had no choice – though all her experience taught her she was ultimately on her own, she had been too long a single girl in an unaccepting world. Sofia grew up here, the partner-hungry ethos got in anyway. Basking in Gabriel's love made her feel better. Think less and feel better. Just like any other addled love-head.

And then of course, anyway, inevitably, because while the world may be without end, happiness never is, it all just went too far. Time passed and Sofia could hide in the bliss of no-change no longer. She had been enjoying herself too much to look where she was going and slipped into the future without noticing she was there. All of a sudden it was the moment to move on. Next issue, next place, new race, no stasis and just don't ever think it doesn't move, won't change. Everything moves all the time. Only the sun stands still.

Sofia left work at thirty weeks. She didn't want to stop, knew that although she had been shocked by her own body changing, intimately involved with every millimetre of difference, that actually, from the outside, she wasn't all that big, did not yet look so phenomenally pregnant. She couldn't be classed as sailing ship huge, she still hadn't been offered a seat on the bus, could have passed for a big five months at anyone's ante-natal clinic. Could have kept going for another few weeks on looks alone. But looks alone didn't work any more, and Sofia was no longer making it on stamina. She was exhausted, bone-tired. Shocked that her body no longer responded immediately to every demand made on it. The bliss time was well and truly over. Every day she woke up late and sore-eye sleepy, she afternoon-napped to make the evening possible, struggled to work and then went back to bed as tired as she had woken. The walk back from the bus stop became too far and she found herself crying as she walked down her street, too tired to do anything but place one foot in front of the other and let the tears drip down her face. She cut back from five night-time routines to four then just three, choreographed more and more for the others to do until she was making only a final appearance in most of the numbers. But it was still too much. Sofia was growing on the outside, but her baby was eating her up from within. There was no energy left. Sofia had to leave because she simply couldn't keep going any longer. Though she did have one hell of a leaving party.

Three in the morning, they closed the club early, wound up Saturday night with the flourish of Sofia's last dance, last chance for tips. And everyone else's evening bonuses went into her leaving pot anyway. A good night's work, the whole evening geared for party flight, dancers giving their all to the punters so they could hand it all over to Sofia. Every woman in the building well acquainted with the far more valuable cache of pocketed cash. Once the last paying customer had stumbled up the steps and out into the street they cleared the glasses, wiped down the tables, set out new candles, straightened the chairs, opened the champagne, and then the night began in earnest. Girls dressed up to party and now Danny dancing for them. The 'Strip-o-Boss' he'd been working on with Caroline every morning that week – Joseph and three other bouncers roped in as accomplices. Dragged in as accomplices they said, but Caroline whispered that Joseph had loved every minute of it. An hour later Joseph slurred the same truth himself in alcohol-honesty. Sofia was showered with baby gifts and personal gifts and house gifts and leaving gifts. Come-back-soon gifts of tiny sexy underwear too, clothes she had all but lost sense memory of. There were plenty of pledges that Sofia could trust to be fulfilled, along with many others, too drunken-offered to be remembered the next day, let alone when she would really need all that promised babysitting in six months' time. Generously given though and, like so many other broken promises, declarations of true love, every word was truly meant in the moment of speaking.

Drinking and laughing and dancing. Really dancing, the four of them. Sofia and Helen and Sandra and Caroline. Dancing for themselves, like it was playing and partying, which of course it was, always was anyway, no matter who they were dancing for, but now much more than that. Dancing for each other too. I show you, you copy, you follow me and then we turn it into yours, into hers, back to ours, and then mine again. Dancing in the way that the dance was originally meant for each of them, before it became job, before the dance was career, when just to be in the movement was the point. When it wasn't about bleeding toes and strained ligaments, applauding audiences and pleasing punters, but purely to please the self. Dancing so the whole body was part of the same game, all just one big game. Moving with a congregation of stunned onlookers and not even caring they were there, reflecting no gaze but their own. Dancing for the hell of the dance, heaven of the dance, no in-between, just the being there, spinning there, holding time in space as long as the music could stand it and keeping going until there was no more to keep going for. Four too tired to keep going. One by one each woman dropped off, leaving Sofia alone. Solo dance, still dance. Quite still, but it was a dance anyway. Held moment, grace note, dropped to the floor with the dying beat, dead beat, fucking exhausted.

There followed tears and kissing and laughing and Joseph vomiting his too many vodkas but promising support anyway and Sandra crying at the latest episode of her straight lady-love heartbreak, Helen home to sleeping babies and sleepier drug, Danny and Caroline professing their undying, drunken lust, and eventually each one climbed the dark stairs and stumbled out into their own dawn. Sofia still not certain that she knew the way to hers.

At a latest night hour that was very nearly the same as day, Sofia waved over Matt's cab and tried to engage him in conversation for the first time ever.

'Morning Matt.'

If he was surprised by her endeavour, Matt didn't show it. He looked at her through the half-open window, said nothing. Nodded his head to Jim Croce.

Sofia bundled her presents and parcels into the back, climbed in after them, 'Crouch End please. West Hill – oh, well you know.'

Matt shrugged assent, put the cab into gear, and drove off.

Neither of them noticed the young man watching them from a dark corner as they drove away.

Sofia settled herself among the parcels and half-opened presents. 'I'm finishing work tonight.'

Matt kept his gaze on the road, ignored Sofia's attempts to catch his eyes in the rear-view mirror.

'I'm pregnant. That's why I'm stopping work. Can't dance any more. Not for a bit anyway.'

Matt changed gear again, increased speed.

Sofia waited another five minutes and then tried again. 'Sorry, I know we don't usually talk, I never want to talk either. Not ever really, not after a night at work I mean. It's just that tonight I'm a bit excited, or probably more sad really, that it's over. My job. For now. For a while I suppose. I sort of never thought today would really come. Can't believe it has actually,' Sofia looked out the window, watched Regent's Park speed past, 'Well . . . anyway, that's it Matt, just that I'm leaving. So I won't see you again. For a bit. Will I?'

Matt said nothing, turned his radio up and responded to his controller's call for a cab picking up in Muswell Hill.

Sofia sat back not sure whether to applaud his strength in sticking to what had become their pattern or to be annoyed that he wouldn't break his vow of silence just this once. By the time he dropped her off, she had decided that Matt was right, she'd made a bit of an idiot of herself trying to get him to talk, was undeniably embarrassed, but Matt was to be congratulated for not bending his own rules.

She handed him a twenty-quid tip after he gave her his receipt, 'Because it's the last time?'

Matt shook his head and started to drive off.

Sofia shoved her hand further through the window, her voice more urgent, too loud for the early street, 'And because I'm sorry for trying to get you to talk?'

Matt put his foot on the brake, took the note and folded it into his shirt pocket. He nodded, smiled and drove off. Sofia heard him singing along with Jim as his cab rounded the corner.

Thirty-six

For the first week after she'd left work Sofia was OK. Not great, but not too bad either. Getting used to it, feeling her way around the now free evenings. Watching TV at night, late and later programmes, getting up with the sun in the morning rather than using it as her signal to go to bed, making spaces in her wardrobe and drawers, throwing out old papers, unused clothes, preparation for all the new things she would need to buy – should she ever bring herself to go shopping for them. Or invest in a Mothercare catalogue. Or, better still, accept Beth's eager offer of hand-me-downs. The twins were growing at an alarming rate, and the minimalist beauty of their parents' pared-down bedroom was severely marred by double piles of milk-stained babygrows, two small Moses baskets, and a huge range of miniature designer outfits that had fitted the babies for just three weeks. Beth could accept the idea that two tiny people might challenge the attempted order of her chaotic life, what she couldn't bear was the encroaching detritus of their discarded weeks. Sofia figured she was safe from the shopping terror for a couple of months yet, at least as far as her own baby's clothes were concerned. Nesting was not one of the text-book attributes she'd developed along with darkened nipples and a belly-to-pubes demarcation line.

As for her own needs, Sofia wasn't quite sure what they were. It was years since she'd had quite so much free time to contemplate them. Not since she'd been obliged to visit a little room off the locked long white corridor. And really, that amount of enforced personal inventory had been more than enough then. And for a long time to come. Sofia had consciously kept herself busy ever since in an effort to stave off the terrors of her own imagination which, when given time to multiply, did so at an alarming rate. Now, however, there was little else to occupy her head. Something she was all too aware of as she lay on the sofa and wondered about her future, all the while trying to push away the questions that plagued her about her baby. Though she believed in Gabriel as an angel and she believed in her pregnancy because it was now a fact of her life, what she had never been able to look at was what her baby might turn out to be. Still didn't know how to, couldn't bring herself to, and so, even in the final stages of her pregnancy, Sofia did her best to ignore the biggest question of all. What a Messiah baby might mean.

Gabriel continued to appear in her flat every evening and stay through until the early morning, sometimes he was there for breakfast, more often he left while she was still asleep. Now that they had evening time together they were beginning to develop a dialogue that went beyond sex and the baby. But not quite far enough for Sofia.

'Where do you go?'

'When?'

'When you're not here, in the mornings.'

'Do you want more coffee?'

'Of course I do. But I want you to answer me as well.'

Sofia shouted after him as Gabriel picked up her cup and walked into the kitchen with it. She waited ten minutes for him to come back, then pulled herself out of bed – the fresh coffee was just starting to bubble under, her toast was warm and buttered, but Gabriel was gone.

The next night she tried again.

'Why won't you talk about where you go?'

'I can't.'

'Can't or won't? Aren't you allowed to?'

'Which question would you like me to answer?'

'All of them.'

'I can't. I can only answer questions to do with you.'

'But it is to do with me. Where you go is to do with me.'

'Why?'

It was on the tip of Sofia's tongue to answer 'because you're mine' but she didn't. Gabriel looked as if he knew what she'd meant to say anyway and then she realised she didn't want to say it after all. She didn't want to give him the chance to deny her. Instead she sighed a tired, 'It doesn't matter, leave it. You know you want to.' Then she turned over and tried to make herself more comfortable. Without Gabriel's back to rest her swollen body on, she was rarely comfortable.

Two days later they were lying together on the sitting-room floor and he tried to answer her question.

'I go away from here because I have to.'

'What?'

'In the morning, I leave you because I have to, it's not good for you to depend on me all the time.'

'Fuck off! I don't depend on you. I don't depend on anyone!'

'No, but if I was here, you might.'

'Bollocks.'

'Sofia, it would be normal. Sane. There'd be something wrong if you didn't start depending on me. Anyone would get used to leaning on someone who was there for them all the time.'

Sofia shrugged, 'Maybe. Or I might just get irritated by you hanging around all the time and lean on you less, have you considered that?'

Gabriel smiled, 'Of course I have.'

'And?'

'That's why I go away.'

Sofia waited as long as she could, but in the end she had to ask, the question burning itself behind her lips, 'OK, but where do you go?'

Gabriel shook his head.

'All right then, let's try it another way, do you go to someone else?'

'Is that really what you're worried about?'

'That you're not rushing off to some other woman? That I'm special to you? Well of course I think about that.'

Gabriel rubbed his eyes, held one hand out just skimming the skin of her belly, kissed her lips with his other, 'Sofia, you are special. That's the point.'

It wasn't much comfort, but it was some. Sofia knew Gabriel well enough to understand it was all she was going to get. And if he didn't fill her night with answered questions, Gabriel was at least there some of the time to help stave off the mounting terrors. Sofia did her best to stay awake with him as late as possible so as to give herself reasons to sleep even later in the morning, little time left to kill in the day. Little, but still too much. She tried a couple of walks in the park, but there were too many frantic pre-school children and their infant-obsessed mothers, and no matter how often she was asked when she was due and did she know what she was having and why didn't she want to know and wasn't it exciting and terrifying and amazing, Sofia just couldn't bring herself to join in the baby chatter. She didn't think she had anything in common with any of them. Of course, she knew it wasn't possible that every one of these women was a happy little housewife with her own blossoming career on hold for a year or so, while a loving husband brought home the low-fat bacon, and the supportive in-laws visited on alternate weekends. Though given that she was park-walking in Crouch End, Sofia wondered if her cliché-terrors really were all that exaggerated. But even if one or two of these women were in a position more like her own, and statistically half a dozen of them had to be, it wasn't likely that many of them were mothers-to-be of the Messiah. If Sofia had felt alone before, her daytime state had now devolved into definite loneliness. Which wasn't likely to be abated by cynically observing the Gap-clad laughter of the One O'clock Clubbers. She decided to give the park a miss. Fresh air was profoundly over-rated anyway, and autumn was far from her favourite season.

The neighbours, however, were determined she should not be alone. Anti-gravity invites poured upstairs from James and Martha, delighted to have a chance to applaud her for finally leaving that job. Their intimate attention was not really the diversion Sofia was looking for, but she finally relented to a meal with the two of them, hoping to shut them up for a while. However, she expended so much energy throughout the evening trying to avoid Martha's meaningful looks, her raised eyebrows, and attempts to get Sofia into the kitchen to sneak a girls' talk about Gabriel, that when she finally climbed the stairs back to her own flat, far from the evening being the relief it was intended, all she wanted to do was collapse for a week in a darkened room. Yes, the food had been great. Better than that, for all her irritating doing-too-much, Martha really was an amazing cook and had provided a brilliant supper culled from a formidable range of restaurant-titled recipe books. Unfortunately, the subtext of the evening also gave her indigestion. Or perhaps it was that the baby too found hiding Gabriel something of a strain. Whatever the cause, Sofia realised that for the time being at least, loneliness might be a more bearable alternative to being cornered into explaining the truth to her ex-boyfriend's new lover and local childcare worker. Sofia felt no desire to add to Martha's concern about the state of her mental health. Let Martha worry about her own visions, Sofia planned to stick to strict angel-ignorance in public.

By her second week off, though, the too-much-time was starting to grate, the necessity of leaving the flat not for work, but for basic provisions becoming a heavier burden day after day. After three weeks away from the job, Sofia found herself weighed down with more than just the baby inside her. The stale air in the flat pushed against her skin from first thing in the morning when she woke and was forced out of bed to pee – burrowing back in as often as possible – until the early evening when Gabriel was with her, evaporating just a little of the dense blue with his own light. Though less and less as the week progressed, her darkness making his light weak and thin. Week three after leaving work turned into four and then Sofia was almost eight months gone. Time became a material wall in front of her.

Autumn was almost past now. The trees behind the bus garage were well over their orange and yellow phase, had been dropping mellow fruitfulness daily, enough to block gutters and drains, sliming up the footpath outside Sofia's flat. Slippery footpaths – another reason not to go out. Sofia added it to sudden showers, nights closing in too early since the end of daylight saving, people with spiky umbrellas, and wind that drove her crazy, whipping up the too-much hair that now hung lank to her shoulders, but she just couldn't face going into the hairdressers' to deal with it. Couldn't face going out at all any more, cut off chunks of unwashed locks when they annoyed her too much and tried to ignore the concern in Gabriel's face when he came in the evenings. Closing her eyes and fucking seemed to achieve it the best.

Except that, much as he happily involved himself in the sex, Gabriel didn't mean to be ignored. He had a job to do.

'I'm worried about you.'

'So am I.'

'You are?'

'Yes. I'm worried about how I'm going to pay the gas bill in the middle of winter. I'm worried about buying nappies – panicking about shopping and about paying for it. I'm worried about a screaming kid keeping the neighbours awake.'

'You've got loads saved, Danny gave you hundreds of pounds' worth of vouchers for nappies and everything else, and you've never cared about disturbing your neighbours – come on Sofia, your neighbours are Martha and James.'

'OK, then I'm worried I'll never be able to go out again.'

'Liar. You don't want to go out. You finished work nearly a month ago, you could have been out every night of the week, instead you've chosen to go out only five times since then.'

'I went to Beth's.'

'To borrow some clothes.'

'I still went out.'

'You stayed for half an hour, turned down her offer of a cup of tea, refused to talk to her about the baby, about me—'

'Snooping were you?'

'If you want to call it that. When she tried to talk to you about your depression you ignored her.'

'Because I'm not depressed.'

'Really?'

'Of course I'm unhappy, look at what's going on. That's not the same as talk-to-your-therapist depression.'

'Beth's also your friend.'

'With two screaming babies who take all her energy. She doesn't need to be worrying about me.'

'Is that why you fled the moment the twins woke up?'

Sofia closed her eyes, 'I'll have plenty of crying of my own to deal with soon enough, I didn't want to listen to theirs as well.'

'OK then, what else have you done? Other than watch TV and sleep?'

Sofia snarled, 'Made sweet passionate love to you.'

'I know, I was there.'

'Sounds like you were bloody everywhere.'

'It's what I do. Anything else? Been anywhere else? Seen anybody?'

'I went to dinner.'

'Downstairs is not out.'

'Gabriel, it's taking me time to adjust, all right? I don't do holidays. I do keeping going. I don't want all this spare time, I don't like not using my body, I don't want to just sit around here all day.'

'So why don't you go out?'

Sofia shook his arm away from round her shoulders, 'That's not what I want either.'

Gabriel wasn't going to be pushed off, 'Beth rang a couple of times, did you call her back?'

'You've been listening to my messages?'

'Yes. Did you call her?'

'No.'

'Sandra?'

'No.'

'Your mother?'

'Guess.'

Gabriel held his head in his hands, pulled his hair back into a frustrated fist, 'This isn't good for you. Look, I know how scared you are—'

'No you don't. You have no idea how scary this is.'

'Then tell me.'

'I can't. It's too big. It's too close.'

'What is?'

'The birth, the baby. I won't know what to do with it.'

'Yes you will, you'll pick it up, everyone does.'

Sofia stared at him, 'Everyone isn't giving birth to the Prince of Peace.'

'Right. No. Good point. So, do you . . . ?'

'Believe you now? Maybe. Probably. I don't know. But if I do believe you, it's even scarier. How the hell do you mother the Messiah?'

'It's a baby first Sofia. You just mother the baby.'

Sofia sighed, 'In that case there's nothing to worry about is there? I'll just carry on as normal, shall I?'

'Yes, but you're not carrying on as normal, are you? You're not doing anything except hiding in here. Of course you're probably bored, you're used to working hard five nights a week and partying the rest. I do realise there needs to be a period of adjustment, I imagine this is the first chance you've had to take some time to think about what's happening to you in years, but you really can't just sit in the flat all day. You need to get out, I mean, when was the last time you went shopping? There's no milk, no bread, no soap in the bathroom . . . it's really not good for you.'

'You're welcome to go shopping if I'm not providing enough.'

'I have been. I want you to.'

'Fuck off Gabriel, you're not my therapist.'

'You're hiding Sofia.'

'I've got a lot to hide from.'

'But you're not eating, you're not sleeping properly, you're not taking care of yourself at all. I just don't think it's good for you to give in to this depression.'

Sofia rounded on him, 'Give in? You think I want to feel like this? You think I actually choose to sleep twelve hours a day and then panic because I'm wide awake half the night? You think I enjoy being terrified of going out my own front door?'

'No, of course not. I'm concerned about you.'

'So am I. And there's nothing I can do about it. I don't know how to shift this. I don't know how to move away from the heaviness I'm feeling – no, not feeling, I'm not feeling anything half the time, because if I let myself feel it scares me senseless – I don't know how to get out. I never have done. I've always relied on other people to guide me back, only this time I can't even tell the truth about what's landed me in this state. Gabriel, there's nothing I can do.'

Sofia stood up, arms wrapped tight around her chest, fingernails digging into her upper arms for the comfort of pain.

Gabriel's response was less than useful. 'I know you feel terrible, but it's not just about you, you have to think of the baby now, Sofia.'

Sofia's arms fell to her sides, she shook her head and walked to her bedroom door, 'Well, that'll teach you to pick a nutter for the mother, won't it? Leave me alone Gabriel.'

She stayed under the duvet with the curtains closed for another day.

Thirty-seven

Throughout most of the pregnancy, Sofia had tried to ignore the inevitable practicalities of her situation – the basics like actually giving birth, and then bringing up the baby, were worries which, like the Messiah question, she'd attempted to dismiss as quickly as they crept into her head. Now, though, it was no longer possible to ignore the future that was hurtling towards her daily. She was physically big. Very big for Sofia – she had enjoyed the sensation of size for a couple of months, started to embrace the possibility of herself as bigger – physically and emotionally – felt herself growing with the flesh. But now the inevitability of birth pressed itself on her every waking moment and, despite her best efforts to hide in unconscious sleep, she was awake most of the time. She couldn't stay asleep, though she did stay in bed as often as she could. In addition to her own terrors of unplanned motherhood and the usual tricks of her heavy depression, now that she had decided to want the pregnancy, she was afflicted with baby fears. What if it wasn't all right? What if the birth was TV-dreadful? What if the baby hadn't been protected as Gabriel had claimed? What if her excesses of the past eight months had somehow managed to harm it, despite his angelic assurances? Silent nights warm beside Gabriel's no-touch skin were close to comfort – but not close enough.

Sofia knew that despite Gabriel's promises of care and guardianship, she really was by herself in this – she would be giving birth, she would be bringing up the baby. She'd be doing it all. Unfortunately, right now, she didn't feel capable of doing anything. Didn't feel at all if she could possibly help it. Sofia wouldn't answer the phone, couldn't bring herself to leave the flat even for the most basic needs; she was alone, hated anyone who tried to make her less alone, and she didn't know how to get out of the dark she was hiding in. Even the possibility of chemically getting out of it was no longer an option – alcohol made her throw up, her meagre coke supply was long gone. As a last resort, she could have gone to James for dope, but that would have meant forced conversation and pretence of normality. Which had now become impossible. The day she'd left work all things had seemed possible, now everything seemed so hard, too big, far too real. Sofia had not envisaged a traditional life for herself, but nor had she planned on single parenthood either. Now, though, fighting her future was no longer an option, it was going to happen anyway. And fighting required effort, for which Sofia no longer had the energy. She had barely enough strength to hide in the dark.

Sofia felt quite prepared just to hide in bed until they came to take her away. Angels or men – either of them in shining white – whoever they might be. Her depression had now progressed so far that it was refusing her even the release of sleep, she was wide awake at three in the morning, denying Gabriel's presence on the end of her bed, and crying silently into the night. From that dark cold, she was ready to give in to the heavy blue. She was actually looking forward to it – abdication of personal responsibility as an alternative freedom. Deep blue settling over her face and skin, heavy dark covering both mouth and nose, Sofia was breathing it in, welcoming the thick no-air inside her flesh as well as in her mind, opening to the darkness simply because she was too tired and heavy and scared to push it away any longer. Because giving in was the only way out.

For three days she lay in her own darkness, not answering Gabriel's questions, not responding to his no-feel touch, ignoring the messages piling up on her phone, refusing to hear James knocking on her door. She dragged herself out of bed only to drink tap water and eat her way through three packets of pitta bread. It was all she had left in the flat and she certainly wasn't going out shopping for anything more tempting. Sofia was beyond terrified and had willed herself into a place where she felt little and questioned nothing. With the event now imminent, her mind couldn't compute the idea of who and what Gabriel said she was giving birth to, she had no reason not to believe that what he said about her child was true, and yet in itself, believing him made no sense. Sofia journeyed down to the non-sense.

She already had herself shut away in a cool white corridor on the other side of the safely locked doors, was preparing to welcome the vision of herself as someone else's problem, when an arc of surprise pain broke over her, shattering light into her face, and ripping wet hurt from far down inside, up to the smooth surface of her suffocating desolation. She hadn't spoken aloud for almost half a week and surprised herself when a gush of pain split her dry throat and spilled into the dark room. Sofia's early labour began hard, fast, and too late to do anything sensible. Like call a midwife or go to the hospital. Not that she had been making any of the pre-birth meetings she was supposed to anyway. Sofia had missed her last few ante-natal check-ups, could no longer bring herself to offer a glowing-mother smile to the practice nurse. She hadn't wanted to be ready for what she didn't understand.

Sofia's waters broke, a more impressive torrent than Beth's disappointing trickle, and immediately her pains stepped up another notch. This was not the slow and steady increase of labour at timed intervals that she had been led to expect from the couple of baby magazines she had forced herself to read while in the doctor's waiting room. It was not the slow increase in dilation she'd seen on every filmed birth screened on docu-soap TV. Sofia hadn't done this before and she didn't know what to expect, but she did know she was having the baby. Really very soon. Between sharp breaths that were both grasping for air and shock at the force of the pain, she tried to tell Gabriel what was happening. She didn't need to. Gabriel was feeling it himself. Gabriel was doubled up on the end of the bed, writhing in agony. His face was as close to pale as it would ever get, his arms clutching uselessly at his stomach, and his mouth clenched, holding in the white noise of his pain.

'Gabriel – what's going on?'

'It hurts.'

'Yes, but why does it hurt you too?'

'Don't know. Haven't done . . . don't do . . . never been in pain . . . before.'

'Never? You've never felt pain before?'

Gabriel stuttered out his answer, 'No . . . I . . . it wasn't like this. I wasn't with her.'

'I thought you were meant to be there all the time?'

'Yes, but I didn't do the same . . . empathy. I mean, not . . . oh, God . . . no. Not before. Not—'

'In love?'

Gabriel shook his head, managed to get over the shock of his pain and bring his eyes level with Sofia's, 'No. Not before. Never felt pain. Never in love.'

For her part, Sofia, now well and truly bought back to life with the advent of her own agonies, took time out of writhing and moaning herself, long enough to laugh in his face, her first smile in almost a month, 'Shit babe, welcome to the real world.'

They kissed. And cried. And moaned a bit more.

There was a two-minute lull in the pain. Sofia suggested Gabriel call an ambulance.

'I can't.'

'Why not? You might be hurting sweetheart, but I'm the one that's actually giving birth here.'

'No. They can't hear me. My voice doesn't work for them.'

'Oh. Right. Oh God – here we go—'

Then another bout of hurting, Sofia pulled herself from her bed to the sitting room, picked up the phone. There was no line. No dial tone. Nothing.

'Oh no, you bastards, you fucking bastards!'

No dial tone, but a knock on the door instead.

Martha's voice outside, 'Sofia? It's me, are you OK? Do you want help? Is it the baby? Sofia?'

Sofia went to the door, let her in, breathing hard, 'Baby's coming and there's no fucking phone.'

'I know. There was a BT van outside this afternoon – you know how it is whenever they dig anything up, they always seem to manage to cut you off at the same time as they fix someone else's line.'

'Yes, but the baby—'

'I know, I mean, we guessed.'

'Who?'

'James is waiting by the phone box – he said if you want him to call an ambulance I should wave out the window.'

Gabriel appeared at the door looking, if possible, even worse than Sofia, 'Yes, quick, do. The baby's coming now.'

If Martha was surprised to see Gabriel she didn't show it, she was all calm professionalism, went to the window, waved assent to James, then walked Sofia to a chair.

Martha turned to Gabriel, 'I can't see you very clearly, and I can't hear you all that well either, obviously your energy's going into something else right now, but I gather you're suffering sympathy pains with Sofia, which makes sense I suppose.'

Sofia started to explain but Martha hushed her, 'You concentrate on breathing, or whatever it is you're supposed to be doing.' Then she turned back to Gabriel, 'Now look, I don't know how long the ambulance will take, and I don't know how long we've got till the baby gets here—' She looked at Sofia, now off the armchair and squatting against the back of it, trying to hold on to something stronger than herself, then turned back to Gabriel, 'The thing is, James will be up in a minute – and I imagine he's not supposed to know about you, is he?'

Gabriel shook his head, torn between needing to help Sofia, his own pain, and his far greater shock at having to deal with Martha who was still talking as she collected Sofia's keys and handbag and wallet, 'OK, not that I understand what's going on either, but I know James isn't the seeing things type, so I don't think he'll be able to see you of his own accord, will he?'

'Ah – no. I shouldn't think so.'

Martha continued, 'Right, well, that's what I thought. So I just want to say that I don't mean to ignore you, but I imagine you don't want me pointing you out to him, I can see that you're in pain, and I'm not being rude here, but I need to make Sofia the priority at the moment – well, we all do, don't we?'

Sofia could have pointed out that now was hardly the time for negotiating the niceties of birth protocol – she didn't give a damn whether Martha talked to Gabriel, ignored him, or walked right through him, she was in far too much pain to care about the delicate feelings of her guardian angel – he with his uselessly empathetic capabilities. She could have pointed this out except that at the precise moment she opened her mouth to have a go at Martha, she was struck by an astonishingly forceful wave of pain – and an unmistakable urge to push.

The ambulance arrived ten minutes later and they just made it to the hospital. Where there were no available beds in the labour ward. Not that it would have mattered anyway, Sofia barely made it out of the ambulance, would have given birth in the car park if she'd had her way, but was forced to hold on just long enough to get her inside the building. The baby was born on a gurney in a lift just between the sixth and seventh floors, two paramedics hurrying her upstairs, Martha's left hand crushed in Sofia's right and Gabriel crouched in the corner, out of everyone's way and in direct view of Sofia's line of sight. Eyes locked, pupils dilated.

James locked up both flats and followed the ambulance to hospital in a taxi, waking friends and family from his mobile as the driver got him there at terrifying speed. He turned down the five quid tip – 'Nah, mate. New Dad, believe me, you're going to need it.'

James didn't bother to contradict him. The driver's assumption didn't feel all that wrong. It was five in the morning when he paid the driver, the beginning of an early winter day, the sky was especially clear for London, and in the east James noticed an incredibly bright star. He watched it for a moment, surprised at its sparkling clarity and then turned back inside to the hospital, better things to do, important phone-calls to make.

As James turned around the star did too, now showing its red light blinking beside the bright white, heading south, early morning Gatwick arrival.

Thirty-eight

Sofia's son weighed just over seven pounds. A couple of weeks early, he was small, but otherwise healthy. From the moment he was born, he cried, screamed, wailed, whimpered and would not be placated. Until Sofia was finally left alone for a moment, curtains closed around her bed, and she was able to hand him over to Gabriel. Then he smiled. And didn't cry again. The child looked mixed race, mixed races, like Gabriel. Dark brown skin, lots of curly black hair and – hers wide and round, his definitely almond shaped – he had a baby version of Sofia's palest blue eyes.

Sofia watched Gabriel holding the now calm, quiet child, 'So you lot didn't think a girl could manage it, then?'

'What?'

'Whatever. Whatever this little one's got coming to him. He's a boy.'

'Yes?'

'I just thought you might have gone for a girl this time.'

Gabriel looked from the baby's face to his mother's, 'Oh. I see. No. It's not like that. You've managed to do this, haven't you? Be the mother? Against all odds, hardly traditional.'

'Yeah, but Gabriel, I'm magnificent.'

'True. The world isn't though. It'll be a while yet before enough people would listen to a girl to make it worthwhile.'

Sofia shrugged, 'Not that I mind, little boys have better clothes anyway. I think I'm probably better with boys.' She held out her arms for her son, took the tiny boy in her arms and stared into his face. She smiled down at his unfocused eyes. 'I never really thought about what he was going to look like.' Then she shook her head and corrected herself, 'Actually, I didn't really think about him at all. I mean other than panicking about if he'd be OK in the past couple of weeks. And . . . the other thing,' She whispered, 'The Messiah thing. But apart from that, I think I assumed, that once the baby was here, imagining it was healthy and all that – then it would be fine. You know, he could take care of himself. I think I sort of thought the job would be over once I'd given birth. Or at least, I didn't think so much about what would come next. Was so freaked about everything else, I didn't want to think about what came next. Crap or what?'

'Not really, even people who mean to be pregnant sometimes forget that the end result is living with the child. And you didn't exactly plan for this.'

'As I've spent the past eight months telling you.' Sofia held out her hand and stroked her son's soft fuzz of hair, 'All that fuss and he's really just a little baby, isn't he?'

Gabriel nodded, 'That's exactly what he is. That's all he is.'

'Yet.'

'Yes. What are you going to name him?'

Sofia looked up, 'Oh. I don't know. What am I supposed to call him, Emmanuel?'

Gabriel shook his head, 'I don't think so. Not even in Crouch End.'

'We could always pretend he's some Hispanic kid from *NYPD Blue*, Jesus pronounced with an H.'

'Bit obvious.'

'Yeah, asking for trouble really.' Sofia held the baby's

hand, kissed it, then kissed Gabriel's arm resting on her shoulders, 'Gabriel's a nice name.'

'Sofia, no! White single mother, mixed race kid, no father to even take him away on weekends, and you want him to be picked on as "gay-Gabriel" for the whole of his school life?'

'Lap dancing white single mother, thank you. I don't know. He's going to get teased whatever I call him. That's what happens. To all kids. For whatever reason. He might as well learn to stand up for himself right from the start. Anyway, for all we know, he could be gay.'

Gabriel nodded, 'Maybe.'

Sofia leaned back on the bed, held her son close to her, 'Do you really not know what's going to happen to him, then?'

'No. I don't. But I'm sure he'll be fine.'

'Did you tell her that?'

'Who?'

'The other mother.'

'She didn't ask.'

'I bet she didn't.'

Sofia closed her eyes, hoped he was telling the truth.

She fell asleep. Gabriel and the baby watched each other.

Because her baby was early and because Sofia had told the hospital that she lived alone, she stayed in for the first day of Gabriel's life. She received a steady stream of officially not allowed visitors, persuaded to grant them access by her lack-of-partner status. And some angelic osmosis that softened the resolve of the staff at the ward entrance, left in place before Gabriel departed for the rest of his day away. Beth arrived with twins strapped on back and front, Pete working on a rush job, and she on her way to attend an out-patients meeting in her part of the hospital anyway.

'So, how do you feel?'

'I don't know. Weird. Better than I did yesterday. I think the labour was a kind of bodily ECT.'

'What do you mean?'

'I'm not depressed any more. Shocked. Surprised, by the baby, by his presence. By what his simply being here does to me, what it makes me.'

'But not depressed?'

'No.'

'Unhappy?'

Sofia shook her head, 'I don't know, I don't think so. Not now. Not really. I'm tired and I ache a bit – no, much more than that, I hurt a fuck of a lot – but really, I'm fine. It's weird. I feel different.'

Beth suppressed a yawn and wiped some milky baby vomit from her shoulder, 'Please don't tell me you feel complete? I don't think I could stand it.'

'No. Not at all. I felt complete before. At least I did before I got depressed. Before the last really bad one, up to about seven, eight months, I felt more in my body than I ever have. I actually liked being bigger. I haven't felt at ease with my body since I was a really little girl. I've fought it forever, beaten it up, hurt myself for my "art"? And then, when there was no point in fighting it, when I couldn't do anything about it anyway, I liked it.'

'That's good.'

'Maybe. It didn't feel like a breakthrough – not in therapy terms I mean. I just felt different about my body. I liked it not for what it looked like, but for what it could do. Just for being mine. I don't think it was about being pregnant, I think it was about feeling like me. Like Sofia. I felt like my body and my mind were the same thing. For once.'

'That's good isn't it?'

'Of course it is, but you know, that kind of ease, it never lasts long. Still, it felt good at the time. And I guess it might do again. I feel different. Weird. Different. Tired. But good.'

Beth stood up to go as her baby daughter started to grizzle, 'Don't worry babe. Plenty of time for it to get rubbish again.' She stopped when she got to the door, 'Um, Sofia?'

'Yes?'

'That man – Gabriel – do you still think you can see him, do you still think this baby is, you know . . .'

Sofia looked down at the tiny child sleeping by her side, 'What? Do I think he's special?'

Beth nodded, jiggling up and down to placate her daughter and waking her son in the process, 'Yeah, you know, what you thought – like a miracle or something?'

Sofia smiled, sidled a safe path around the question, 'Beth, it's fine. I'm not crazy. But yeah, he is pretty miraculous. I mean, doesn't everybody think that about their own kid? Fairly normal behaviour for a first time mother, isn't it?'

When Beth had gone, Gabriel opened his eyes and looked up at Sofia. And though she knew he wasn't yet able to focus, it certainly seemed as if he knew her.

Sofia was woken by her son screaming. As she clawed her way up from exhausted sleep, she struggled to work out where she was. There was a baby wailing to her left and a man staring into her face and calling her by name, except it wasn't a friend, it was a punter, that punter, the one who'd come in for the new floorshow, the man who'd hassled her outside the club. She couldn't understand why the club was now so well lit or why she was dancing alone, dressed in a hospital gown, flapping open down the back, or why there was a baby screaming at the side of the stage. When she did understand, she felt even worse. The man calling her name, standing over her, smiling, was no punter, not here anyway, though he was the man she'd knocked into the gutter that night. He was also, quite obviously, a doctor. Someone she probably would have met at the birth had her baby had a better sense of timing. Then again, perhaps the baby did have a perfect sense of timing. Perhaps the baby knew exactly what he was doing so as not to arrive when this particular doctor was available.

The man smiled down at her, 'Fancy meeting you here. Who'd have thought?' He smiled again and this time she knew he was laughing at her.

Sofia was frantically wondering what she should do, explain the situation to one of the nurses who was with him, ask to have another doctor do whatever this one was supposed to do, or just get up and out of there. Certainly she had no intention of letting him touch her, despite the fact that he was already leafing through her notes.

He put the file down and smiled again, leaned in closer to Sofia, 'Calm down, it's all right, I don't do ladies – just babies. I'm here to look at your son. His lungs are certainly healthy enough though, aren't they?'

The man took her child from her, both of the nurses were off at the other end of the room and Sofia didn't know what to do. Every part of her rebelled at the thought of this man touching her child and yet she couldn't explain why, couldn't expose herself or the child to a room full of strangers. She was forced to sit there, as calmly as possible while the doctor poked and prodded her son, every now and then looking up at Sofia to smile, his eyes noting her body beneath the hospital gown, the tired face, the nervous hands fiddling with the sheet.

He filled in various sheets on her forms and then held the baby out to her, half-whispering, 'A fine healthy specimen of a boy. You really do have so much to be proud of. I expect you'll want to take extra-special care of him, won't you?'

Gabriel didn't stop screaming until the doctor handed him back to Sofia and went to the other women in the room, both of whom had come in with their new babies while Sofia was sleeping, and who now lay just screened from each other by thin yellow curtains. Sofia held the child close to her and waited, cold and rigid, for the young doctor to leave. He walked past her bed on his way out, turned and looked at her, 'I hope you're coming back to work soon? I've really missed you.'

She heard him whistling as he walked down the corridor.

An hour later Sandra, Caroline and Helen were standing around her bed, each woman unveiling the delicious gifts they'd brought, a lavish display of perfumes and silver spoons, baby clothes and tiny, sexy Sofia clothes for when she fancied dressing down again. She was grateful for their presents, but more grateful still for the raucous laughter and ludicrous jokes and brash baby appreciation that swept away her insecurities on a wave of trashy insights into the nature of young men punters, those who turned out to be paediatricians in particular. It was a bravery that lasted until the minute they left and returned as soon as Sandra's high-heeled clipping died in the corridor. Sofia was immensely grateful when her own Gabriel returned to his place at the foot of her bed and she felt safe enough to fall asleep, just as her baby did beside her, knowing he was watching over them both.

The next morning another doctor arrived to pronounce both Sofia and her son well enough to leave, Martha and James arrived within the hour to pick her up, and mother and baby went home.

Thirty-nine

An hour after she climbed out of the cab, Sofia's parents arrived with armloads of roses, chocolates, baby clothes, and an excessively generous cheque. When her father asked her what she wanted for her son, Sofia heard herself repeating everyone else's clichés – happy, healthy, loving, kind. And was pulled up short to realise that behind her spoken words were the less perfect feelings she'd always suspected other people of having – true, she did want health and happiness for her son. Of course she did. But she knew she also wanted him to be clever and funny and witty and good-looking and charming. And intelligent, sporty, musical. He was a day old and all she wanted from him was that he was perfect. She attempted a brief moment of rationalisation – certainly being pretty seemed to help everyone else, there was every reason to believe an attractive and intelligent Messiah might be more successful than an ugly one. But she couldn't even fool herself. Thirty hours into her son's life and she was already proving herself as imperfect as her own parents. When they left that afternoon she gave them particularly grateful kisses goodbye. Then they got back on the M4, promises to return at the weekend, and a three-hour traffic-jam drive to help them adjust to their new, third generation status. And get used to the fact that it hadn't crossed their minds their grandchild might not be white.

The next week was exhausting and exciting and alarming. Sofia didn't have time to be depressed, she could barely manage to understand what she did feel, between learning how to feed her son and working out what to do with him and trying to interpret what his cries meant and entertaining the constant flow of admiring visitors – and then trying to get rid of them so they could both sleep – and leaning on Gabriel to give her a break whenever he could – which was never when anyone else was around. She had only just got used to the idea of uniting her own spirit and flesh, and now she was having to turn around again. For the time being at least, all of her belonged to baby Gabriel. And for the time being at least, Sofia figured that was all right. When she had a moment to figure anything at all.

Just over a week after Gabriel's birth, Sofia held a naming party for her son. It was a repeat of the wedding celebrations, with the same guests, although this time Sofia was no longer pregnant, Caroline and Danny spent all day in each other's arms, Sandra brought the sexuality-shy boss lady with her and Helen brought her kids too. Though she was happy to leave them to Martha's ministrations while she played top-tease with Katharine's sons. Sofia's mother and father were additional guests of honour, proudly showing off their grandson to the world. And their video camera. And their digital camera. And the old instamatic. And the nice lady who was a complete stranger in the newsagent's over the road. Beth's twins didn't cry once all afternoon – possibly because they weren't the centre of attention now there was a new baby and people didn't insist on poking them all the time. For her part Beth had decided she'd put aside her Sofia-concerns in favour of allowing both herself and Pete to play properly for the first time since the babies were born. She'd spent the past week expressing and freezing milk for the babies, they made sure everyone knew what to give them and when, and then launched herself at the party champagne with a willingness that had even Caroline muttering dire hangover warnings. And Sofia revelled in the attention both she and her baby received. It was a cold afternoon, but warm and bright in the middle of the party that took over both of the flats and all of the people.

This time, Sofia and Martha tidied up that evening rather than the following morning, only a week of motherhood and Sofia had already learned to grab every opportunity that her son was asleep to conquer another monumental task that couldn't be accomplished with a baby in her arms. Like having a shower. Or brushing her hair. Or sitting down. Baby Gabriel was exhausted after all the fuss, it looked like he might well sleep for a couple of hours, and Sofia planned to make the best use of the time. Planned, but didn't succeed.

They had just piled up all the dishes, Sofia was hunting for rubber gloves, when Martha, who was surprisingly not completely sober, let out a huge sigh.

'Um, Sofia, I need to tell you something.'

Sofia, head in the under-sink cupboard replied a muffled, 'What?'

'You should sit down. There's a bit of a problem.'

She removed her head from the cupboard and looked up, 'What?'

'Or it might be a problem. It isn't yet. I think. And I may be able to help, but I think you should know.'

'Martha, what are you on about?'

Martha fiddled with a plate, picked at a piece of stale French bread,

'Something's happened at work.'

'Are you all right?'

'Yeah, I'm fine. It's not me, it's about you.'

'What?'

'There's this doctor, from the hospital, he knows one of the women who work with me – he told her you were working when you were pregnant, that he'd seen you, at your work, and he said he was concerned about you when you were in hospital too, and look I shouldn't be telling you any of this really . . .'

Sofia stared at Martha and the words came flooding out of the social worker's mouth. 'You know, this is really not something I should be doing, but they ran a check on you – I looked in her files when she was out at lunch, which I have to say is something I've never done before, ever.'

'Get on with it Martha!'

Martha nodded, prompting herself with her bobbing head, 'Anyway, I'd heard her mention your name – I thought she was going to ask me about you, but she didn't say a word, she just went straight to the records, and there is information on you Sofia, about Beth, you being her patient. And now that this doctor's told her about your work, and that you were still working while you were pregnant, and they know you're alone . . .'

'What about patient confidentiality, how the hell can they know about me and Beth?'

'They don't know what you were seeing her for, but there are accounts that you were hospitalised, that's a matter of public record, and well, there's your job . . .'

'They can't complain about that, loads of women at my work have kids!'

'Yes, of course, it's just how your name came up – how he brought you to their attention and, I mean it's clear to me this doctor was just stirring, but . . .'

'Yes?'

'Well, obviously I shouldn't really say anything to you, though they do know you're my neighbour, so I can't imagine they didn't think I'd talk to you, but well . . . whatever the protocol, I don't really care what I'm supposed to do, not in this case. We're not close, you and I, but I do consider you a friend and I know this is a special situation – that man who's with you – I don't know what to make of that – if he's real or if you make him up and I see him because you believe in him, or what – maybe he is just in your head and I'm only adding to that, to your fantasy.'

'He is real Martha.'

'Yes, right, but anyway, you really don't want my office to know about him do you? I mean, what could you tell them? Oh God, I'm really sorry Sofia . . .' Martha's rambling speech ground to a halt as she looked around for wherever Gabriel might be and realised she could neither see nor feel him near, 'Anyway, I thought you ought to know. You probably need to be careful now. You know, just in case. Well . . . maybe you should think about going away?'

Sofia stared at Martha for a minute, then turned and went into her bedroom, picked up her son and climbed into bed with him. Martha tidied the kitchen and the rest of the flat, made Sofia a cup of tea and took it in to her. She offered sympathy and any help she could give, Sofia cried and held her child. Martha left after a while and then Gabriel was on the end of Sofia's bed.

'What am I going to do? What if they want to take him away? Did you know this was going to happen?'

Gabriel shook his head, 'No. Really, I didn't. I only knew when she told you. But maybe Martha's right. Maybe you should go away, just for a while, give this all a chance to blow over.'

Sofia shook her head, tears muffling her voice, 'Yeah right, like where? You and me take the kid and flee into Egypt?'

'Not quite. Katharine's family have got that place in Ireland, she and Zack already said you were welcome to have a break there if you wanted, you know they still feel they really owe you, I'm sure they'd like to help.

You've got savings, enough for a year maybe, if you're careful.'

'But I'm meant to be going back to work. Danny wants me to start on the new choreography next month, he said they'd book a rehearsal room so I can take Gabriel and everything!' Sofia's voice came out in a little girl whine as she realised how much she might be missing out on.

Gabriel nodded, 'I know, and you can probably still do all of that – in a while, once things have blown over. Just not yet Sofia . . . things change.'

Sofia picked up her son as he started to whimper, distressed by the tone of her voice, she switched to soothing mode – in attitude if not in truth. 'Yeah. Don't I know it. Come on little boy. Come to Mama.'

They planned Sofia's future that night while baby Gabriel slept beside them. The next year anyway. She would speak to Zack in the morning, Gabriel was sure the cottage would be available – and it would be a safe retreat. She'd get James and Martha to sublet her flat so there was somewhere to come back to when she was ready – and so that she'd still feel a connection with London, so that Ireland wouldn't be too cut off. And she would leave as soon as possible. As Gabriel pointed out, for all her openness this evening, Martha really was ingrained social worker through and through, if things had gone far enough for her to feel she needed to alert Sofia, then the sooner Sofia was out of there the better. It did occur to Sofia that perhaps this too, was meant to happen. Maybe Gabriel had got it wrong, maybe she was only meant to give birth to the baby, and perhaps its future wasn't to do with her.

Gabriel was certain in his denial, 'No. Definitely not. I don't know what's coming, I know very little really. But I do know for a fact that you are meant to be the mother. This baby's mother. All his life.'

Sofia heard the certainty in his voice and realised that, anyway, she had no choice. Gabriel was her baby now, she'd chosen to be his mother. Not chosen when Gabriel first asked her, but chosen through time and growing – and, as with so many seeming choices – through lack of any other option. He was her child and she was tied to him. She had made what had happened to her become her choice, a new life bought with present hindsight. Sofia could no more let someone else take Gabriel from her than fly. So she'd flee.

It was late, close to morning, when she asked the terrible question. Terrible because she thought she probably already knew the answer, because she knew Gabriel wouldn't want to say. Make the future real by naming it out loud. But she had to know for definite, so she asked him anyway.

'Gabriel, are you coming with me?'

Gabriel's silence was enough of an answer, his tears on her face were a more burning contact than she'd ever had with his no-touch skin. He held her and couldn't speak. They kissed, lips and salt water.

Sofia lay wide awake in the middle of her bed, solid night heavy in the room, baby on her left side, angel on her right. In the morning Gabriel slowly kissed her swollen eyes to sleep. When the baby woke her an hour later, Sofia knew she was now alone with the child.

Forty

They lived in Katharine's house in Ireland for Gabriel's first eighteen months. He started to crawl there, and then took his first stumbling steps. He learned words and pictures and how to drive his mother crazy. He was sweet and infuriating and exhausting and normal. He gained weight at the right stages, completed the baby milestones at the right ages. And though Sofia watched him constantly, there were no signs that he was anything other than an ordinary little boy.

After the first few months, once she had established some sort of routine, Sofia took on a few local girls as students. She didn't have the qualifications to teach them for exams, but she had the inclination not to be lonely with only her son for company, and she certainly had the desire to earn. Besides that, in a village of two hundred people, a single mother with a screaming child was very interesting. This way the mothers could bring their daughters to her for a dance class and then report back what she looked like, what she seemed like, what she was doing there. There were plenty of interested parties, but no one ever found out what she was doing there.

Time passed, it rained. Sometimes when Sofia came home late with Gabriel strapped to her back, and her home was unusually dark or empty, she caught herself looking hopefully for the shine of luminous angel blue. The borrowed house stayed resolutely dark.

When Gabriel was nearly two Sofia ended her self-imposed exile and returned to London. As soon as she'd set herself up with a reliable babysitter – paid for three nights' care, and accepted Martha and James' offer for the other two, she returned to the club to work, took up where she'd left off. It was surprisingly easy to return to work and though she was always tired, it wasn't impossible. The young doctor had never returned to the club, nor did he make an appearance when Sofia came back. She continued to work there for two more years, gradually easing out her evening work in favour of choreography for the other women and taking part in the easier-to-do shows instead of so much floor work. She continued to watch Gabriel closely – as did Martha and Beth – and he continued to be ordinary. The angel stayed away.

When Gabriel turned four Sofia gave up work at the club and began teaching full-time. But this time she wasn't teaching little girls and their unreasonably proud mothers, she was teaching grown girls who wanted to become dancers just like her. Sofia had been good at it, she had skills to pass on, and there would always be work for these young women. Certainly Danny's three clubs were doing very well. It was a good move, she knew what she was doing and she trusted herself to do it well.

Gabriel grew into a sweet-natured, funny little boy, only prone to the occasional temper tantrum when he couldn't get his own way, or when his childish abilities meant he wasn't yet able to do something he wanted. And he wanted to do everything. On his seventh birthday Sofia and Gabriel went down to Danny and Caroline's country house for the weekend. They'd had three children in quick succession and, as Gabriel was a couple of years older than their eldest, it meant he had playmates who hung on his every word. Something he seemed to enjoy more than a little.

It was a cold morning, the country air crisper, the frost deeper than the London version Gabriel was used to. Sofia woke to the sound of children playing in the field outside her bedroom. She pulled her curtains back to call out to Gabriel to keep the others quiet until Danny woke up. Though he had managers in all three clubs, he still stayed in town most nights, coming home with Caroline at three in the morning. Danny wouldn't appreciate an early morning call from four screaming brats even if three of them were his own undisputed angels.

A narrow river ran through the bottom of the property, fenced off for safety where it grew into a small pool and made a delicious swimming hole on hot summer days. Fenced off, but not impossible to gain access for a handful of determined small children. Sofia was just about to shout out that he should come back from the edge and bring the little ones back right now, when Gabriel stepped out on to the water. Walked across the water to the centre of the pool. Sofia looked at the morning light glaring off the surface, trying to make out if it had frozen over in the cold night. She ran downstairs and out into the field, grabbing Danny's jacket to cover her as she ran. By the time she got outside Gabriel was skating across the water's icy surface, the other three children watching, urging him on. And Sofia watched in horror as he held his hand out for Caroline's youngest Rebecca, only two years old. She was about to scream at her son for being so stupid, risking a tiny girl on what had to be thin ice. Risking himself on thin ice. But as she got closer she realised it wasn't ice her son was skating on. It was water. Cold water lapping across the top of his boots, splashing against his legs as he played. Sofia stopped in her tracks and watched, horrified. And as Gabriel held his hand out to the other children, they too giggled and laughed and walked across the uncertain surface, until all four of them were dancing on the water.

Sofia stood still, her constant fear finally confirmed. Then, in the thin morning sunlight, she felt her skin grow warmer, experienced an ease and comfort she'd not known since her son was a week old. The mist on the cold ground beside her shone a pale, luminous blue. Sofia held out her hand and closed her eyes, felt a tall man's hand in hers, his arm warm around her. They stood together, he watching over her son and she, eyes closed, smiling at the angel behind her eyes. When she looked again, he was gone, and four small children stared up at her, this crazy beautiful woman standing barefoot and grinning in a frosty field.

Gabriel smiled at Sofia, 'Don't worry Mama, we were only playing. It doesn't mean anything.'

Sofia nodded and held him close to her, then she took them back into the warm kitchen for pancakes and hot chocolate. The water in the wide pool flowed on behind them.

After that morning Sofia watched her son grow. And waited.